To Nana

Many thanks for the tickets for Big Step. Hope you enjoy it.

Love

Suzanna Bartaba

THE DEVIL'S CUP

by

Suzannah Zerfahs

IMCC Ltd

First Published 2006

In association with

IMCC Limited
Riverdream,
Taggs Island,
Hampton,
Middlesex.
TW12 2HA
imcc.sz@gmail.com

ISBN 1-4116-7879-6

This book is dedicated to
"The Esher Dissident Faction"
for their support, friendship
and social prowess.

THE DEVIL'S CUP

There is danger for he who snatches delusion from a woman

PART ONE

The Letter

CHAPTER ONE

The envelope was addressed "strictly private and confidential". When he slit it open it contained a single sheet of thick, quality paper from a solicitor, whose address indicated a prestigious street in London. It requested that Simon contact them in order to hear something to his advantage.

He frowned over the words and handed the letter across the breakfast table to his wife.

"What do you make of that?" he asked.

"You've been holding out on me, do you have some very old, millionaire relative tucked away somewhere?" She turned the paper inspecting the back. "Pukka paper anyway."

"Rich old rellie, huh! That would be some luck wouldn't it? Couldn't come at a better time, but don't get your hopes up."

"But still ..." Donna, halted in her routine of clearing away the breakfast plates; "... something to your advantage usually means something like a legacy, doesn't it?"

Simon discarded the envelope and tucked the folded letter into the back pocket of his jeans, as he rose from the table. He wiped the crumbs from his hands on the tea towel, and gulped down the last mouthful of tea from his Bart Simpson mug, a Christmas present from one of the children. Picking up his car keys, mobile phone and some loose change from the end of the kitchen counter he absently-mindedly kissed Donna on the cheek.

"See ya later," he told her. "I'm probably working through this evening, I'll call and let you know for certain, when I can."

"Don't forget to call about that letter too, it's gotta mean something good, surely?"

Simon double slapped the pocket of his jeans, "Sure thing." He tried to sound bright about it, but he had a sense of uneasiness about the letter. It was true enough if it was some sort of legacy then the timing couldn't be better.

Simon and Donna had been married almost eighteen years, they had four children; the eldest Suki was just about to start university, with all the costs that involved. Her sister, Peta, wasn't far behind her, in September she would be starting her 'A' level courses. The twins were active boys and tore through trousers and shoes at an alarming rate.

For years Simon had worked at the Rowley Max factory in Cowley, on the outskirts of Oxford, which produced components for electrical heating systems. It was mindless, often dull work, but until recently the rate of pay had been good and there had been plenty of opportunities within his shift system for overtime. He had always been first in line to accept whatever had been on offer. That was up until the imminent closure of the factory was announced. Now he had to supplement his wages by whatever means he could find.

Although he would have said that generally they were a close family, there were times when he felt he was nothing more than a weekly wage packet. He left for work early and arrived home late and exhausted. He could go days without seeing the boys, Ronnie and Ryan, who at seven years old, were tucked up by seven thirty each evening. Suki and Peta sometimes raised their eyes from Big Brother to grunt an acknowledgement as he entered the room, before shushing him at his attempts at conversation. He would wander rebuffed into the kitchen, where Donna would be looking tired and harassed behind a mountain of ironing whilst she watched a re-run of *"Frost"* on the portable.

Simon would sigh, remove himself to the backroom, click on his computer and blast a few aliens to smithereens. It wasn't a satisfying existence but it was safe and safety was something he appreciated now. Obliterating aliens was as exciting as he wanted things to be for the moment.

When Simon arrived at work he was saddened at the depleted workforce. Since the closure had been announced the atmosphere had been depressing and each week there were more and more gaps as people moved on. He exchanged a few jokes with Quassi, the guy who shunted the trolleys from one part of the factory to the next, before helping a couple of his workmates with a stock take of RF143 components. Until now he had been philosophical about his work, it had paid the mortgage, it had paid the bills, it was not what he would have chosen to do; he was smarter than his work might imply. What had started as a holiday job when he was a student had become a full time job as a matter of need when Donna had fallen pregnant with Suki. Almost two decades later he was still letting his mind wander down alleys of dreams which he had no real intentions of following. After all, dreams didn't put food on the table, and neither would Rowley Max for much longer.

In the past, when he wasn't too tired, he had scribbled stories, which he never seemed to have the time to finish. He knew the name of every bird that flew and the few that didn't. He could recognise the call of most English species. His holidays had been spent hiking or taking the boys camping. He and Donna rarely got so much as an evening to be alone together. He accepted with resignation that life was sometimes hard and often mundane, but it had never seemed so until that summer two years ago. That summer had turned things on their head. Since then he craved peace and routine. Instead each day was filled, to some degree, with self recrimination and regret; with a pile of "what ifs" beside his bed which caused him no end of guilt.

As he worked through the morning he considered the letter folded in his back pocket. It burned like a brand and gave him a feeling not of hope and excitement as might be expected, but a slight chill of fear. He could not reason why exactly, except he had no rich relatives, he was as certain as he could be of that. His family were sixth generation descendents from Russian immigrants, who had escaped hardship and persecution. Simon had spent many months researching his family tree. When the 1901 census had become common property on the Internet he had been one of the first to log on, only to be immediately frustrated when the site crashed, and was closed down to be reprogrammed to cope with the phenomenal number of hits which no-one had predicted. When it was once again up and running, he found an unexpected amount of information of a generation of shoemakers, who had settled in the London district of Shoreditch. His research led him to previously unknown relatives and family links who pooled information with him, via e-mail and faded away just as fast when the research was completed and they found they had no actual common ground. There had been an almost manic interest in genealogy in the country at large at that time. As far as his search into his family tree could provide the answers, rich relatives he felt, were probably thin on the ground.

When the bell sounded, echoing loudly around the half empty factory, Simon made his way amid a small throng of men and a few women, towards the canteen. Around him chatter and catcalls flew back and forth regarding the match on television the previous night.

"See the match last night Simon?" someone called.

"Nah!" Another voice responded," I expect he was watching some cookery programme." It was well established Simon was not a sports fan. He took the banter in good part, whilst being aware that he was not really quite 'one of the lads'. He never joined the Friday night gang, who finished the day shift and poured across to the Working Mans Club, to drink away part of their weekly wages. The people at work had long since stopped asking him to join them. Sometimes he still thought it would be nice to be asked, but he knew he would always refuse and he supposed they knew it too.

During the tea break, Simon chatted to a couple of the girls from packing, he always found it easier to talk to women. He was aware that by doing so he was ignoring the letter, typed on the very thick and fancy paper, which formed an obvious oblong through his denim pocket. He could not explain his reluctance, could not or would not, not even to himself. He knew that Donna would be pacing at home, watching the clock for his tea break time, eager to know what could possibly be "to his advantage", and still he ignored the letter until with a sense of relief the bell rang again, seemingly longer and more persistently, calling them all back to work. All around him paper cups were left scattered on the Formica topped tables; cigarettes were almost desperately inhaled with a final gasp before being ground out in tin foil ashtrays. People licked the last of the doughnut sugar off their finger tips and with a few moans and groans made their way back to their various sections.

CHAPTER TWO

By lunchtime Simon could no longer ignore the letter. He had picked up a message on his mobile telephone from Donna, who even in a text sounded furious with him for leaving her in suspense. He took himself off to the roof of the factory and sat with his back against the wall. Beside him the huge air conditioning fans rotated with almost lazy insolence, filling the air with the dry smell of rubber and dust. He pulled down his overalls to reach his back pocket, not bothering to pull them fully up again but knotting the arms around his waist as he sat cross legged and let the sun warm his head and shoulders. He smoothed the letter flat, and read it through not once but four times before finally pressing in the central London dialling code. His finger hit the cancel button. Simon's heart was racing, his stomach turning somersaults, he took a couple of deep breaths and once more tapped in the number, this time getting to the very last digit before again pressing cancel.

"For Christ's sake get a grip," he said out loud to himself, before punching in the number more forcefully and this time listening to the ring. Almost immediately a precise and clipped voice answered.

"Sylvester, Markham and Tweed, how may I help you?"

"I ... I've had a letter," Simon stuttered out, "from a Mr Markham."

"Can I take your name sir?" the no-nonsense voice requested.

"Koweski, Simon Koweski," he replied.

"One moment Mr Koweski, I'll put you right through." There was a click on the line, a moment of silence then a man's voice, deep, an older man, well educated sounding, 'very public school' thought Simon, his nervousness increasing.

"Ah! Good morning, Mr Koweski, thank you so much for calling," the voice was smooth, like dark treacle, rich and confident, with only a slight quiver to give any indication of the speakers age.

"I received a letter from you," Simon started to say.

"Yes, I rather thought you might," the voice responded. Simon thought it contained a faint trace of mockery, it continued, "else why would you be calling, why indeed?" Simon was certain now the character at the other end of the line was ridiculing him in some way, he felt a twinge of annoyance. He hadn't wanted to call the damned number, he was doing so because Donna was hard to live with when she had a bee in her bonnet, and this seemed to be a particularly large bee as far as she was concerned.

"Well, could you tell me what it's about?" Simon requested.

"Yes of course, but I am afraid I cannot discuss such a delicate matter over the telephone." The voice had lost its trace of humour now and sounded as Simon supposed a solicitor ought, official, curt, secretive. "I wonder if it might be possible for you to call into my offices in the near future."

"Well, I'm not sure," Simon hesitated, "I don't travel into London much these days, I have work commitments, you know?"

"Yes, Mr. Koweski, I understand it may be difficult for you, but I really cannot discuss such a matter over the telephone. I shall need proof of your identity you see, to establish that you are who you say you are."

"Well I got the letter didn't I?" responded Simon, with some exasperation.

"Yes, forgive me Mr Koweski, but in my business we learn to be cautious, and as I say ......"

"You can't discuss it over the telephone," finished Simon with a hint of sarcasm.

"Quite! Now I wonder if this coming Friday would be good for you, say at 11.00am?"

"Yes, yes I suppose that would be okay. I suppose I can manage that," replied Simon, wondering how he could afford to miss a shift and lose a days pay.

"Fine, splendid, then I very much look forward to meeting you on Friday. Thank you for telephoning Mr Koweski."

"Thank you," responded Simon, not knowing quite what he was thanking the elderly solicitor for. He sent a text message to Donna, explaining briefly and went slowly back down the fire escape his boots making metallic echoes on the fretwork spiral stairway. He re-entered the factory, through the double swing loading doors and meandered to his work station, his brows knitted as he pondered the conversation. Mr Markham had certainly given nothing away.

The week slowly crawled around to Friday. It couldn't crawl slowly enough for Simon; the sense of foreboding would not leave him. He replayed the events of two years ago over and over in his head and wondered why he should be linking the two things together. He felt that somehow in someway there must be a connection, and that he was about to be exposed. His reasoning told him it couldn't be, but his guilt was rearing its head and he could not provide any other explanation.

Donna informed him she would accompany him to London. Simon could not persuade her otherwise without arousing her suspicions. Peta offered to take the boys to school and pick them up and she encouraged Donna to take a day off and spend it window shopping.

"You never know mum," she said, "if we are going to be millionaires you might do some real shopping."

"Yeah right!" Donna responded. "Still it'll be a change to have a day in the city, and to spend a couple of hours not clearing up after you lot," and she grinned at Peta affectionately.

On Thursday night Ryan awoke with a fever and was soon being horribly sick. Donna sat with him through the night sponging his forehead until he finally fell into a flushed sleep. In the morning Simon took Donna a cup of tea but she could hardly prise her eyes open.

"We have to leave in an hour," Simon told her.

"What? I can't. I'm sorry. I really don't think I can. I'm shattered, and anyway I need to keep an eye on Ryan." Donna told him in staccato sentences through layers of sleepiness.

Simon attempted to keep the relief out of his voice. "Well, maybe I should stay here with you?"

"No, don't be silly, you have to go." Donna waved him away and turned her face back into the pillows. "You go," she mumbled into the fabric.

Simon, with some reluctance, left the house. His car had been giving him some trouble but this morning it fired into life first try. He put it into gear, slowly pulled away from the kerb and wended his way down the lanes before joining the M40 motorway at the Thame junction and heading for London. He travelled in the slow lane, in no hurry to reach his destination. Driving through the deep cut of the chalk hills in the direction of Wycombe, he would have, on another day, admired the sky hung in muted blues right down to the ploughed fields, where flocks of birds circled and dove and circled again, but this day Simon hardly noticed. He tried to listen to a CD, but the one in the slot was an old one of Suki's and the constant thumping of the beat irritated him. He switched to Radio Four and listened to some old windbag of a professor droning on and on about global warming and the effect on the iguana population. Simon felt, even given his current state of mind, this was not ever going to be riveting listening; he flicked the switch to *'off'* impatiently.

When he reached town he found a car park and hoped to goodness Mr Markham wasn't going to keep him long, the cost of parking in London was exorbitant. The day was warm, one of those balmy late spring days just before the season tips full into summer. A gentle breeze stirred the air. Given other circumstances Simon could have enjoyed the feel of the sun on his face and the thrill of being in London. He had walked all though these parts many years before. For a little while London had been one of his obsessive interests. He had explored every street, every alley, read books on ghost sites, trawled around The Tower of London, the museums in Exhibition Road, Harrods, (though only to look). He knew Threadneedle Street and Downing Street, Kensington

High Street and Notting Hill. He had loved the vibrancy, the bustle, the multi-cultural feel of the city. He knew its history, he knew why Mayfair was so named, and he had stood outside the Abbey National which was Sherlock Holmes fictional address. He recalled the many happy occasions he had spent exploring, eating noodles in Chinatown, at a surprisingly clean and incredibly cheap café, where all the diners sat on wooden benches at a long trestle table. Where, as soon as his bowl was empty, the proprietor would bustle the hapless patron out demanding, "You go now, you finish, you go now," for there was always a demand for places. He hadn't been into London for many years but it all came back to him as he proceeded along The Strand, before turning off a side street.

Then there it was. He was standing in front of Sylvester, Markham and Tweed; a discreet brass sign told him so. The dark oak door was polished to a mirror like sheen, the steps leading up as white as if they had been new painted that morning. Not a speck of dust dared to despoil the black wrought iron railings, and behind the façade, Simon could sense, although not see, an aura of calm, which no crisis, however desperate, could rattle. Taking a deep breath he proceeded up the steps and rang the bell. The door was opened almost immediately by an elderly porter.

"Simon Koweski for Mr Markham," Simon announced, almost bowing with some deference toward the man's uniform as he spoke.

"Yes Sir, Mr Markham is expecting you. If you would care to take a seat here, I will inform him of your arrival," the old man gestured towards a green, leather, button-back sofa, which had the appearance of comfort, with that cracked, aged look which good leather sofas should have. Simon sunk into its pungent depths, and ignored the stack of Country Life magazines on the mahogany table in front of him. He gazed around the wood panelled room and wondered just how much polish Sylvester, Markham and Tweed must get though in a year.

He didn't hear the woman enter; the thick pile of the carpet muffled her footsteps. He jumped when she spoke. "Mr Markham will see you now," she advised him.

He leapt up to follow the neat, immaculate figure in her prim grey business suit, with her hair in a short grey bob. Her Hermes scarf, tied artfully at her neck, giving her the only splash of colour. Simon felt decidedly uncomfortable in his rather creased cargo pants and t-shirt, but it wasn't like he'd had much choice. He followed the secretary into an old fashioned lift, where she slid the concertina door shut, without making a clang, and they rose up two levels.

"Nice day," commented Simon in an attempt to break the silence.

"Yes Sir," came back the polite but discouraging reply. Simon raised an eyebrow and sighed.

Exiting the lift he followed the straight backed woman along a corridor, his feet sinking into the deepest carpet he had ever experienced. This was not a run of the mill solicitor; this was a company who would be charging bankrolls by the hour. Simon's curiosity was aroused and although he still felt uneasy he began to feel a little more confident that this was nothing to do with the events of two years ago, this couldn't possibly be. This was just *too* much.

CHAPTER THREE

Simon was ushered into a large room, the overwhelming tone of which was wealth and good taste. Bookshelves lined the walls, great tombs of law, leather bound and gold embossed. Even though it was a warm day a real fire crackled in the huge, York stone fireplace, beside which were placed two burgundy coloured, high-back, leather chairs. From behind the widest desk Simon had ever seen a man came forward, his hand extended. He was taller than Simon might have expected, although slightly stooped, his hair white, his expression benevolent although his eyes were sharp.

"Thank you for coming Mr Koweski; I'm Markham, Neville Markham. I'm so glad you could make it." They shook hands. Simon was aware of the callous' on his palms compared to the softness of Mr Markham's manicured hands. "Do have a seat," Markham gestured toward the fireside chairs. Simon would have preferred to be as far away from the fire as possible, he was already feeling hot and uncomfortable, but he took the proffered seat dutifully.

"Can I offer you some refreshment Mr Koweski, some coffee, tea, perhaps? I usually have a little something myself at this time."

"Yes, thank you, coffee would be good," Simon answered.

"Ah! Splendid", replied Mr Markham in a pleased voice, Simon felt it was as if he had performed some marvellous trick. "Coffee for two please, Miss Simmons." Mr Markham spoke to the grey-clad woman, whom Simon had not realised was still waiting with infinite patience for instructions. She inclined her head and withdrew.

"Good journey?" Mr Markham enquired. Simon figured that he was not going to launch straight into business until the coffee was served, so he sat back in his chair and agreed that it had been a good journey. They chatted for a few minutes, through Miss Simmons return, then as she poured from a silver coffee pot and distributed the richly dark fresh coffee between them. When the door had closed behind her Mr Markham fixed Simon with a look. "Well young man, I expect you are wondering what all this is about?" he enquired.

"I'm wondering," said Simon, with a hint of irony, "if you have the right person."

Mr Markham laughed gently. "Well now, did you bring some identity with you - a passport perhaps?"

"I don't have a passport; I have a driving licence, is that any good?" Simon fished into the side pocket of his cargo pants as he spoke, and produced a bedraggled, limp, pink sheet of paper, which bore signs of having been mangled by the dog. Mr Markham took it, showing no obvious display of distaste at the scruffy, smudged offering. He examined it carefully.

"Well that seems to be in order," he said handing it back to Simon.

"Well now I have been instructed," Mr Markham intoned in an emotionless voice, "to pass on to you this envelope." In saying so, he reached to the table beside him, and picked up an A4 sealed envelope.

"Instructed by whom?" Simon asked.

"I am not at liberty to say." Mr Markham responded.

"Has someone died?" Simon tried a different tack.

"I am not at liberty to say."

"Do you know the contents of this envelope?" Simon asked feeling more and more puzzled and more and more uncomfortable.

"Yes." The one word answer provided no clues.

"Can I open it now?"

"My client left no particular instructions."

Simon ripped the seal of the envelope. As he did so Mr Markham rose and walked to his chair at the other side of his desk, giving Simon space and re-establishing a more professional distance.

Pulling the contents from the envelope Simon found a single sheet of paper, it read: *Dreams, Holt Lane, Sheldon, Oxfordshire. Tomorrow.* There was also a key, nothing fancy, an ordinary latch key. Simon rose and walked to the front of the old solicitor's desk. He flapped the letter toward him, and brandished the key with his other hand. "What is this? What does it mean?" he asked his voice rising on a note of impatience. "I hate puzzles."

"Do you Mr Koweski?" Markham's tone was inquiring and Simon was struck by the fact the man in front of him knew more about him than he was letting on. He obviously knew for example that Simon, far from hating puzzles, loved them: crosswords, number puzzles, all sorts. When he was camping with the children, after they were asleep, by way of relaxation he would work his way from front to back through puzzle books,: enjoying breaking the codes, beating the systems, and this man, this tight lipped solicitor, seemed to know that. He stared into the older mans eyes but Markham's expression had become blank.

"Will I find the answer at this address?" Simon asked more calmly.

"I am not at liberty to say. Now if there's nothing else Mr Koweski ..." Mr Markham rose and extended his hand and Simon had no choice but to take it, shake it, and turn to follow Miss Simmons, who had once more shimmied into the office with not a sound. In the reverse journey down in the lift Simon made no attempt at conversation, his brows were knitted in puzzlement. On leaving the offices of Sylvester, Markham and Tweed, he walked with slow concentration toward St. Paul's Cathedral. Spying a coffee shop he decided to risk the car park exceeding the small amount of cash in his pocket, and even blow a further two pounds of his money on a coffee, strong and black. The coffee shop was crowded. He asked a woman if he could take the spare seat at her table and on her acknowledgement sat down opposite her as she once more raised her newspaper, placing a barrier between them. Time and time again Simon read the address on the paper Mr Markham had given him, and time and time again it offered no further clues. His eyes glazed over as he stared into the middle distance, brought back to the present situation by the woman at the table rustling out the pages of her broadsheet. As he stared at the page facing him, without really seeing the words, suddenly something focused. His eyes caught the date at the top of the page, 14th June. That made the next day 15th June.

"Oh Christ!" It was only as the woman peered from behind her paper he realised he had spoken out loud. "Sorry," he apologised. But his thoughts were racing. Could it be? 15th June? It couldn't just be by chance could it? 15th June? He had known. Deep in his heart he had always known that there had to have been a connection, it was too much of a coincidence. 15th June - but how? The swanky solicitor – how? No, surely it was a coincidence? Surely he was just a bit on edge and really 15th June was purely a fluke of fate. But he knew, as he had really always known, it wasn't. Dear God, what was he going to tell Donna now? He could tell her it was a mistake that the letter hadn't really been intended for him after all. She wouldn't believe him, he knew she wouldn't.

He did not know afterwards how he managed to get through his night, he knew however he was glad he hadn't had to go straight home and face the barrage of questions that was bound to come, following his meeting with Mr Markham. He had driven away from the car park with no change in his pocket, his telephone turned off, and he had just driven, with no purpose. He ended up in Denham, where the traffic was heavier. Swinging off the main road he travelled down a side street until he saw a park. Pulling over to the kerb he got out and walked as aimlessly as he had driven, head down, seeing nothing and acknowledging no-one. In his head he played over and over again what had happened that day two years ago in the Ashmolean Museum, where he had gone to browse. Two years ago on 15th June. The months afterwards were glorious summer months, the days brighter than they had ever been in his life before, the colours more vibrant, plants, birds, flowers everything bloomed or sung with extra gusto that summer. He trawled through his brain and although he had a memory for minute detail, in none of his recollections could he assimilate those thoughts with the posh solicitor. Of course he had always suspected wealth, but not that sort, not Sylvester, Markham and Tweed level of wealth. But then it came back to the date – why else the 15th June?

Simon eventually had to go to work, he was working evenings for a minicab firm and he knew he had long night ahead. He finished just before dawn was breaking. He was exhausted, not from the physical work, or the long day and night, but because his mind would not be still. Simon drove home in silence along the quiet roads. On arriving he was pleased to observe the house had not yet erupted into life. It was too early for any movement. He undressed on the landing and crept into the bedroom, cautiously pulled aside the duvet he climbed into bed next to Donna. She turned toward him, mumbling in her sleep. In seconds he too was fast asleep.

When he awoke, without even looking at the clock, he knew it had to be around eleven. The impact of the day hit him. He had decided to tell Donna it was all a mistake, that it was nothing to do with him and that would be an end to the matter. He lay back on the pillows practising phrases which might make it sound sincere. Donna was climbing the stairs, he heard the familiar creak. He took a deep breath ready for the lie.

As she entered the room she put his mug of tea on the bedside cabinet. "Hi, Sweetie," she bent over him and placed a kiss on his ruffled hair. "The mystery deepens eh?" she was waving the letter with the address on it toward him.

"You've been through my pockets?" Simon shot at her accusingly.

"Of course I've been through your pockets, I was putting on washing," replied Donna frowning in her response. "Did Mr Markham say anything other than what's here?"

"No." Simon was abrupt, his mind once more racing; there was going to be no escape.

"So get up, let's go see what it's all about. Peta says she'll look after the boys. Ryan is much better this morning, and it shouldn't take us more than an hour or so round trip. Come on, get up, aren't you in the least little bit curious?" Donna pulled the duvet off Simon as she spoke, leaving him sitting in his boxers, trying not to spill his tea.

"I've got to shower," he told her.

"Well don't be all day. I've got to get back in time to take Ronnie to a party, and Ryan if he's up to it," in saying so Donna turned from the bedroom and left Simon taking deep breaths, as he tried to still the beating of his heart. What was he going to do? What was he going to find? What the hell was he to tell Donna?

Simon spent a long time under the water jets, the smell of the peach shower gel cloying his senses, making him feel more nauseous than he felt already. If only he knew what they were going to find at the address he'd been given. If only he knew whether it really was anything to do with anything?

Donna shouted from downstairs, "For heavens sake hurry up in there, we'll never get going at this rate."

"Well that wouldn't be such a bad thing," thought Simon, but he turned off the jets and towelled himself dry, looking in the steamy mirror as he did so. He thought he looked older - older even than yesterday. He pulled in his stomach and once more resolved that he should do more exercise before it spread even further. Then he let out his breath, and his stomach and it protruded into its more natural and more comfortable position. He decided that having a six pack was not all it was cracked up to be and it was personality that counted. "Yeah!" he exclaimed into the mirror, "all fat blokes say that!"

He found on entering the kitchen, Donna at the sink, Ronnie and Ryan at the table drawing and Peta was scribbling Mrs Peta Williams, Mrs Robbie Williams, Robbie 4 Peta. "Still in lurve then Pet?" teased Simon.

"Leave her alone Simon," Donna admonished him as Peta threw him a black look.

"Want some toast?" Donna asked. Immediately three arms shot into the air with cries of, "I do, I do."

"I wasn't asking you lot, you've had breakfast," she looked toward Simon, but he shook his head.

"Nah, a coffee would be good though."

"Okay, but as soon as you've had that we're off. What do you think the great mystery is at Sheldon then? There's nothing there really, just a few cottages, not even a shop or a pub."

"I don't know. We don't have to go you know. I'm sure it's all some wild goose chase. That solicitor didn't really say anything."

"Then why give you the address? Aren't you in the least little bit curious?" Donna asked.

"No, not really, I'm sure there are a million things here that need doing."

"Since when did you suddenly become so keen? Come on, get a move on, I told you we have to get back for that party for the boys."

Half an hour later, coffee drunk, teeth brushed, Donna and Simon were in the car and heading along winding lanes toward Sheldon. As Donna had said, it was nothing more than a tiny hamlet of Cotswold stone cottages and a few barns.

"Stick a CD on," Simon told her. "I think there's one of those compilation ones in the glove box." Donna pushed the button to ON whilst she rummaged. The first beats of a track thumped out. Simon thought he recognised it but he couldn't place it. Then suddenly it clicked, it was a track by the band *Establishment*. It wasn't the same thumping beat that he had turned off the day before. He pressed the reject button and the CD slid out from its slot. It wasn't a pre-recorded CD, it was the sort where the girls down-loaded tracks from the Internet. "Didn't know the girls were into Establishment," he said, half turning toward Donna.

"No, neither did I but its fine, leave it on." She pushed the CD back in its slot. After the long thumping intro the words suddenly filled the car.

"My house is your house,

My house is our house"

A chill crept through Simon. "When were they in the car?" he demanded of Donna fiercely.

"Who?"

"The girls, when were they in the car?" Simon was gripping the steering wheel tightly, his knuckles bone white.

"I don't know. Why?" Donna was looking at him as if he had just fallen from Mars.

"The CD - when did they put the CD in the car?"

"I don't know, the other day I expect." Donna answered with some impatience.

A feeling of horror was creeping over Simon, he knew the CD hadn't been there the day before, and as the words continued to beat around the confines of the car they filled his head. Each verse was full of more implications, and then the chorus kicked in: *"Gotta have you in my life"* and a voice from two years ago came back to him, *'You will always be there in my life Simon, won't you?'* and he had answered, *"Yes, I'll always be there."* But he wasn't. For the past year and a half his guilt had been tearing him apart. Six months of sublime happiness and eighteen months of regrets and self recriminations, and now there was a CD in his car and he hadn't put it there. He was driving to a village he didn't know, to a house he hadn't heard of before yesterday, to find ... what?

"Are you okay? Simon, are you okay?" Donna's voice was frantic beside him. "Slow down Simon, look at the speed you're doing," she was tugging at his arm. Simon flicked his eyes to the speed dial. Christ, he wasn't aware his old jalopy could even go that fast; he eased his foot from the accelerator and watched the needle drop. The sweat stood out in beads on his upper lip and he wiped it away with the back of his hand.

"Sorry," he mumbled, "sorry." The track had finished and no more came to replace it, just one track on a strange CD, one track about '*always being in my life*'.

CHAPTER FOUR

All Simon's instincts told him to turn around and head straight back home, but Donna was beginning to get really excited. If Simon hadn't been so distracted he would have been in seventh heaven. This was picture postcard England. The verges were full of flowers, the smell of wild garlic hung in the air, it was totally intoxicating. The few houses they passed were chocolate box pretty with thatched roofs and traditional cottage gardens, vibrant with early honeysuckle and bluebells. As they entered Sheldon itself the black and white thatched houses were replaced with traditional stone and slate roofed workers cottages, most probably still tied to the local farmers. They found Holt Lane just the other side of the tiny hamlet and followed the single unmade track. To either side of the road cows grazed unconcerned in hummocky fields and the air was full of birdsong.

"Simon, isn't it all so pretty?" Donna asked him excitedly.

"Yeah, lovely," Simon's response was gruff.

"What's the matter with you? You love this kind of thing, you love the country and thatched cottages and not seeing another soul around and you're being absolutely .... well ... so off," in her annoyance she struggled to find words.

He was prevented from his retort by the sign ahead, '*Dreams'* it said on a wooden board. They turned into the track and followed it up the ridge of a small hill and as it tipped over the other side, there below them was a house. A new house to be sure but so perfectly sited, and so perfectly designed to fit in with the surrounding country, set as it was into the side of the hill. Donna and Simon turned to look at each other in silence as he stopped the car on the ridge.

"Who do you think lives there?" Donna asked, not able to keep the excitement out of her voice.

"Well there's only one way to find out," Simon spoke resignedly as he shifted the car back into gear and they rolled forward. "This was it," he thought to himself. They crunched into the wide, gravelled, carriage driveway and pulled up. The house seemed deserted, no-one came to open the door, no dogs barked as might be expected in this isolated part of the country, the windows all remained tight shut.

Alighting from the car they rang the doorbell. It peeled out behind the silent façade, but no footsteps were heard, no click of a latch being turned. Simon fiddled with his keys in his pocket. Curiosity was now eating at him. Against his better judgement he pulled his own house keys from his pocket and selecting the new one amongst them he inserted it into the lock. It turned smoothly and the door swung open.

"Where did you get that?" Donna asked.

"From Mr Markham, it was with the letter."

"Do you think it's all right to go in?" Donna asked tentatively.

"Yes, otherwise why give us a key?" Simon stepped over the threshold with Donna behind, clutching his t-shirt like a child afraid of being caught in some misdemeanour. As they took in their surroundings they both drew in their breaths.

"Wow! It's amazing," Donna spoke first. Indeed it was. They were standing in a hallway, the floor of which was black and white chequered marble, the walls the colour of rich clotted cream and to each side pale wooden doors stood closed. Straight ahead a wide staircase lead upwards, branching out each side half way up, thickly carpeted in midnight blue, dotted with gold fleur de leys, framed with intricately turned banisters. "Can we look around do you think?" Donna asked in a stage whisper.

"Probably," Simon was feeling less and less certain why he had actually been pushed into this bizarre situation, but Donna now was becoming carried away with ill-concealed inquisitiveness. She stepped toward a door on the far left and turned the handle. The door opened onto the kitchen.

"Oh My God!" she exclaimed. "Would you look at this!" The kitchen was huge, filled with warmth from the Aga, three walls held base and wall units, all pale cream Shaker style with brass knobs. Donna's shoes clicked on the wooden floors as she turned a full circle marvelling at such luxury. "What wouldn't I give for a kitchen like this?" she spoke rhetorically. She ran her fingers along the cold dark marble of the tops, around the sweep of the sink and over the brass taps. "It is just so stunning," her eyes were shining. In the centre stood an island with a second sink, "What do you think they have two sinks for?" she asked Simon.

"Vegetables," answered Simon distractedly.

"How the hell do you know that?" Donna exclaimed in surprise.

"What? I don't know." How the hell did he know? Echoes of a conversation, a laughing voice, *'you must have a vegetable sink – it's compulsory'*. "I guess I read it somewhere," he told Donna.

At the far end of the room stood a large scrubbed pine oblong table with eight wheel-back chairs each with a plump, yellow cushion. Following the sweep of the room it opened onto a casual seating area with large squishy sofas and a giant flat screen television on the wall. There were bookshelves, which were bare of books and low tables free of clutter.

"Do you really think we should be in here," Donna asked again. "Maybe someone should be meeting us or something."

"I don't know," Simon told her in genuine puzzlement. "Why give us a key unless we were supposed to let ourselves in?" So they continued to look around, from room to room they wandered; each room was perfect. They could find no fault. They opened up doors to a formal dining room, a lounge and a library. All were fully furnished with beautiful furniture and the windows draped with rich, elaborate curtains. Other doors opened to reveal cupboards and the cloakroom. The final door was to a study; again unfilled bookshelves lined the walls. A flat screen computer stood idly on the desk, a multi-coloured ball bing-bonging back and forth across the screen. Finally they made their way up the stairs, feeling to go upstairs was even more intrusive but unable to resist, Donna due to awe and curiosity, Simon because increasingly he was filled with horrified fascination. At the top of the stairs they looked at the shut doors which stood like a circle of huge dominos around the gallery bound by the turned wooden rail. Seven doors, all identical, all firmly shut. The first one Donna opened was a cupboard, deep and wide with hanging rails and shelves down one side. "Hey, look, this is about the same size as the twins' bedroom at home," she told Simon on a laugh. "What do you think the next one is?" she asked, turning toward Simon, her hand on the handle.

"A bedroom, one of six," he answered in a flat voice.

"You don't know that, it might be another cupboard." She swung the door open to reveal a pretty girls room, all pale pinks and yellows, a real girls room, in the far corner another door opened onto a white tiled shower-room. "Well would you look at this," gestured Donna excitedly, "it has its own bathroom. It's obviously a girl's room from the decoration and it has its own bathroom. Could you imagine our lot with rooms like this, they'd die for it wouldn't they?" Not stopping for an answer she spun from the room and onto the next, exclamation after exclamation followed. "They all have bathrooms," Donna called.

"Yes, I rather thought they might," answered Simon under his breath.

Then she reappeared on the landing. "You have got to see this," she pulled at his arm and led him into the main bedroom. The feeling of sumptuous luxury was everywhere, from the thick carpeting to the silver satin quilt, piled high with beautifully embroidered cushions. Doors leading off revealed two bathrooms and two dressing rooms. "Look his and hers," Donna told him, as indeed they were. He walked the expanse of the room and sat down on the bed. Donna was immediately by his side pulling him from the designer perfection of the covering, straightening it back out where it had indented. "Don't, you mustn't mess it up," she hissed at him, reverting back to her stage whisper.

When Donna had had her fill of exploring they made their way back downstairs. "Let's look outside," she pleaded. Taking a key from a hook beside the back door she opened it onto a wide terrace and before Simon could stop her she was tripping down the steps. The house was cut into a hill and immediately below the terrace was a second terrace, "Simon, come here, come quick," but he didn't hurry. He knew what Donna had found, he knew it was a swimming pool, with Grecian pillars and hung with vines. He knew it with absolute certainly, for everything else had been just as he had once described should he ever be lucky enough to win the lottery, why wouldn't this be too? And so it was. Directly beneath the main terrace was a pool where the sliding doors could be opened or closed dependent on the weather. The water was a blue shimmering invitation of opulence, with the slight gaudiness of its Grecian theme done with such exquisite good taste that instead of being an eyesore it looked like a well executed joke.

"Oh my God!" exclaimed Simon on a groan. "Oh my God! Come on," he beckoned to Donna, "haven't you seen enough?"

"I can't wait to tell the kids all about it," she was saying.

"There's nothing to tell," Simon told her angrily. "Let's just get out of here."

"But what's it all about? I still don't understand."

"Neither do I, now let's go." Simon was pulling her back into the house.

"We had better close all the doors; I'll do the ones upstairs. I just want one more look at that bedroom." Before Simon could stop her she was dashing back up the stairs once more. He locked the back door and replaced the key and started to close the doors to the other rooms. At the study door he paused half way through pulling it shut. The coloured ball was still bing-bonging across the screen. Pushing the door wide again and with a furtive look over his shoulder Simon went to the desk and cautiously, as if it might be red-hot, he touched the mouse. The screen saver disappeared and instead, in bold blue letters, he read the words, *WELCOME SIMON, TO YOUR NEW HOME.* Simon leapt back as if he had been hit, just as Donna came in behind him; over his shoulder she read the words.

"What the *hell* does that mean?" She demanded.

CHAPTER FIVE

Simon and Donna stared at the screen, her with confusion, him with mounting trepidation.

"What does it mean Simon?" Donna demanded once more.

"I don't know," Simon hissed back at her through clenched teeth.

"But it says it's your home," Donna was looking from the screen to Simon trying to make some sense of it.

"I can see what it says, but I know as much as you," Simon's brain was working at double quick time but coming up with no answers. What the hell was he supposed to say? That he suspected he knew who had done this? That he had done wrong and this was the consequence? That this was some bizarre twisted fantasy? He so wanted to be somewhere else, anywhere else but here.

"Touch it again," Donna told him, but Simon remained frozen to the spot, who knew what would come up on the screen, what incriminating words. But Donna moved forward and left clicked the mouse. The 'welcome' message fragmented and was replaced by a screen set out as a letter. Taking a deep breath Simon read the words aloud.

Dear Mr Koweski,

By now you are no doubt very confused, however I am pleased to be the bearer of good news. An anonymous benefactor has instructed me to advise you that this house, in which you currently stand, along with all fixtures, fittings, furnishings, etc. is, from this date forth, 15th June, 2002, yours to own and in which to reside. As a condition of acceptance you may do as you will with the property, with the exception of letting or selling the said property, for a minimum period of five years. In order that you may enjoy 'Dreams' you will find an envelope in the top right hand drawer of the desk which contains further papers for your perusal and benefit.

Your obedient servant,
N. Markham.
Sylvester, Markham and Tweed.

Simon pulled open the drawer. Inside lay a folder, tied with pink legal ribbon, he undid the single knot and pulled out a sheaf of papers. Inside were the deeds of the property and a bank statement. The Bank was Coutts of London and it was made out in his name, in the credit column was listed the sum of one million pounds. Simon fell back into the desk chair, his hands shaking, the papers slipped from his grip and fell to the floor. "Jesus Christ!" he exclaimed in a low voice.

Donna was hopping about from foot to foot. "What is it, what on earth is it?" Not waiting for an answer she scooped the papers from the floor and read, as Simon had done, the bank statement. Letting out a whoop of absolute joy she flung her arms around his neck, raining kisses down the side of his face as he sat there as unmoving as a statue. His lack of reaction began to register and Donna pulled back.

"What, what is it?" she demanded.

"Donna, think about it. People don't go around giving out mansions and a million pounds spending money to other people and certainly not to people like me. It's crazy. It just doesn't happen."

"But it has happened," she answered logically.

"Yes, but we ... I ... can't accept this. I can't accept an anonymous donation of a house and money. From whom? For what? It doesn't happen to people like us. People like us work and struggle and somehow we survive. What the hell am I supposed to do in a house like this?"

"Well I don't know. Stop the struggle. Write. Become the author you've always wanted to be instead of just talking about it. I don't know why and I don't know how. Of course I'm curious but I'm not going to look a gift horse in the mouth. Simon you know the factory is in trouble, you know your job is about to fold, we are about to lose our home, in a few months we could be on the street, I don't know why this has happened. Simon you are a good, kind man, somewhere, somehow you must have done a good deed, maybe for some eccentric old bloke who remembered that and has left you this by way of a thank you. Maybe that lady who's shopping you carried out to her car was really the heiress to Woolworth's and she's repaying you for a single act of kindness. I don't know why, but I do know that this is a dream, huh! It's even called '*Dreams*', it's a dream come true, you can't turn it down. Think of it as fate. Think of me, think of the kids, what a chance for us all to get out of the hutch we live in now, to this," she gestured the expanse of the house by spreading her arm.

"Donna, see sense. People don't give you millions of quids for carrying a bit of shopping ...."

"They do if they're eccentric," cut in Donna sulkily.

"I didn't realise you felt we lived in a hutch," Simon tried a different angle. "It's what we bought together, I thought you were proud we had escaped from that bloody estate and had made something for ourselves. The kids will be leaving one by one, before you know it they'll all be gone it won't seem such a *hutch* then."

Donna was not to be swayed. "Of course I'm proud of what we've built up. We did get out, we have great kids, we've managed - but I'm tired of *managing*. I'm tired of not being able to buy a new dress because the kids need shoes. I'm tired of shopping in lo-cost stores just to stretch the pounds. I'm tired of eating mince when we could afford steak with this sort of money. The girls are always complaining that their room is hell because they're on top of each other, even the bloody dog hasn't got enough room to lie down. Simon, look at this, look around you, this is a palace, it's a bloody palace and you want to say no to this?" Donna's voice was full of pleading and exasperation.

Simon felt he was fighting a losing battle. He ran his fingers through his hair, what was he supposed to do? Should he own up? How could he? If he did that it would be the end of Donna, she would kick him out, his kids would hate him, and he could barely afford to keep them all now. He would certainly struggle if he had to find somewhere separate to live for himself, he just wouldn't manage, nor would he want to. "Let me think about it," he heard himself saying to Donna.

"Thank you, thank you," she flung her arms around his neck, it was the happiest he had seen her in months, the weight of drudgery, of every day life, seemed to have lifted from her face.

"I only said I'd think about it," he told her, trying to curb her exuberance.

"I know, but you'll do the right thing, I know you will." Simon knew he had lost. With a feeling close to dread for what the future might hold he knew at that moment he had no choice but to accept the house, the money, the change of lifestyle and whatever consequences it might bring.

"Don't tell the kids yet," he told Donna as they were driving home.

"Why?"

"I need to get my head round this a bit first," he answered.

"But you're not going to change your mind are you," Donna asked with a slight uncertainty in her voice.

"I just need to come to terms with it," he answered flatly.

"Okay," she responded, pulling her knees up and hugging them within the restrictions of her seatbelt. "Okay, it's not everyday you become a millionaire so I guess you can take a while to get used to it – only not too long." She was grinning from ear to ear, mentally already on a shopping trip with the girls. In her minds eye her hands were full of carrier bags. Not the flimsy ones like the supermarket supplied, no, the posh ones, the ones made of glossy card with rope handles; the ones like Liz Hurley could be seen carrying in pictures in the *News of the World* magazine. A million pounds, a million bloody pounds. Who cared where it had come from; suddenly life had become very much easier.

CHAPTER SIX

"What are you doing?" Donna asked as she walked into the bedroom later that same day.

"Getting ready for work," Simon replied, pulling on a clean pair of jeans.

"Simon, you're a millionaire, you don't need to work!" Donna's exasperation was clear.

"Will you keep your voice down," Simon hissed at her, "you know everyone hears everything in this house."

"All the more reason to live in the other one then," shot back Donna triumphantly.

"Yes," Simon said, trying to contain his anger, "you've made your point." He tied his laces with suppressed fury. He couldn't wait to get out of the house. He felt everything was bearing down on him.

He had one of those journeys whereby he couldn't remember one single second of driving, he was on autopilot. On reaching the factory he was three quarters of an hour before his official night-shift starting time, so he made his way to the office, which was closed but not locked. The computers were on idle, so he pulled up a chair and logged into his private Yahoo e-mail address. Choosing his words carefully he taped in the familiar address, which he had not used in over a year but which flew from his fingers as it had done so often prior to that. In the message box he wrote; *I need to speak to you, urgently, please return contact as soon as possible, Simon.* His finger hovered over the send button. What if it wasn't her? What if he was making a mistake? Then he thought of '*Dreams'*, the dreams they had shared, the conversation about his perfect house, the CD in the car, the date, there were too many coincidences, so he pressed 'send' and sat back. The screen flashed back at him that he had an incoming message. He went to his inbox and there was the message he had just sent, returned to sender, address not recognised. He checked, he double checked, it was correct, there was no doubt about it, it was correct – she had shut down her mailbox. "Shit!" He spoke aloud into the empty office. "Shit, shit and double shit!" Hanging his head in his hands he had never felt more trapped in all his life.

PART TWO

From The Beginning

SASHA

I didn't know I was capable of such feelings.

That day in the Ashmolean I was just browsing around, killing time really, I spent all my days trying to use up the minutes and the hours. Have you any idea how long a minute can seem? How long an hour takes to tick round?

Nigel, my husband, is a Management Consultant. He has his own business, Enderson-Zee; he has prestigious clients, private banks, government departments, international companies who need an image and his rare expertise. He saves them vast amounts of money and in doing so he makes vast amounts of money, which in turn enables him to spend vast amounts of money. We have an extremely grand house. Not a home, but a house, full of white sofa's and white rugs because Nigel likes to exhibit his wealth and white is the best way of doing that in the house. We drink only the best wines, the cellar is always full. The racks forming abstract pictures, a Bridget Riley dotscape of coloured foil tops. Most nights Nigel eats in town with his colleagues (or so he says). I, on the other hand, know my soap stars inside out and back to front, they have become a surrogate family to me - so boring has my life become.

Nigel went to Stowe and he talks with plums in his mouth, although sometimes he throws in the odd rhyming slang, which sounds totally incongruous but which he thinks makes him one of the lads, a bit like Guy Ritchie, really it makes him sound a total prat. I was not exactly bowled over by him in the beginning, but he was rich, handsome and available and I did not intend to be poor. I came from a pretty miserable background, and I couldn't wait to get out. I didn't know my *fois gras* from my *gross point,* but I learnt, and I learnt fast. When I left school, I traded on the one resource I possessed, my looks. I worked at shows and exhibitions, one of the mindless girls who parade their assets in the hope of selling a car or a boat or a holiday villa, so that the fat, greasy jerks who bought the car or boat or holiday villa at least went away with the impression it would help them to pull girls who looked like me. I wasn't really so mindless, I was learning all the time.

I didn't intend to do that kind of work forever but it paid well and I got to attend some prestigious events: The Open, Formula One, The Cheltenham Gold Cup, all the sort of places where one rubbed shoulders with the rich and famous and there was always the chance of a date or even better marriage. I met Nigel at Glyndebourne, where I had been invited to a corporate party held by one of the big software companies. He was, still is, handsome. He was, still is, rich. He was fun for a while and I suppose for some people he still is, only not for me. He started ignoring me a long time ago and he has never had much time for Annabel, our daughter – note, only the one child.

Annabel is beautiful, why wouldn't she be, she has beautiful parents. She is thirteen now, long and leggy like a young filly, she has my blond hair and Nigel's hazel eyes, with a smattering of freckles across her tipped up nose that makes her look a mischievous, happy person. She was fun and happy before Nigel insisted on boarding school. She hates it, I hate it, Nigel expects it and whilst he is still paying the bills and funding our lives what choice do we have?

So the reason I was in the Ashmolean that day was because I was bored. BORED! BORED! BORED! I have long since stopped letting my life revolve around clothes and shopping, there are only so many pairs of Jimmy Choo shoes a person can wear, only so many Prada trousers needed in one wardrobe. I can't buy anything else for the house; anyway I would be buying to cater to Nigel's taste not my own. Sometimes I dream of a life on my own, if I had my way I would move to a cottage with American Country furnishings, lots of muted checks and the smell of cinnamon drifting through the stable-door. I would live in jeans and carry my shopping home from the village store in a real wicker basket. I would not have monstrously sized crystal vases which the florist comes to refill every Wednesday morning with flowers which owe more to the hothouse than to nature. Oh no, I would have bunches of daisies in beautifully old, and maybe a little chipped, ceramic jugs. I would grow crocuses in old tea cups and tie the stems of my daffodils with raffia before plonking them in a jar. Nigel would die of shame if he saw a daisy in our house.

So having outlived the shopping experience I turned, as many a bored housewife has before me, to self improvement. I have done courses on art appreciation, Spanish and English literature. The more I learn the more I realise I do not know. Where I used to fill my days with facials and pedicures I now hunt out exhibitions and galleries. I trawl my lonely way through the echoing rooms to improve the void between my ears by comparing long-dead artist's perceptions of The Madonna. I am fascinated by The Virgin, what a lonely woman she must have been. I see it in her eyes. Artists make her sad and I share her sadness.

The physical side of marriage was never great with Nigel, I think his public school buggery left more of an impression on him then he would ever own up to me. I live my strange, sterile, celibate life. I do not disgrace my husband, I play hostess when I'm needed, I attend functions when requested; I am little more than a paid escort. I prostitute myself for a lifestyle and to keep Annabel in ponies and prestige. I have been poor, and despite my idealistic, wistful country cottage dreams I will not be poor again.

That day in Oxford I parked my Lotus in St Giles and wandered the streets, looking at, but not really seeing, dreaming spires. I took a circuitous route and found myself in front of the massively impressive frontage of The Ashmolean, the oldest museum in the world, in fact the first collection to coin the word museum. Ascending the steps I walked into its cool interior, my pumps making squeaking noises on the stone floor. I wandered from room to room, trailing my fingers along chrome framed, glass display cases, seeing nothing and caring less, until I came to the Chinese Room. There a small soap stone seal caught my eye, not because the seal was anything to write home about, not to my untrained eye anyway, but for the words inscribed around it which the museum had very kindly translated onto a card. I read them once, twice, and a tear sprung to my eye, *"In the cloud shrouded cottage, set before the flowing water, one can forget the troubles of the world"* – beautiful!

I stood there for a very long time picturing the cottage, a delicious little stream tinkling through a garden full of love-in-a-mist, poppies and cornflowers and me in a white dress, with a glass of Champagne, (my only concession to my present life), as birds sung and bees droned around me, my sense of wellbeing slid off the scale. The reality of course was that I stood with my hand flat on the display case, my palm making a damp impression on the glass as a tear slid down my cheek before splashing onto the case.

I was aware of someone beside me, he handed me a tissue and asked if I was okay. A stranger - a complete stranger asked me if I was okay. No one had asked me that in such a long time. To my shame my tears fell thick and fast and I gulped and sniffed and tried to turn away and apologise and thank him for the tissue, until nothing came out right and I laughed at my own stupidity.

"Ming always has that effect on me too," he said.

"Yes," I answered, "I really should stop coming in here." I hiccupped and finally gave a real smile.

"Can I get you a coffee or something, just 'til you feel better?" he asked me. Well part of me thought it was ridiculous and I wanted to escape as fast as possible, but part of me wanted to spend just a little time with this guy and his unsolicited kindness. I could go days without speaking to another human being. The part of me that wanted to spend a little time with a caring stranger won over and I nodded agreement. He took my elbow and guided me through a guard of honour of classic statues, who stood mounted in recesses in the dusty pink walls, watching our progress with their blind eyes, as we made our way toward the coffee shop.

"Why don't you go get cleaned up a little," he suggested as we passed the ladies, "I'll fetch the coffees."

Again I just nodded agreement and turned right into the toilets. My nose wrinkled in distaste at the stark grey, not very clean, room. Trying not to touch more than I had to I peered into the cloudy mirror. What a mess, my eyes were red and my cheeks burning. I washed my face and thanked heaven that I hadn't had mascara on, for I would have been a regular panda if I had. Having done the best I could without keeping my rescuer waiting, I made my way to the café and looked hopefully around. He was sitting in the second recess, two cups of coffee on the wooden table in front of him. He stood up as I approached and I was able to get a proper look at him. I think he had the kindest face I had ever seen. He wasn't good looking in the conventional sense, but he had all the right features in all the right places, his eyes were stunning, the bluest eyes imaginable, framed by long dark lashes. His hair was a dark, rumpled mess of curls, his mouth turned up at the corners, a mouth of perpetual happiness. He was slightly on the heavy side, maybe twenty pounds overweight. His clothes were clean, old and well worn and not a designer label in sight. He had on old trainers and jeans with worn-white knees. I guessed from first impressions he was five or six years older than me, maybe early forties.

We sat on the uncomfortable brown vinyl seats and drank our coffee and talked as all around the clatter of cutlery echoed off the vaulted ceiling and bounced back from the terracotta floor. We didn't flirt, there was no physical contact; he told me about his wife, his family and asked about mine. He explained that he worked in a factory and although he didn't say it in as many words I got the impression he was pretty hard up. I kept the information I gave out to a minimum. I didn't want to swank over my designer life. I told him about my gallery visits and my efforts to self educate, having, for reasons I didn't go in to, not made the best of my schooling. We laughed easily together and in no time the incident by the Chinese seal which had brought us together was forgotten and my tears totally dried. We shared a second cup of coffee, which I insisted on paying for. I was glad he accepted I was thoroughly enjoying his company. He was down to earth, said things bluntly. Things I would never have owned up to in a million years. A lifetime of conditioning had taught me to hold my tongue, but he came straight out, with no guile, no false front. As he said himself, 'what you see is what you get'. I liked him. I liked him a lot, which doesn't mean I fancied him; I liked him - as a friend. I didn't have friends. I was sorry when the second cups of coffee were finished but thought it would be a little over the top to suggest another, so with a mounting sense of disappointment I rose as he did to leave.

"Are you sure you're going to be all right?" he asked, as we made our way up the stone steps to pavement level.

"Yes, of course. It was only a silly five minutes. I'm fine, really I am." I wanted so much to ask if we might ever see each other again. Every fibre of my body wanted him to ask for my number, not because I fancied him, really it wasn't that, I had just enjoyed talking. Talking to one of my own kind had been much more enjoyable than I might ever have imagined, talking to someone who didn't base all their conversation around the mighty dollar. But he wasn't asking, he was starting to wave, starting away from the steps to peal off in his own direction.

"Simon," I called after him. He turned, "I ... I just wanted to say well ... thank you ... again." Stupid dumb fool, why couldn't I offer him my number? Well I knew full well why, how could I ask him to ring the house, or my mobile for that matter, it just couldn't happen. I couldn't risk Nigel finding out, it might be just the excuse he was looking for and I wasn't going to leave on those terms.

"S'okay." He smiled and waved and turned away again.

"Simon?" Once more he turned. "I will probably be here next week if you fancy another coffee." There I'd said it. A shadow of something seemed to flicker across his face. Oh God, I'd blown it. Then he was walking back toward me. "I just ... it's only, if ..." my words were stumbling over themselves in my embarrassment. "I mean, I don't ... it's just ... I ... well, I've enjoyed talking to you, I'm not trying to ... well ... you know." He put up a hand to stop my incoherent flow.

"I work shifts. I won't be free next week."

"Oh, well, okay, don't worry, it was only if ..." Hope dropped like a stone, my cheeks were flaming, I could feel them. The upturned corners of his mouth seemed to be mocking me, I wanted to turn and run and hide.

"But in two weeks I think I'm off, although I can't promise. If I get offered extra work I'll take it," he said.

"Yes, yes of course. Well if we're here, we're here and if we're not, we're not, no big deal, right?"

"Right!" But I think we both knew it was a big deal and we would both be there come what may.

SIMON

I love the Ashmolean. I love the little bits of people's lives which are there forever. People who lived thousands and thousands of years ago who have left a mark in the world. People who never dreamed that a pot, a plate, a hair slide would be being looked at across the other side of the planet by an ordinary man like me; a man who wonders now about them, what they had been when they had owned these little trinkets which capture time. Or maybe because I live in a house that is always chaos and noise, with four kids, a Labrador who likes to sprawl, and a cage full of hamsters that I find the museum is a sanctuary of calm?

Most of the time home is fine, in fact most of the time I'm at work, but when I do pitch up home I'm warmed by my family, even if it can sometimes feel like I'm little more than the bloke who pays for new trainers.

I met Donna through a friend, we hit it off immediately. She was warm and bubbly and I knew even from the first meeting that she was the one for me. I had to break off my engagement to Sally, but to tell the truth I wasn't heartbroken and I don't think she was either.

My mum and dad weren't around. My dad had buggered off when I was about three; I didn't even really remember him. My mum met Terry soon after, he didn't like me being around, I used to stay at my Grans and eventually I stayed so long that there was no point in me going home. It was sort of accepted I'd never go back to my mum, and certainly never live under the same roof as Terry. Gran lived on the Blackbird Leys Estate, a vast sprawling mass of 50's houses and tower blocks, ugly and void of personality. It was always rough but I made my way okay, mostly because of being Gran's grandson. She could be a formidable woman when roused. I avoided the gangs and pretty much kept myself to myself. I worked hard at school, and what friendships I did have were mostly forged because I let people copy my homework. I was determined to get to college and to get away. I had high hopes. I had dreams. Then I met

Donna and my dreams changed but I was still determined to get to college. I worked at Rowley Max in the holidays and I saved what I could. After giving Gran some I'd put most of the rest toward books, I wasn't much of a one for going out. Then Donna fell pregnant, we got married and she moved in with me and Gran. My savings went on the pram, the cot and nappies instead of books and my pattern of life changed – I stayed at the factory. Don't get me wrong, I loved being married to Donna, loved having Suki, she was such a cute baby, the sort of baby that old women stop and coo over. I'm a great believer in fate and destiny and it seemed my fate was not to qualify as an engineer but rather to weld computer boards which engineers could use.

Peta followed Suki two years later.

Living with Gran was difficult, two women under one roof is always hard but especially when they both had strong personalities. Gran was forever criticising the way Donna looked after the girls. Every week Donna took a percentage of my wage packet and tucked it away in the building society, 'Our Escape Fund' she called it, she had plans of her own and part of her plan was that one day we would have a home of our own. I must say the idea appealed – no one in our family had ever owned their own house before, as our savings grew so did our ambition to achieve our goal.

Then Gran had a stroke, a bad one, she never came home from the hospital and the Council in all their compassion gave us two weeks to vacate her house, so we were pushed into a decision sooner than we might have been otherwise. We found our house quickly, pleaded with the Council for an extension to stay until we completed, which they granted and so it was we managed to escape the increasing violence of Blackbird Leys and make our home in Fallgrove, a village south of Oxford. Fallgrove still retained its village appearance along its main street. White washed, timber beamed cottages sat with their footings planted in the very edge of the stream, and traffic still stopped for ducks to cross the road to get to the village pond. There was one old lady who had never been further than the neighbouring town, and when at ninety she died her house was as it had been a century before, and the one before that. Behind the façade of the old and rural, was a new sprawling estate, little boxes, housing little families like us. It may not have been our perfect dream house but it was a long way removed from Blackbird Leys. We loved it. In time we had the twins and the place was bursting at the seams but it didn't matter, it was full of love and laughter and I was contented with my lot. The walls were always covered in bright childish paintings, the corners piled with plastic toys and we felt we belonged in a real community.

I had always been a bookworm. I think the only time Donna and Gran agreed was when they were teasing me over my "book learning", as they called it. I was someone who became obsessed with projects, like the family tree, or my exploration of London, but once it was done it was done and I was ready to move on to the next thing. I never explored Oxford the way I did London. I think it's that age old thing of having it all on your doorstep and I just sort of knew it. There was always a thrill of excitement as I crossed from Cowley and passed over The Magdalen Bridge but it was so far removed from what I knew that I felt in awe of all the learned people who inhabited the rooms beyond those hallowed, yellow, sandstone walls. However I did visit the Ashmolean periodically. I was walking through the Chinese section on that particular day when I saw her. At first I thought she was a girl, so slim was her figure, but she wasn't, she was a woman. The thing that struck me most was not her beauty, although she was stunning, but her stillness. She was standing with her hand flat on one of the central exhibit cases. I watched her through the glass of a freestanding display, pretending I was looking at a Chinese horse as I looked past it to her. I stood where I was and watched her. I'm sure I must have stood there for at least five minutes and she never moved a muscle. I was curious about whatever she was looking at which must have stirred her to stand so lost in reverie. As I watched, a single tear slid down her face and landed on the glass.

I hate to see people upset. I fumbled in my pocket and found a tissue; it was clean, if a little scrunched up. I walked up to her and offered her the Kleenex. The flood gates opened and to my surprise tears poured from her eyes as she gulped and tried to thank me and tried to stem the flow. I just wanted to put my arms around her and say "there, there" as I would with one of the children, but of course I couldn't do that, so I offered her coffee instead.

We talked. We talked easily, the sort of conversation which is really enjoyable but afterwards it's hard to recall any of it. I felt comfortable with her. She bought the second coffee, which was nice of her and then it came time to leave. If I had of been a single bloke I would have asked her for her telephone number there and then but I wasn't a single bloke. Still I had a sinking feeling in the pit of my stomach when we parted on the steps to go our separate ways. Then she called my name, it sounded like honey on her lips. She was stumbling over the words, wanting to make an arrangement but not able to do so and I so wanted to help her out but I was assailed with a feeling of guilt over Donna and the kids - understandably. To have encouraged her words would have compounded that feeling. But then she said she'd be back at the Ashmolean and I told her I couldn't be for two weeks.

I knew as I walked away that, guilt aside, I would move hell or high water to be back there in two weeks.

SASHA

My life is pretty bloody miserable, miserable and lonely. It's a mystery even to me why I stick with it. I suppose part of it is pride, I don't want to own up to having made a monumental mistake. Part of it is because on the good days I enjoy the wining and dining - well I did, I think perhaps I'm not that shallow any more. A large part of it is for Annabel. She may not like being at her school but she is getting the finest education and if I had my chance over then I would love to have been forced to study harder and make the most of whatever brain power I had. The final reason, mercenary as it may sound, is for the money. Nigel may have his faults but being mean isn't one of them. He allows me to spend whatever I like on whatever I like and he never queries it. It's why in the years we have been together I have managed to siphon off a little fund of my own, well when I say little, it now runs into a couple of millions, not that I have 'borrowed' millions from him but what I have 'borrowed' I have invested wisely (with the help of a man who knows about these things). If I left Nigel I might have to own up to my little nest egg and that could lead to all sorts of difficulties. So, I do what I do and hope that it doesn't go on indefinitely, just perhaps until Annabel is ready to fly the coop.

I haven't had sex in twelve years. We tried a couple of times after Annabel was born, in an effort to produce the heir, but Nigel always had problems in that area and quite frankly I would rather go without than succumb to his limp fumbling. Twelve years is a long time, but Nigel has been an experience I am not keen to repeat.

Twelve years may be a long time but I don't think any of that twelve years has gone by as slowly as the last two weeks, I almost resorted to putting big red crosses through the days on the calendar, like they always seem to do in movies, but didn't want Nigel asking what they were for, so I just count them off in my head. Every time I think of that Thursday, and believe me I think of it *all* the time I am filled with such a feeling of warmth – goodness I hope he turns up for the two week date – well when I say date I know it's not really a date, but still.

SIMON

There has been a good run of overtime at work. As always I have taken each and every hour offered. We just couldn't manage on my basic wages, or rather we could but there would certainly be no extras and we've just about got to the stage where the children are old enough now where Donna and I can sneak out for a few hours. Sometimes we go to the cinema in Oxford, but mostly we just take Rosa, the dog, for a walk across the fields or something. We could both do with the exercise to be honest. I didn't seem to notice the extra pounds I'd piled on until I met Sasha that day. Suddenly now I'm aware of my gut hanging over my jeans and I wouldn't mind losing a bit. Not because of her but because it would be more healthy.

I've thought about her a lot, more than seems reasonable for someone I've only met once and shared a coffee and a few tears with. She was so different. She hadn't let herself go. I could see her clothes cost a bit of money. She only had on jeans and a shirt but you could just tell from the fabric they were quality and when she turned to go I saw the name on her jeans was Versace. She had on some bangles, I think they were gold, everything about her was understated and she looked so clean, her hair shone, her teeth were white as white, her nails were long, not too long, and thank goodness not painted in some garish colour, just slightly shiny.

I have been offered overtime for that Thursday when we said we *might* meet; well not meet, but just bump into each other. I turned it down. You should have seen the foreman's face - I thought he was going to fall off his chair. I tried to play it down but I think I actually blushed when I thought about why I had turned it down. I had to move away quickly before anyone noticed; I had to blow my nose to cover my face.

SASHA

I took a long time to get ready that morning. I laid in a hot bath beneath a hill of bubbles. The water was silky smooth and I ran my hands from my shoulders to my ankles in one long slow sweep, lifting my leg high out of the water, and I felt a stirring of something I had not expected to feel, the stirrings of something I did not entirely recognise.

I dressed with care, found an old pair of 501's in the back of my wardrobe which I haven't worn in so long but which are the least pretentious of all my clothes. The day was warm, I didn't need more than a short sleeved t-shirt, just a plain white one, cut quite low. When I looked in the mirror I was pleased with the effect. I appreciated my figure, my long legs, and my stomach, flat and hard from the thousands of sit ups over the years, and my full bust. When I was a teenager the other girls at school had teased me for having a figure like a Barbie doll but I know they were only jealous, it's a good combination skinny with boobs.

I slipped on some loafers and picked up the car keys. I wasn't taking my car, much as I love driving my Lotus I didn't want Simon seeing it, it really is very flash. I was taking the au pairs car, the Fiat. Not that we have an au pair any more, she left when Annabel went to school, but we keep the car because the housekeeper uses it for the shopping. I drove into Oxford and parked in the same place as the other time. When I climbed the steps to The Ashmolean it was a little before eleven o'clock. Although I'd said we might bump into each other there had been no mention of where. I pondered for a while and considered and dismissed waiting in the entrance or the coffee shop, both of those seemed just too obvious, and what if he didn't show, what a saddo I'd look being stood up. But of course he was going to show, I knew he would and I knew just where to wait. I made my way to the Chinese room.

"In the cloud shrouded cottage, set before the flowing waters, one can forget the troubles of the world", the words were still just as beautiful, even after staring at them for about an hour they were just as beautiful. I think the attendant thought I was plotting to steal the thing I stood there so long. In the end I took a writing pad from my bag and scribbled some notes to make it look as though I had a more genuine interest in it. While I was copying down the inscription I felt a hand flat on the small of my back, it sent electric signals through me that made me catch my breath. They flew to the very core of me. I closed my eyes, inhaled deeply and turned and there he was. I think my grin hit both ears and his mirrored it.

"Hi," I said. I didn't know quite what to do, whether to shake his hand or double air kiss as I do with people normally, in the end rather awkwardly I just kissed one cheek. "I'm glad you could come." He nodded back at me, the smiles eased off our faces and he looked into my eyes so deeply I thought he was examining my very soul. "No overtime then?" I asked, trying to break the silence.

"I turned it down." He was still staring at me.

"Oh!"

I was trying to control my breathing the way you do when you are really aware of it. I could feel my chest heaving as I tried to slowly inhale and exhale without sounding like a steam train, counting in for ten, out for ten.

He broke his gaze. "Coffee?" he suggested.

"Sure," I was glad to have something else to think about, walking without stumbling took my mind off my breathing.

In the coffee shop I ordered a peppermint tea, if he did kiss me, not that I expected it, but if he did I didn't want coffee breath.

As the previous time we talked easily. The conversation turned to his past girlfriends.

"There was Sharon," he told me, "she was two timing me for ages and I didn't know. I would buy her stuff and she would enjoy it with this other bloke. Then Nicola, she was fine but she started buying all those wedding magazines and leaving them lying where I couldn't fail to see them so I called that a day. Fiona, she was Scottish and only ever wanted sex where there was a chance of being caught, very exciting for a while but not every single time and bloody cold in the winter. Sally – I was engaged to her, she was sweet, but then I met Donna and Sally sort of paled into insignificance. Donna was the one, I knew straight away it was always going to be just her."

"What are you doing here then?" I asked him, looking straight into his eyes.

He stared back at me, searching my soul once more, "I don't know," he answered truthfully. "What about you?"

SIMON

I was racked with guilt all morning. I took a long shower, longer than normal. When I went downstairs for a cup of tea Donna was in a bit of a grumpy mood, "I hope you haven't used all the hot water," she fired at me, "what were you doing in there?" She didn't need an answer, she was just letting off steam, but her bad mood made me feel even more guilty, like she knew I was up to something. "What are you up to today?" she asked.

"Up to? I'm not up to anything!" I answered. I am such a bad liar, I've never been able to tell lies and get away with it, nor ever needed to.

"What - are - you - *doing* - today?" She asked very slowly as if she were talking to someone who didn't have English as their first language.

"What? Oh! I thought I would go back to The Ashmolean, I wanted to see the .... The Chinese Room again." No point in lying I thought, at least later I could tell her about my day with some degree of truth.

"Right, can you be back by three to wait in for the gas man, he's supposed to be checking that valve on the boiler. I have to take Ronnie to the dentist."

"Yeah, sure, no problem," I finished my tea, collected my bits together and left the house. As I started the car I breathed a long sigh, it wasn't relief it was the sort of sigh men must have breathed before they went over the top at Marne. I was going in. I could tell myself as much as I liked that this was friendship, nothing more, totally innocuous, totally innocent, but it wasn't. If it was why was my heart beating so fast? Why hadn't I told Donna? Why was I feeling so excited? I felt like a teenager again.

Over coffees we talked about my previous girlfriends and laughed about my mistakes. Then she looked straight into my eyes and asked me why I was there, with her, and I had to say "I don't know." That was the truth. I didn't know why I was there, I was doing everything I swore I would never do, betraying my wife, my children and my principals just by sitting there with her. However much I tried to justify to myself that it was nothing more than sitting and talking I knew and she knew that there was electricity flowing between us that could have powered half of Oxford.

"What about you?" I asked. "Why are you here?"

"My life is very strange," she answered slowly. "I don't work, I don't need to, Nigel, my husband, wouldn't like it." She was picking her words carefully, choosing what she would tell me and what she wouldn't. "I saw you that day and something connected. I .... No-one is ever kind to me these days. I provide a service for Nigel." I raised an eyebrow, she laughed, "No, not that service, Christ, definitely not that service!" There was a hint of bitterness in her voice. "I don't have any other family, my parents are both dead - I was an only child. My daughter is away at school, my husband hardly knows I'm there unless he needs someone to hang off his arm at some 'do' or other. I don't make friends easily. I suppose I'm ..."

"Bored?" I filled in the sentence for her.

"Yes, I'm bored," she answered, "but that's not why I'm here with you. If I wanted to relieve my boredom that way I could have slept with half the City by now, but I haven't. I'm here because ... you were kind to me ... I liked talking to you ... like talking to you ... and ... well ... you make me feel like me again," she finished lamely.

I studied her, her eyes were full of sadness. I wanted to hold her, as I had when she had cried. I wanted to sweep away the pain in her life and hug her tight and tell her that I liked her too. I reached across the table and took her hand, it was soft and warm, she hesitated for a second then wrapped her fingers through mine and we were connected.

SASHA

When his hand reached across the table to mine I wanted to stay there forever. I wanted to keep my eyes locked with his, swimming in blue pools of ecstasy as the warmth from his fingers, rough and calloused as they were, caused a heat to rise in me that I had never felt before, not with Nigel and not with the few fumbling encounters I had tolerated in my teens. My chin rose a little as I gazed back at him, I breathed deeply through my nose, I reached my other hand across the table just as he did the same so our four hands were layered one across the other, fingers moving, linking, unlinking, revolving slowly around each others, moving with exploratory tenderness as if they were making love, which indeed they were.

The world around us faded away. We were the only two people on earth at that moment, sound and vision blurred. There was only the depth of his gaze as he climbed inside my soul and read my need and answered it with his own, without actual words. We seemed to sit there for hours, his thumb stroked the inside of my wrist and I was lost in sensations so powerful I knew my legs would not bear my weight if I tried to stand. At that moment my knees would be too weak, would buckle and I would surely stagger and fall. I cradled both his hands in mine, palm up. Rough, workers hands, not totally clean, washed but with the lines ingrained from his labours. Calluses punctuated where his fingers met his palms. I drew his hands up, lifting them gently and leaning forward I kissed each of his palms, his hands were beautiful to me, and despite the rough skin his touch was gentle, warm and tender. I lowered them back to the table as slowly as I had raised them. I looked back to his face; his funny upturned mouth looked happy but in his eyes were tears.

I jerked my hands away from his. "I'm sorry, I'm so sorry," I spoke to him in anguish.

"Let's go." He rose from his seat; it scraped back on the floor making a grating noise. I too rose, terrified I had upset him so dreadfully, terrified all of a sudden of losing him.

"I'm sorry." I said again. In answer he took my hand in his and we walked from the café in silence. "What did I do?" I finally plucked up the courage to ask as we stood outside on Beaumont Street, "I didn't mean to upset you."

"You didn't upset me. You're beautiful. That was beautiful. I didn't mean to be soft back there, it was just, this thing, whatever it is that's happening between us is so powerful, and I don't seem to be able to control it. It frightens me and I don't seem to be able to stop it."

"Do you want to stop it?" I asked.

"No." He answered simply. My heart leapt with relief. "But," he went on, "my head is screaming at me to do the right thing and my heart is screaming at me to follow you." I said nothing. "I don't think I could stop this even if I wanted to." He halted in our slow meander along the road and he gently turned me towards him. He put his arms around me and pulled me to him, holding me tight, in a hug which seemed to bind us together. "I've wanted to do that from the first moment I saw you," he whispered into my hair.

"What took you so long?" I teased, and I heard him exhale as if accepting his fate.

SIMON

When I drove home that afternoon my head was in turmoil. What the hell was I playing at? It wasn't too late. Where was my honour? Where was my will power? In the end all that could result was a bloody awful mess. Wasn't it better to walk away now, before more people got hurt than just us two? But I knew I wouldn't walk away. I was falling fast. This wasn't about sex, this was not a quick bunk-up out of working hours, this was not some predictable but exciting shag with a beautiful and willing woman, who would walk away from me as fast as I would walk away from her. This went far deeper. This was a meeting of minds, a meeting of spirits such as I had never experienced. For God's sake I hadn't even kissed her and I was smitten in the way Mars would throw himself at Venus, or Samson at Delilah, I was so smitten I was even thinking in bollockology. What the hell was I talking about, what on earth was I thinking of? I was driving home to Donna and the kids. I was going home to wait in for the gas man so Donna could take Ronnie to the dentist. I would get home and maybe start the preparations for dinner, watch a bit of television, and cuddle up to Donna on the sofa as I did so and then to bed with *my* wife, in *my* house, with *my* children all sleeping soundly in their beds, not knowing what a complete and utter bastard their dad was. Because although nothing had happened in the accepted sense of the word, the truth was I had betrayed them all already in my very thoughts and desires. Christ I felt like a first class shit.

SASHA

I drove home in a cloud of happiness. I have never experienced such tingles, such absolute pleasure. I longed and longed for Simon to kiss me but he didn't and somehow that added to the whole joy of it because he obviously wasn't rushing me for a quick wham bam thank you mam! Well I knew he wasn't anyway, it was all too powerful for that.

I didn't feel any guilt. Don't get me wrong, I didn't want to get caught out, how seedy would that be? But I didn't have guilt, although I knew Simon was being eaten up by his. We agreed not to exchange telephone numbers, neither of us wanted calls to show up on the bills, either on our home numbers or our mobiles, but I did give him my e-mail address which is password controlled. He didn't give me his, I think he needs to set up one which the family don't have access to. I checked my e-mail as soon as I arrived home – stoopid eh! – But I was desperate. A minute apart from him is already torture, my mind won't think of anything else and it has been racing down avenues it has never raced along before. My fantasies range from tender moments to complete and utter abandonment and for the first time in my life I have stirrings which previously I have only read about and never really believed in.

Nigel rang to say he was bringing people home for supper. I changed and showered but I didn't throw my clothes in the hamper, I don't know if I have the smell of Simon on them but it feels like I do and I want to keep that for as long as possible. He smells good; his aftershave is woody, masculine. When he held me to him I breathed deeply and the softness of his neck on my cheek made me turn my face into him and absorb the essence of him. I didn't care that his clothes were not smart, that his shoes were scuffed. I didn't care that his hair had been badly cut or his hands were rough. I loved the feel of his skin, I loved the fact his stomach wasn't toned, I felt I could sink in to him, he was a comfort zone.

When Nigel came home his gym-toned body grated on my nerves by comparison. His Nutter suit was perfect, even after being worn all day it was immaculate, his hands beautifully manicured and totally devoid of sensitivity. Not a hair was out of place, he didn't drop his aitches when he spoke, his manners were faultless, he was so damn perfect he should have been in a catalogue. I pecked his cheek as he came through the door and resisted the urge to swipe the back of my hand across my lips to wipe away the sensation of him. I poured him and his guests chilled Dom Perignon and I asked about their day. I think his guests were impressed with his caring and devoted wife; I played my part – because that's what I get paid for!

At the end of the evening when we approached our separate bedrooms Nigel courteously thanked me, as he had thanked the housekeeper for staying on for the evening and as he had thanked the chef, taking the trouble to go to the kitchen to do so. All his staff thanked and appreciated. I climbed into my bed, between the cold Egyptian cotton sheets and I snuggled my face into the t-shirt I had worn that day and willed myself to smell Simon's scent mingled into the fibres. I pulled a pillow down and held it the length of my body and imagined I was snuggling into his soft, warm skin for the night, and that's how I fell asleep.

SIMON

If I could press the guilt aside I was flying, I could hardly focus on anything. I had sat curled up with Donna and watched some detective show on television, Donna loves police dramas. I had stared at the screen and not a thing had gone past my eyeballs. I was replaying over and over again my day. I had breathed in Sasha's perfume as I had held her tight, felt her breasts press into my chest, felt my desire rise. She smelled so clean, like delicate flowers, it took all my will power to pull away, I wanted more of her, I wanted all of her, but I also wanted to savour every moment, that's why I didn't even kiss her.

When the television show was over Donna rose to go to bed. We left the girls watching Graham Norton and climbed the stairs. When we were tucked up Donna cuddled into my back, her hands stroked down my stomach a clear sign she wanted to make love. I didn't seem able to rise to the occasion, which was not usual. "I'm sorry, I'm tired," I told her. She sighed, but was determined, she dropped butterfly kisses down my back, her hands smoothing over my hips and down my thighs and I tried to focus my mind on what she was doing but there in the forefront was Sasha, her face, her body, the intensity of her gaze, and before I knew it my erection had kicked in. Donna made a sound of appreciation and rolled me toward her, we made love, or rather she made love to me and I was making love to a woman I had never even kissed. As I reached my climax I wanted to scream out Sasha's name.

One more betrayal!

It was two days before I had a chance to set up a new e-mail address. Suddenly whenever I wanted to work on the computer I was assailed by children needing help with homework, or who wanted the computer to research some school project. I kept going back to the screen but there always seemed to be someone lurking over my shoulder asking what I was doing. In the end it was midnight before I finally got peace enough to set up a Yahoo account and send a short message to Sasha advising her of my new address.

The next morning when Donna was walking the kids to school and before I had to be at work I sneaked a peak at my new account and there it read '*you have 1 message*'. My heart jumped. When I opened it up her words spilled out, warm and funny, she wrote well. She told me she had slept with her pillow and her t-shirt and I could almost hear the ironic laugh she must have given when she asked how ridiculous that was. The thing with e-mail is that it breaks down barriers quicker than happens face to face, so I had no hesitation in writing back just how much I had missed her and that I couldn't stop thinking about her. I really felt about sixteen again, all that heady excitement of discovery and anticipation, it was pretty bloody wonderful.

SASHA

Sex had never been important to me. I had snogged a few boys at school, but I wasn't one of the crowd who lingered around the bike sheds honing their sexuality for future use. The boys I had kissed had been as shy and as inept as me, but most probably for different reasons. People always expected me to be good at that sort of thing, because of my looks I suppose. When I met Nigel I was not a virgin, but that had been through no fault of my own, mind you I suspect Nigel was, although he never owned up to as much. Or at least, if he was not a virgin, he was a novice where girls were concerned. It's not a subject that we have ever discussed. Our wedding night was fairly awful. Nigel drank rather too much, perhaps to get him through the ordeal. I was a bundle of nerves and in the end it was short, sharp, painful and messy and I hated it. During the first few months of marriage we sort of had an unspoken agreement that we would try for a child, Nigel then would have proved his manhood to the world. He hoped for a boy, was disappointed when Annabel was born, lived his own life pretty much, with just the occasional endeavour for a second baby when he arrived home drunk enough to contemplate trying. Attempts soon fizzled away to nothing. He left me and Annabel to cope as best we could with the aid of two Norland nannies and he worked longer and harder and dined out as much as possible. I wasn't sorry. Nigel may have been a good looking man, he may have had the body of Adonis, he may have been a good provider but when he climbed into bed beside me, as he did occasionally at the beginning, well my skin sort of retracted and I recoiled from his touch. That is why when I met Simon I was overwhelmed by the sensations he caused in me. I had never thought of myself as a sexual being and suddenly it was pretty much all I could think about. I wanted to romp. I wanted to give myself up to wild abandon. I wanted to explore every inch of his body, to familiarise myself with the very maleness of him and I found the thought very frightening. I was such a novice and he had four kids for Gods sake, he obviously knew his way around and I didn't want to appear a fool. I didn't know how to pleasure myself, how on earth was I going to excite him?

When his first e-mail arrived my heart jumped in my chest. It didn't say much, just basic information about his new address and that he was finding it difficult to find the space to write. I sat down and wrote back immediately, I was chatty at first, trying to be witty and entertaining but as I got more into it I found I was telling him about feelings, I even told him about sleeping with my pillow and t-shirt. Somehow I knew he would understand. That's the thing with Simon, I feel no embarrassment, I feel as if I could say just whatever I like and he won't judge me or think me silly, so that's why I told him how I'd slept. I didn't mention meeting again, I wanted him to be the instigator.

I was on tenterhooks until I received a reply. When I did I laughed out loud. He said he had missed me, really missed me - I was thrilled to bits. He asked if I was free on the following Monday and whether I would meet him in Maidenhead. He said he knew it sounded a bit sordid but he didn't want to run the risk of bumping into anyone he knew and the chances were if we met in Oxford he could. We fixed a time and a place and I hunted through my wardrobe to find something suitable to wear. I tried on about a dozen things, flinging them carelessly across the bed as I discarded each item of clothing for being not quite right. I was still trying to dress down and my clothes were so well cared for by Mrs. Bobbitt, the housekeeper, that everything looked as expensive as it was. In the end I decided it would have to be the 501's again and a different shirt.

On the Monday I drove to Maidenhead in the Fiat, much to Mrs Bobbitt's puzzlement, I told her she could use my Lotus but she shook her head in horror at the thought. I pulled into the car park Simon had given me directions to and there he was in a beaten up old Escort. A grin spread across my face when I saw him. He passed me a parking ticket he had already purchased from the pay and display machine and I stuck it on the screen. As I climbed from the car he pulled me to him and gave me the biggest cuddle, I half wondered if we could stay in the car park all day just like that.

SIMON

I couldn't even wait for her to climb from the car, I just had to hold her, and she felt every bit as good as I remembered, if not better. When Sasha had locked her car, which was a surprise to me, I had expected her to drive something a little more up market, I took her hand and we walked down toward the river. We didn't say much, but kept turning to look at each other as if trying to imprint each others features on our memories.

There was a bench facing out toward the water, I led her to it and we sat and cuddled like teenagers, watching the Canadian geese as they waddled up the bank. I couldn't wait any longer; I turned her to face me, put my fingers gently under her chin and guided her toward me. When our lips met it was in the softest, most gentle of kisses. All the delicate flowers of her scent seemed to be on her lips, her breath was sweet as honey. When I pulled away she raised her fingers to her lips as if testing them, and her eyes were full of wonder.

"Again?" I asked her, and she nodded dumbly, coming to me as if testing that it was as good as she had thought the first time. This time my lips parted, my tongue explored her lips, pressing them apart, I was drowning, drowning in desire and longing for her, pulling her toward me fiercely now, trying in our awkward position to merge my body with hers, kissing her with ferocity, with a fevered passion, my hands running over her back, wanting her so much, until we broke apart, both gasping for breath, our chests rising and falling as if we had run a five mile race, knowing that what was happening between us was unique in both out lives. I pulled her roughly back to me and hugged her hard; holding her to me and wishing it were possible to hold the moment forever.

All day long, until it was time to part, we were touching, whether it was hands as we walked, our bodies as we cuddled, our lips as we kissed, I couldn't be even an inch away from her. When the time came to part it was hell. We said goodbye then came back together for a final kiss, then said goodbye again and held each other tight. Eventually we had no choice, I had to go, had to get back to Fallgrove and reality, to go back and play the devoted husband and father, and I was both, only this thing was happening as well and I was fast spiralling out of control.

SASHA

When we parted I wasn't sad, I was floating on clouds of happiness. I laid in my bath later that night and my body was a different body to the one I had seemed to previously own. This body was a mass of tingles and nerve endings all jangling to be satisfied. This body had life. I could feel my heart beating. See my pulse jumping. I could feel the blood pumping round, rich, red, vibrant blood, pumping close to the surface, pumping its way to all my repressed sexuality, pumping its way to my very womanhood, pumping to my dreams of Simon, my hopes and needs. This was being a woman, this is what I had missed all my life, had never known, never experienced until now. The feeling was incredible; it was undiluted passion, a force so powerful that I felt out of control of my own body. I felt I would burst if I did not relieve the pressure. I climbed from the bath and wrapped in a robe. I made my way downstairs. Nigel was still in town. I poured myself a glass of wine and flicked on the computer. I clicked on to Simon's address and I told him. I told him just what I was feeling, just how much I desired him, how the sensations in me were strange and new and I didn't know what to do. I exposed my ignorance in such matters because I could, because I could tell him anything. I told him about the feel of the pumping of my rich red blood around my body and as I wrote it became stronger, more intense. I wanted him there. I wanted him to touch me, to take me, right there on the floor, I told him all that and pressed the send button. It was almost as if I were in a state of suspension, disconnected from the normal world, some sort of ethereal being floating in time and space, not part of this world nor part of the next. In the same state of disconnection I climbed the stairs.

In my bedroom I let my robe fall to the floor as I stood in front of the mirror and examined my reflection. Staring back at me was a woman I didn't recognise. I saw the inside of my thighs were wet, that had never happened before, I wasn't sure if it was right, but it felt right. When I climbed into bed my pillow was once more my night time companion.

When I awoke in the morning I was mortified. With cringing, shame-making clarity my e-mail from the night before came back. I raced downstairs to see exactly what I had written but Nigel was in the kitchen waiting for the coffee to filter. I couldn't dash straight to the screen so I wandered into the kitchen and we exchanged pleasantries as almost-strangers do. When he had finished his coffee and left for town I dashed to my study. The computer was humming with life, I moved the mouse and entered in my password and there was incoming mail. Before I went to that I re-read my words from the previous night – Oh yes, they were every bit as descriptive as I had remembered. What was Simon going to think of me now? Whatever had got into me? I didn't even know I knew things like I had written to him. What had I been thinking about?

SIMON

Sasha didn't talk about her home life, in fact when I came to think about it I didn't even know where she lived. She had given the impression that she didn't have 'relations' with her husband, to coin an old fashioned phrase. Although she never said, I also got the impression she was slightly naive, which considering how she looked was surprising. She could have had her pick of men. I saw such longing in her eyes I was certain she had depths even she didn't know she could go to.

When I checked my e-mail I was excited to see mail in from Sasha, but not as excited as I was when I read it. There on the screen was her naked soul and she was offering it to me, fuelling my fantasies with her desires. Just sitting reading her words provoked a reaction in me which meant I had to stay sitting at my desk and think of all the most boring things I could, but it wasn't easy. The pictures she had conjured up of her slim, golden brown body spread on a rug in front of the fire kept pressing the times tables I was trying to recite from my head. Her arms reaching up to draw me to her, her mouth hard on mine, our skin touching our full length from our toes up as we entwined and moved as one, was too powerful an image to dismiss easily. I wrote back. I wrote back in all my throes of lust, telling her how much I wanted her, what I would do with her, to her, for her. What I wanted her to do to me. How when we climaxed together we would be higher than the sky and I wanted to be the one to take her there and be led there by her.

When I finished I went for a shower, it was the only thing I could do, but I took her with me.

SASHA

We talk. He asks me what I want and I tell him.

"Do you want me to touch you?" he whispers in my ear.

"Yes." I reply, the very question sending sensations through me that stir fires inside. Hot molten liquid like the over spill from a volcano seems to flow through my body, as his warm breath tickles on my neck, and his words wrap around me, caressing me and teasing me.

"Where?" he asks.

I tell him. I describe in minute detail what I would like him to do. His breath becomes ragged as I press my body against his, and he tells what he would like. I ache with wanting. We snuggle on the bench by the river, or walk arm in arm along the road. When I go home the feeling is still with me.

I could offer to pay for a hotel, I have the money, but something stops me. Maybe I don't want to offend him, but I think more than that, I love the sensations he arouses in me, and I'm scared the reality would be awful, like it was with Nigel. I have learnt how to achieve my own release and then I tell Simon. I go home to my bed, pull the sheets right up to my chin and in the secret place beneath the covers, I let my fingers slide over my slippery wetness until wave after wave of the most exciting sensations wash over me, they flood out from the very core of me. I e-mail Simon and tell him everything and he seems to like that, it seems to excite him as much as it does me.

I sometimes have wondered if it is quite normal – this verbal gratification. When I asked Simon, he simply said, "does it feel good?" and my answer was a resounding "Yes."

Whenever he takes me to such highs, that feeling of other worldliness seeps into me, until I seem to be floating above myself, not quite of myself, and yet more aware of my physical being than at any other time in my entire life. I never want the feelings to end.

SIMON

I whisper into Sasha's ear all sorts of things I would like to do with her. My fingers entwine with hers as I listen to her breath coming in shorter gasps, and I see the pupils of her eyes grow large and black with desire. I want so much to really be doing all the things I have described to her, but I suppose I am afraid of the depths of my betrayal. I justify to myself that talking about it is not as bad as actually doing it – but really I know it is, because the effect it is having on me is all consuming. I live and breathe Sasha. I take longer and longer showers and she comes to me in a vision. She takes me to all the places we describe together. It is a total betrayal, if not in the physical sense, then most certainly in the degree of longing our times together provoke.

And then she stunned me. We were walking by the river in Maidenhead, hand in hand, when she turned to me, her eyes wide, her lips slightly parted and my stomach leapt with desire for her.

"I love you," she said simply. My own eyes must have widened in surprise, for she looked suddenly very uncertain, vulnerable. "I'm sorry," she stammered out, "I shouldn't have said it."

"No," I hastened to reassure her. "No, it's okay to say it, but I can't say it back. It's not that I don't want to, I do, but I feel guilty enough with what's between us. To tell you that would be just another step and this is already so overwhelming, and my guilt is eating me up inside. Does that make any sense?" I finished lamely.

"It's okay." Her voice was husky; her hand came up to the side of my face and cupped it gently. I kissed her, kissed her deeply, and I knew despite my reluctance to commit verbally, that I loved her too.

SASHA

It didn't matter to me that Simon wouldn't say he loved me, I knew he did, I saw it in his face. I admired him in a way for hanging on to some of his moral code. I was glad I had told him. It was the first time in my life I had ever told anyone, other than Annabel, that I loved them, and I *did* mean it.

Annabel was home from school for the holidays. She had gone horse riding with a friend for the day, which was why I was able to spend a few hours with Simon. He should have been doing overtime but had left work after his night shift on the pretence of feeling unwell. I supposed he would use the same lie to his wife - I didn't ask - he didn't say. This would be my last opportunity for a few weeks, until Annabel went back to school. The thought of not seeing Simon for three weeks was excruciating.

Annabel seemed to have had a change of heart about school, she was full of it. In fact, the more she talked, the more I could see her father coming out in her, and I wasn't thrilled to see it.

As the holidays progressed we seemed to be bickering more and more. I put it down to hormones, to the fact Annabel was a budding teenager, but it was more than that. Some of the things she said cut me to the quick. In one blaze of temper she told me I was common, an upstart, that she was embarrassed to own up to me being her mother. She said she was proud of her father who was better educated, better spoken, better adapted for *her* sort of life. Those weren't her actual words but that was the gist of the thing. I was stung to the very core. I carried my pain secretly, I could not own up, not even to Simon, that my daughter thought me cheap, a free-loader, but her words penetrated and spun circles of disgust in my head. She grew further away from me and my dreams began to veer more towards a life with Simon, and a better future than the pitiful one I had now. I imagined us in a little house, a house with American Country finishes, me baking cookies and him chopping wood for the winter fire. I wouldn't take my millions with me, I had found something better. I would leave with only my personal possessions. I supposed I would have to find a job. I didn't know what I could possibly do, but I must be able to do something. I didn't share my pipedreams with Simon; I hugged them to me, a secret, that one day I would surprise him with. I thought of it like pushing aside the wrappings of a Christmas present that has taken time and effort to procure, as you wait there is that heady anticipation because you know the recipient when they finally see what has been offered, is going to just love it.

So when Annabel dropped her ice cold comments in my lap I switched on the dream in my head, and ran away to '*the cloud shrouded cottage set before the flowing water*', and I forgot my troubles.

I had to go and make myself do things otherwise the temptation was to sit all day on the computer and pour out my feelings and needs. As I occupied myself with other things my brain clicked round like a Dictaphone, endlessly composing words to be relayed when I got back home. Every little thing I saw I wanted to describe, maybe it was because the world had never shone in such glorious Technicolor before. I had never appreciated the vividness of the greens and blues and whites of the landscape and the skies. Sunsets had never before produced such a fireball of oranges and yellows as the great ball of blinding light sunk in a red glow below the horizon. Birdsong was sweeter, children playing made me smile; they seemed to touch a romantic streak in me which placed them all in a Lucy Atwell setting. I gave coins to beggars on the street, and smiled at them, seeing them for the first time as people and pitying them their misery. I saw an old couple shuffling along the road, hand in hand they walked, projecting an image of fifty years of devotion, and I wanted to go right up to them and hug them both.

I imagined Simon and me fifty years on, shuffling along still hand in hand, our love having sustained us through the difficult times that were sure to come, when he finally told his wife it was over between them, and he wanted to be with me and only me. And it would happen –

it had to happen. All the sneaking around, the stolen moments and the furtive e-mails would have to end soon, because this thing, this wonderful, magical, heavenly thing that existed between us was too big to ignore, too powerful to be pushed aside.

Now Annabel has returned to school I will talk to Simon, tell him that I am ready to give up everything to be with him, to devote myself totally to him. To finally set aside my fears, and experience the reality of our lovemaking, to wake up beside him each and every morning with the heat of our bodies mingled beneath the sheets. To be made love too, any hour of the day or night is a thought too intoxicating to bear. To be able to just do the simple things: cuddle up and watch television together, or go to a movie or a restaurant and not live in fear of being seen.

I am ready to tell Nigel that I cannot be his arm candy any longer. I need a life. I need Simon.

SIMON

I think Donna is starting to suspect and I am a bad liar, my face betrays me even if my words try to convince her all is well. She asked why we no longer seem to make love. What could I say? I couldn't tell her that I have been making love every day, beneath the shower jets. I tried the night she mentioned it to become aroused and please her, but my mind was on a different body and I couldn't stop myself making comparisons.

Donna is not stupid, she doesn't watch all those detective shows without picking up a few tips – my overtime is down, but I still seem to be out of the house as much. Why do I spend so much more time on the computer? I bluffed my way through her questions and I felt like a heel.

What had she ever done to deserve this?

Nothing - absolutely nothing! There was such hurt in her eyes, and without words such accusation and I knew then I had to make a decision.

I've been seeing Sasha for almost six months, six golden, life changing, exhilarating months, and I never looked into the future but rather took each exciting day as it arrived. I was caught up on the rollercoaster ride of thrills when we were together, and was plunged into the depths of longing for each moment we were apart. But it is not real. It is amazing, it is way beyond my wildest dreams, it is my wildest dreams, but as I looked across the kitchen at Donna, with her spreading figure, the body that had borne my four children, nursed and nurtured them, supported me in my role of husband, father and provider, the anvil of guilt, which had for so long been precariously balanced over my head, fell, finally hitting me with a gut wrenching reality check.

I loved Sasha. I was elevated onto a different plain with Sasha, but I loved Donna more, differently, more realistically, more lasting. Idiot that I was, I was on the brink of losing my wife, my children and my home. I have never been kicked in the nuts by a horse, but I bet it feels something like I am feeling. Like a fucking, stupid, low-down rat. I knew then, I knew at that moment, with alarming clarity that I had to do the right thing before we all got hurt, before Donna got hurt, I could at least get that right. I would hurt, Sasha would hurt, and I was not looking forward to that but it was as if I was climbing from a thick cloud and the mist was clearing before my eyes. I was not a horrible person, on the contrary I always thought I was a pretty nice bloke, but for the last six months I had been living a life of deceit and dishonesty, and suddenly it was leaving a very sour taste in my mouth. Christmas was almost upon us and the boy's excited chatter as we decorated the tree all added to my burden of guilt. I stood outside myself and looked at what I had become.

When I checked my computer later that evening there was happy mail from Sasha. It didn't help. I replied. I arranged a meeting and I went to bed with a very heavy heart.

SASHA

Having made up my mind that I was going to make some life altering changes I e-mailed Simon in a very happy mood. I was pleased when he fixed up a new meeting, I was desperate to see him, it was probably going to be our last chance before Christmas. I wanted to share my news with him, to let him know I was ready to come to him. It would be my present to him. He would be pleased, I knew he would be, it's what we wanted; we had met in mind, in spirit, in dreams, now it was time to join our whole lives together. How could he not be happy?

I took the Fiat to Maidenhead and waited in the corner of the car park. I was there first. I bought the parking tickets from the Pay and Display machine while I waited. When his car pulled in my heart gave that now very familiar leap. He wasn't smiling as he usually was when we saw each other after an absence. He climbed rather heavily from his car. My thoughts immediately raced to the fact he must have told Donna, this was going to be so much easier if he had broken the ice. I tried to suppress my happiness in the light of his serious face but it wasn't easy. He took my hand and in silence we walked toward 'our' bench by the river. As we walked I began to feel the first stirrings of trepidation. When we sat down, on the cold slats, I didn't cuddle into him but turned to face him.

"What's the matter?" I asked.

He took a deep breath. "Sasha," he took my hands, he couldn't meet my eyes. My blood ran cold. "Sasha," he said again, "I ... this has to stop. I can't do it any more. I'm sorry, I'm so sorry." I sat stunned, looking at him. I had heard the words but the impact of them didn't sink in. "Sasha, do you understand what I'm saying to you?"

Did I understand? Did I understand? The pain shot through me like a knife. I rose from the bench and walked away a few paces.

"Please don't do this to me," I said in a small voice as I turned back to face him.

"Sasha, I would give anything not to hurt you, but this has to stop. I can't do this to Donna and the kids anymore. I just can't. You have to understand, please understand. I'm torn in two. I do love you, and I do want to be with you, but I just can't." There were tears in his eyes. He had said he loved me. He was trying to leave me and he chose now to tell me that he loved me.

"You can, you can do it. You don't have to be with me, just let's carry on like we've been doing. Just don't leave me, please." I was begging; I threw myself down onto my knees in front of him clasping his hands, tears streaming down my face. "Please," I pleaded, "please." His hand came up to stroke my hair and a quiver of hope rose in my chest only to be dashed away.

"I can't Sasha. It's over." He rose from his seat, trying to make me rise, but I wouldn't be helped up. I looked up at him with desperation. "I'm sorry," he said once more, and he walked away. I watched him go, his shape blurred through my tears, he never looked back.

"SIMON," I screamed to his fast disappearing shape. I saw him hesitate but still he never turned around, he just kept on walking, walking away, walking out of my life. "Simon," I sobbed into my hands, the tears poured from my eyes, "Oh God!"

SIMON

What had I done? I had replaced one guilt with another. I so nearly went back as I heard Sasha's anguished cry but if I had turned and gone to her I couldn't have walked away again - and I had to walk away.

I drove around for ages before finally pulling into a lay-by along the wooded road and I cried, cried like a baby, cried like I had not cried since I was a small child - if then. It would have been so easy to tell Sasha I had made a mistake and that we could continue, but then I thought of Donna, and while she didn't drive me wild with passion our love was safe, certain, secure and I didn't want to be an absent father. I had not known my own father, barely knew my mother, she was just a blousy figure who only appeared at Gran's whenever she needed money or if Terry had bashed her about just a bit too much. I wasn't going to be the sort of parent my children thought of with disgust and loathing. I would be there for them and if being there meant giving up Sasha, then that was how it had to be. But it hurt, it hurt like hell, and I prayed I would be strong enough to cope.

It was a long time before I arrived home but when I did Donna's sharp eyes detected my still slightly red nose and eyes.

"You okay?" she asked me, her gaze penetrating.

I turned my face away. "Yeah, I think maybe I'm coming down with something. I think I might just go to bed." I turned to leave the room.

"Simon," she stilled my exit. "We're all right aren't we?" If anything could have made me feel any worse that was it. She knew, or maybe she didn't, but my guilt made my shame even deeper. I climbed into bed and laid in all my misery wishing sleep would come and knowing it wouldn't. When Donna came to bed some hours later I feigned sleep. She climbed in beside me and whispered into the night, "I love you Simon." A tear slid from my eye and puddled on the pillow.

I threw myself into work. Made a pretence of enjoying the Christmas celebrations. I functioned. I tried to put on a good front at home but as soon as I left the house the sorrow, which now seemed an extension of my soul, lay heavy inside. Sasha and I had shared so many feelings and thoughts that everyday I was assailed by memories. Words from songs took on more poignancy, films all seemed to be about lovers parting, I couldn't look at the sky without remembering her words, her descriptions. Life was hell.

SASHA

My grief was like bereavement.

I don't know how long I sat huddled by that bench, when I finally rose my knees were stiff, my legs cold. The sleeve of my jumper was wet where I had repeatedly wiped my nose, I don't remember walking back to the car or driving home. The following days I was like a zombie. I didn't see Nigel, he came and he went. I lay in my bed. He couldn't abide illness and Mrs Bobbitt told him I was unwell so he kept his distance. If I had had my way my bed would have been a Tracey Emin style installation, but Mrs Bobbitt came and turned me out each day to change the sheets and administer warm soup. I ate as a child does whilst she stood over me. She was kind. I hadn't realised before what a kind woman she was. I tried to smile my gratitude to her but smiles would not come. Tears came in abundance. In a moment of lucidity I wondered if they could possibly run out before I ran out of grief, they had to, my grief would last forever.

I didn't understand it, we had been so happy. I had decided to leave Nigel and be there for Simon, how had I come to that decision and he had decided it was over. It was his wife's fault. It had to be. I bet the little bitch had confronted him, given him an ultimatum, made him choose and with all the ammunition of all those children how could he afford not to agree. What choice did he have? I began to see it from his point of view, began to see how she must have manipulated him. It wasn't his fault and it certainly wasn't mine but it didn't stop the aching inside.

It was two weeks before I could function again. I missed Christmas totally and I didn't care at all. Nigel stayed in town and had Annabel to stay with him at the flat; Mrs Bobbitt told them I was too poorly to be much use with the festivities. I was forced out of bed to cope when my period came, had to bath, had to be clean, so I washed my hair, put on clothes and those simple acts had a surprisingly good effect on my spirits.

I checked my mail, there was nothing from Simon, but that didn't mean I couldn't mail him. I didn't want to accuse, I didn't want to plead, so I just sent a simple message asking if he was all right.

The next morning there was a message from him. He wasn't all right but he was doing what was right. He was worried about me, he was missing me but he had to be strong.

I wrote back, I agreed. If I stood any chance of winning him back I had to be cool, bide my time and be cool. He loved me, he had told me he loved me, he couldn't walk away, I would reel him back in, slowly, gently, sweetly, he wouldn't even know it was happening, he would just come back to me willingly because he couldn't live without me and then his wife could go and look after her brood and Simon and I could be happy together.

I began to believe that there might be hope. I didn't bombard Simon with mail, but every five or six days I sent a small caring message and his replies came back, short but revealing. He was finding it as hard as I was to be apart, he didn't actually say that but I knew that was what he meant. I was encouraged. Then one day, when I was feeling just fine and thinking I very soon would have him hooked I received a final mail – Goodbye, he wrote, please don't contact me again. I tried, straight away I tried but his e-mail address had been blocked. I wept bitter, frustrated tears, tears hot with anger at this second rejection. It had to be her, it had to be. No-one had made me feel the way Simon had, I couldn't give him up I just couldn't, he should have been mine now. Weeks slipped by. Annabel had a couple of exeat weekends; she came home still aggressive towards me, although now with the surliness of teens, shrugging her beautiful shoulders with condescending distain whenever I tried to talk to her. Nigel actually took her into his London office one day, suddenly he was the bloody hero father and I was out in the cold. Poor, uncultured mummy, with her aspirations and her social climbing, she wouldn't understand, I could almost hear them laughing behind my back, their two heads close together, excluding me, shutting me out. Well to hell with them both, I had someone who loved me, he just needed to realise he couldn't live without me, that's all!

SIMON

There was something a little bit scary about the e-mails Sasha started sending. At first I thought she was genuinely concerned and I answered her as honestly as I could without compromising my resolution to be a decent husband and father.

I started paying more attention to Donna, actually taking her out and buying her flowers. She greeted my attempts to woo her with veiled suspicion, but when she saw I was genuine she unbent a little toward me and we began to laugh again as we had before Sasha. I still missed Sasha, sometimes achingly so, but it was getting easier. Then the mails started and there was just the tiniest hint of something I couldn't quite identify which made me feel wary. In the end I blocked my account. I wrote a brief, but to the point, goodbye to Sasha, felt a bucketful of regret and sighed with relief that I could now put a line under things and do my best to put her out of my mind. I had dabbled in madness for a while, I really felt that now, I had been bewitched by her beauty and her innocence, I had had temptation put in my way and I had succumbed like a weak and feeble man. I had sipped from The Devil's Cup.

As usual life was a struggle financially but we managed, I was using less petrol anyway. Days went past, weeks became months and Sasha was history. I still felt pangs of love, lust, a dull ache when I thought of her so I tried not to think of her. I was beginning to be happy again.

As I pulled out of our road yesterday I nearly collided with a bright red Lotus with tinted windows. I had seen it in the village a couple of times but I didn't know who it belonged to, possible just a visitor. It was a dream car, it flashed into my head that it was the sort of car Sasha should have driven instead of that little Fiat, but the thought vanished as fast as it had appeared. The car veered but it appeared to be all right, I drove on and it slotted in behind me. I slowed down to let it pass but it slowed down with me so I accelerated on, half watching the long, low red machine throbbing along behind me, it really was a beautiful looking piece of kit and the boy in me lusted after it and the realist in me knew I could never aspire to such lofty heights. The car stayed tucked in behind me all the way to my work, as I pulled in the factory gates it opened up its engines and roared off into the distance, a definite thing of beauty.

SASHA

I saw them together, Simon and HER! He was pretending he was happy, laughing at something she had said. She was a lump, blown up with so much child bearing and probably a crap diet, she looked like a chip buttie sort of a woman - a slob, with her ill fitting clothes, her fat arse squashed into her cheap jeans and her horrible hair. She reminded me of the sort of women who I saw every day in my childhood and I had detested them for being so common, with their loud voices and their stupid ways. He was holding her hand, like he had held my hand, only of course not the same; it was all I could do not to jump out of my car. Not the Fiat any more but my car, my beautiful sleek, sexy car. He looked straight over at the car, but of course could not see through the tinted windows. I stared back at him, stared into his eyes, "Simon, Simon, Simon," I groaned out, his name catching in my throat as a sob rose. He pointed out the car to *that* woman and they both made admiring sort of gestures, then laughing they turned away and continued down the road.

The next time he nearly saw me was when I had given up hope of seeing him from my stake out position that day. I couldn't park close to his house, it was too obvious, but I had checked his car was outside and then I had taken up my position in the village, which was the way he came when he walked the dog. I was heading home when he pulled out of his road and nearly bashed into me. I braked hard, the car skidded a little on the loose shingle, but I recovered and when he realised I was okay he drove on and I followed. My heart was thumping as he slowed to let me pass, I slowed, he speeded up, I speeded up, I watched his face in his rear view mirror, getting close enough to see his well remembered features but not so close that he became suspicious. I followed him all the way to his work before I peeled off and feeling totally exhilarated at the prolonged sighting I manoeuvred the car fast through the country lanes singing at the top of my voice one of my favourite *Establishment* songs, '*In My Life*'. As the words filled the car, bouncing around the interior it came to me. The lead singer's voice was deep and seductive as she sang '*My house is your house*', as she repeated the line I sang as loud as she was, for the germ of an idea was forming in my mind. I knew what I must do. I was giggling inside. It was such a stupendous idea. I looked at it from all angles to find the negatives but as far as I could see there were none. I would get Simon back. I would build him a house, his house.

One day we had sat in a coffee shop in Maidenhead and discussed what we would do if we won the lottery. I had made up some stuff, because the lottery didn't mean anything to me, I already had the glamorous lifestyle he imagined money could buy and it was pretty shitty, but he told me in great detail about his dream home. He had described a bedroom and a bathroom for all his small army of children, a playroom with a huge plasma television and squashy sofas to sink deep into. As well there would be a huge fitted kitchen, big enough for everyone to fit round a table. He took me on a verbal tour through every room before we ended up with the swimming pool, complete with Grecian pillars and hung with vines. Even at the time I had thought the pool sounded just a bit tacky but I had smiled at him as if he had exquisite taste and bitten my tongue. If I built him a house he could move, leave his crumby job, and not feel so pressured to provide for his family. He could pursue his dream of being a writer, he wouldn't have to work. I would give him a bank account to supplement his lifestyle. When he saw how settled everyone was he would be able to leave them, give them the bloody house and come back to me. He wouldn't feel guilty then because they would all be provided for; he would have money to pay, whatever her damn name was, her monthly alimony. He would have time free to come and see me and eventually he would know that our being together was the best thing. *'Gotta have you in my life'* I sung out as I rewound to the same track over and over again.

It started off as a fantasy but the more I thought of it the more I liked the idea. It would work, I was sure it would, of course I couldn't let him know it was from me, not at first anyway, maybe not ever, but when he was better off that would be one obstacle out of the way, it wouldn't be then like he couldn't afford to leave *her*. Maybe when it had happened I could bump into him accidentally and he would be so excited about the changes in his life he would tell me, we would sit over coffee, as we so often had before, and he would describe how an anonymous benefactor had bequeathed him a house so like his dream house it was uncanny. I hugged myself tight, chuckling, the laughter bubbling up in me, laughter I hadn't felt since the break up. I couldn't stop, I was so happy; I had some direction again, if only I could stop laughing. Wasn't it stupid? I wanted to but the laughter wouldn't go away, every time I was close to stopping I thought of Simon and his joy at his equivalent lottery win and back it came, gurgles of laughter until the tears were pouring down my face and my stomach was cramping with the pain of it.

SIMON

Donna and I really were happy again. The relief at having no complications in my life, no guilty secret, no excuses to make, felt as though an enormous weight had been lifted from my shoulders. Donna seemed happier too, the old Donna came back, or maybe she was always there and I just hadn't seen her for all those months when I had been blinded by unreality. She seemed to be taking more care with her appearance, she had her hair cut into a sleek bob, and she lost some weight and looked sexy as hell in her new jeans. I was proud walking down the street with her and we held hands like courting teenagers. Even the struggle with finances didn't seem such a heavy burden.

One day I was walking through the village and I saw the beautiful red Lotus, but I wasn't envious, interested yes, because that's the sort of thing blokes are interested in, but not envious, I had everything I wanted. I walked over to have a closer look. The windows were as dark as any I'd ever seen, but because of the way the sunlight was bouncing off I detected a movement inside the car. I went to knock on the window and ask if I could have a look at the dashboard. I tapped gently. The engine of the car roared into life, a deep growling tiger of a roar and with wheels spinning it sped off. I had to jump back to avoid having my toes run over. A shiver of fear ran through me. For a fleeting second I felt ice settle around my heart, I couldn't be sure, it could have been the light, but just for a nano-second I thought I had caught a glimpse of hair so blond it seemed the sun shone out of it.

I walked back across the street and into the post office cum general store. "Have you seen that Lotus parked outside?" I asked Mike behind the counter, in a would-be casual voice.

"What Lotus?" he replied, looking over my shoulder to see into the road.

I too turned around, "Oh, it seems to be gone now," I told him, "but I've seen it around a few times, I just wondered who in the village had won the jackpot and splashed out," I tried to keep my tone light.

"No-one I know Simon, and you know news spreads like wildfire through this village, now what can I get you?"

I walked home slowly, clutching the newspapers and bread under my arm, unable to shake off the feeling of apprehension.

"Are you all right?" Donna asked when I got home. "You look like you've seen a ghost." That just about felt right.

I kept my eyes peeled after that but I didn't see the car again, and it wasn't a car that was easily missed. As the days slipped by I told myself I had been mistaken and it had been a trick of the light and eventually the feeling of unease left me as the routine days ticked slowly round.

SASHA

He had nearly seen me. That wasn't how I wanted it to be. I had revved up the engine and driven off as fast as I could. My gift idea was starting to take shape and I didn't want to spoil it now by bumping into him too early. I resolved not to sit in the village any more. I would have to forego quick snatches of seeing him for the greater good. I had found an isolated plot of land and it couldn't have been more perfect. There was a decrepit old building set in the middle, an obvious knock-down, but the fact there was a house there already made things very much easier. It was nestled into the hillside with woods stretching out behind and a tiny stream running through the trees. I wouldn't have minded living there myself. Actually that was a better possibility, a better dream, when we finally got back together he could just pay off '*whats-her-face*' and he and I could live in his dream house, although I'd have to re-do the swimming pool to something a little more tasteful.

Sylvester, Markham and Tweed had been recommended to me by my broker when I had started to invest some of the money I had *borrowed* from Nigel. I had spoken with Mr Markham on the telephone on numerous occasions but we had never met. I made an appointment to visit his offices and he couldn't have been more charming. I dressed up. Gone were the 501s', I wore a mid-blue Dolce and Gabbana dress, simple but reassuringly expensive, with a small cropped jacket to match. I wasn't a fashion victim. I had found a look which I favoured and I worked with that. I teamed it with mid heel black court shoe and packed my few bit and pieces into my Lulu Guinness bag. When I arrived at Mr Markham's offices I was treated with the respect which my understated wealth deserved.

I outlined to Mr Markham my intentions. He seemed a little concerned, shocked even. "Is there any reason why I cannot do this?" I asked him.

He sat back in his chair across the fireplace from mine; his finger tips pressed together forming a steeple as he tapped them to his lips in contemplation. "No ..." he said slowly, "it is just a very unusual direction."

"But perfectly legal?"

"Oh Yes, I see no legal complications, but you perhaps should be aware of the tax implications."

"Well then, that's fine," I told him. "Perhaps you could draft the papers according to my instructions." I handed him a slip of paper with Simon's name spelled out. "I will be in touch soon, when building has commenced and I have some of the finer details which need to be inserted." I stood to leave and he rose with me, holding out his hand.

As I reached the door of his office I turned, "I need not say again, I'm sure Mr Markham, but at no time, in no way, is my name *ever* to be mentioned whilst you are acting on my behalf. As always you should not forward any correspondence, I will call you periodically."

"I can assure you that I will carry out your instructions to the letter," he inclined his head towards me and I took my leave.

Having found the parcel of land I now set about finding a builder who was qualified to achieve the quality I required from the plans my architect had drawn up. My architect was not a man I could readily warm to but he knew how to grease palms and I handed him thick parcels of banknotes in order that the Council would approve the plans in record time. I needed a builder who could follow my instructions to the letter. I found money does talk. I promised an inflated payment if the work was started immediately and bonuses if it was completed within the specified time frame. I estimated a year. It was a long process, but it would be worth it and anyway, a year would bring us round to June and what better time to present such a gift, what a perfect anniversary present.

I visited the site every day, and became quite offay with builders parlance as I learnt all about footings, damp courses and drainage. The day the wet concrete lorries arrived and poured in their loads for the foundations was hugely exciting. The thick grey liquid came spilling out of their bellies and spread and settled. I watched from a safe distance as the builders worked fast to rake it level before it set. It was taking shape, my dream, Simon's dream, it was all coming together. I was feeling so alive, so excited, at the prospect of seeing how thrilled he would be, how excited he would become when he knew that the drudgery of his now-life would be ending. I had to calm myself down because there was a danger that the gurgle-laugh would start again and I didn't want to be standing there next to Mr Nicholls, my builder, and not be able to stop.

As well as checking on the builder's progress each day I also had to shop. Furnishings and finishes had to be purchased and my years of retail therapy were paying off as I trawled through furniture stores to find exactly the right pieces. My handbag was filled with swatches and colour samples; I tucked them away at night into the back of my wardrobe lest Nigel caught a glimpse of them on one of his rare visits home. Nigel was spending more and more time at his flat in town, the one he had bought for convenience when he was working late, but really I knew it was more than that; I wondered sneeringly how many 'friends' he entertained at his flat. The distance between us had widened to an unassailable breech, but that was absolutely fine by me, it was a huge effort now to be even moderately polite to him. When he did show up at the house Mrs Bobbitt saw to all his domestic needs and I kept my distance. Annabel seemed to prefer to holiday with her friends, she skied with Gemma, went on a yacht to the Bahamas with Amelia and it was with some reluctance she now only came home for her exeats, if she couldn't secure an invitation elsewhere. Those weekends she now spent with Nigel, he took her to the theatre and out to dinner, at restaurants totally unsuitable for a thirteen year old girl, or was she fourteen now? I suppose she was. I was *persona non gratis*, she didn't want to know me.

I hadn't realised what hard work it was building a house, well not the actual building of it but quite how many decisions had to be made.

My head was spinning with the choice of taps, floorings, door furniture and a thousand other little details. Mr Nicholls suggested an interior designer and for a moment I was tempted, but I dismissed the notion. This was my project, mine, my gift to Simon. I still wasn't sure if I would ever tell him, I would have to see how things went, but if I ever did I wanted him to be proud of me for having achieved so much of it on my own. So I continued to dedicate my days to the monumental task, with my eye on the future.

SIMON

Things were really good at home between Donna and me, it was far more than I deserved and when I looked back and realised what a hash I could have made of it all my shame ran deep.

However such is life that when one thing goes well another thing comes along to kick you in the teeth just to make sure that you aren't getting too comfortable. It seemed in the world wide market, sales of electronic components were down. A small recession the papers said, a blip the bosses at Rowley Max called it, but while we were 'blipping' the overtime was cut, first to a minimum and then to nothing. For years we had relied on my overtime payments as part of my wages, to lose it now meant we were going to struggle.

"How are we going to manage?" Donna asked me in a desperate voice as we lay in bed that night.

I took her in my arms and held her tight, "I don't know Donna, but there are more important things in life than money."

"Yes, yes you're right, we'll manage somehow," she held me back as tight as I was holding her and a flood of warmth spread through me for her.

It was a struggle. At first all the luxuries stopped, I didn't bother with things like a daily paper any longer, every penny helped. Donna had always been a prudent shopper so there wasn't much to be shaved off the weekly food bill but crisps and snacks went by the board and the kids had to fill up with bread if they were hungry. There was no more *'snap crackle and pop'* we all ate porridge," more healthy anyway," said Donna as the kids turned their noses up in disgust. We were never going to starve but it was hard. I obviously had more time to be at home, the poor dog had never been so well exercised. I walked that dog everywhere. I couldn't stay shut up in the house, I wasn't used to it. The countryside was beautiful; as the months passed I saw it turn from the dull browns and greys of winter into a green and pleasant land. The farmers prepared their fields. Rich earth turned in wet clods behind their ploughs and in a few weeks shoots began to appear. Lime green at first in their spring newness, then darkening as they gained strength. In no time it seemed the countryside had been painted from a child's colouring box as the lurid yellow of the rapeseed covered acre after acre, filling the air with its pungent and slightly repulsive smell. The wild flowers grew in abundance and I would often sit on a fallen tree and lose myself in their delicate beauty, as Rosa ran hither and thither, pretending she was the best rabbiter in the whole world and never catching a thing. She began to lose weight with her increased exercise, I began to lose weight. I felt fitter than I had done in years, my skin tanned and my shoes wore down.

One day I arrived home, no one had realised I was back, I heard Donna and Suki shouting at each other. Suki had always been the most argumentative of the children. At first I couldn't hear what they were saying but as I drew closer I caught her words.

"It's so unfair mum, everyone's going."

"Suki, I've explained about ten times now. I've said no. We can't afford to help you with the tickets, we just can't. We've all given up things. I know it's hard but you'll just have to get over it."

"I hate this family. I'll never get another chance." Suki stormed at her and I heard the door bang and the thud, thud, thud of footsteps on the stairs before the door upstairs was slammed with equal vehemence.

When I entered the room Donna was furiously polishing the wall unit, her anger finding its vent in the rapid circular movements as she worked her way along the shelf until there was a scramble, an attempt to catch the flying ornament, and a smash of china on the floor. "Oh Shit!" she exclaimed and to my dismay she burst into tears. I rushed to her side, she jumped slightly. "I didn't hear you come in," she threw at me almost accusingly.

"Sit there," I told her, "I'll go and put the kettle on – tea's the great healer," I tried to joke. Whilst the kettle boiled I swept the broken pieces of the ornament into the dustpan, it was shattered into too many pieces to repair. It had been a baby in a cradle. It had been the gift I had given Donna after Suki had been born. I understood exactly why she was so upset. I went back into the room with mugs of tea and sat down beside her as we both silently sipped at the warm brew.

"I was talking with one of the guys in packing the other day," I told her, "he said there might be a chance for some minicab work for me through a mate of his."

"You don't have to do that Simon. You never know who you'd pick up."

"Donna," I told her, "I'm big enough and ugly enough to look after myself."

"Not so big now," she said poking my trimmer waistline.

"But still ugly eh?"

"Yeah, still ugly," but she was smiling again now and she nudged me with her shoulder to let me know she was joking.

It is the most bloody awful job. I'm out half the night, and that's after my day shift at the factory. Pick-ups are normally drunk and the language is nearly always foul, the jokers pathetic, although they think they're funny, and there is always the threat of someone throwing up in the back of your motor. I hate it and I hate that I'm so bloody tired all the time. I don't tell Donna, I just hand her the extra money and fall into bed and sleep. I think its helping, I'm too knackered to even notice.

I am no longer aware of the changing of the seasons and Rosa has almost forgotten what rabbits look like, the days are long and the nights longer but neither of them in a pleasant way.

Then Rowley Max started making layoffs. Rumours were rife and we all waited to see where the axe would fall next.

SASHA

It was all taking shape. The builders had done an excellent job and each new stage had been thrilling to watch as out of nothing a huge shell had grown, at first breezeblock grey, then plastered, and finally painted and looking like a proper house. When the flooring was laid it really did look absolutely gorgeous. I made sure I always slipped off my shoes so my stiletto heels did not damage the new wood. As I wandered from room to room to inspect, my fingers trailed along the shiny wooden handrail of the banister, along the doors of the fitted wardrobes, along the sink and shower cubicle which would soon be Simons. In the mirror I almost felt I could see his reflection as he leaned slightly forward to shave, his face whited out with foam. I leaned back against the towel rail and I watched him, he winked over at me. I walked forward to cuddle into his back and my legs bumped into the side of the unit top, Simon's image evaporated. "Silly," I admonished myself, shaking my head, for he had seemed very real.

I had enormous fun when the furniture began to arrive, making sure it was all in the correct rooms, all angled just so. The lady from the curtain shop hung the drapes, with their swags and tails set perfectly. I made up beds myself, fluffing up quilts and pillows. Simon's bed was like a prop in a film, huge, swathed in its silver satin cover, a mountain of embroidered pillows resting against the antique brass headboard. I tried not to think of *her* in it as well, but that would only be for a short time. When I came to live here, when Simon finally came to his senses and got rid of '*The Elephant Woman*' I would replace this bed for one of our own, unsoiled by *that* woman. As I stood admiring the effect I wondered which side would be Simons, closest to the door probably, that's what men did. I smoothed my hands over the cover and murmured his name.

"Simon," I whispered, as I climbed between the sheets, pulling them up to my chin. "Simon," I whispered, as I moved my hands across my body, cupping my breasts, spanning across my flat stomach.

"Simon," I whispered, as I unzipped my jeans and let my fingers slide inside my panties. "Simon," I called into the empty house, as he lay beside me watching me as my back arched and he brought me to a shuddering climax. "Simon," I whispered, as I lay there in his arms, my eyes closing as I breathed in his musky, male smell. One day. One day soon.

SIMON

The axe did fall.

Rowley Max was set to close down and the hundreds of workers would be joining the dole queue. With a mixture of guilt and relief I remained as one of a skeleton staff, my hours cut to part time and my wages slashed too. I continued with the mini-cabbing, working all the hours I could, straight from the factory, weekends, and all for little more return than I had been getting when I was doing only nights. By the time I had paid out for petrol and given the owner his percentage I wasn't left with enough to cope. The owner assured me it would pick up with the summer coming and the promise of the airport runs, but it wasn't coming fast enough. The mortgage slid into arrears. One month, two months, three months and I wasn't able to make the payments. I hung my head in my hands in despair. It wouldn't be long and the building society would repossess the house. I felt absolutely wretched, at the end of my tether, what had I brought Donna and the children too?

Then the letter arrived from Sylvester, Markham and Tweed.

SASHA

I was on tenterhooks all day. 15th June. I knew that Simon would make the connection; I thought that had been rather clever on my part. There were times that I thought it wasn't going to happen, for a while the builders had been delayed by rain, then the curtain lady had messed up on one of the rooms, I had to kick up stink about her redoing them, but she couldn't afford not to, my order was too big for her to mess me about. She could be not paid for any of it or she could do as I had originally ordered and get the thing done on time. In the end she saw it my way.

I wished I could have been a fly on the wall and seen Simon's reaction when he first saw everything, it was all as he had described as we had sheltered in *The Coffee Pot* in Maidenhead, one wet and windy day. That had been a good day, we had snuggled together and it was as if we had been planning our own home. I know sometimes I had had to bite my tongue when he had said something I thought a bit naff, like the swimming pool, and I had had to put him right on a few things, educate him, like on the sink for vegetables, but on the whole he hadn't had bad ideas and now I had seen them through to fruition and added my own touches I have to say it all looked fine, excellent in fact. But how I wished I could have seen his face.

I toyed with the idea of putting in a camera linked to the computer, but the thought of seeing *that* woman with him just made my blood boil, he needed to get that sorted and sorted soon if we were to have any chance. I bet his jaw dropped when he saw the message on the computer screen and I bet even more he was stunned when he saw the bank statement. That was so brilliant, giving him enough to fund his new life, to take away the worry. I felt like a fairy godmother. He could buy a new car, invest some, spend some, maybe I would get Mr. Markham to suggest ways in which the money could be used to his advantage, after all when we got together I didn't want to be poor and quite frankly I didn't have a lot of my own money left now. As always with these projects whatever the first figure is it is best to double it. I hadn't quite run to double but I had certainly spent a lot more on furnishings than I originally intended. I think that Simon would have been just as happy with cheaper finishes, probably wouldn't have known the difference, but I wanted him to have the best, he deserved it. When I moved into '*Dreams*' I would work on revamping his wardrobe, educate him about men's fashion, I could picture him in some beautiful linen trousers and a crisp white shirt, so sexy, so sophisticated, he had potential, he definitely had potential in that area.

SIMON

I couldn't stop Donna and I couldn't find a way of getting out of the nightmare. It didn't matter which way I looked at it I was stuffed. If I owned up to Donna about Sasha I would be history. There was no way she would condone my betrayal; although I had never actually slept with Sasha who would believe that? Who would believe a woman could, in this mad and convoluted way, sort out a house and a bank account with more zeros than that, for a man she had not at least been shagged stupid by? What a fool I had been, what a sad, idiotic fool!

For the last eighteen months not a day had gone by when I haven't berated myself for my behaviour, or haven't felt a deep remorse and an even deeper regret. My one saviour was that Donna had never found out and I hadn't had to face those consequences, but now here I was, caught like a rabbit in the headlights of a fast moving vehicle, and I felt I was on the verge of being splattered. If I told Donna I would be out, if I didn't accept the house Donna would want to know why, and what could I tell her? We were so far in debt that we were in danger of losing everything, maybe even splitting up the kids. Christ – what could I do?

The next morning Donna had told the children. I came downstairs to wild excitement. I was furious with her. I had wanted more time, ostensibly to get used to the idea, but truthfully to find a get out clause. They were all clamouring to go and visit the place; I felt I was being dragged deeper and deeper into the quicksand. The thing with quicksand is not to struggle and hope for rescue, so I stopped struggling and bowed to what now seemed the inevitable, however instead of expecting rescue I rather thought the quicksand would end up sucking me down and to my last bubbling gasp I would be waiting for escape and knowing I was in too deep for help to ever arrive.

When I was showered and dressed I telephoned Mr Markham, he confirmed the house was mine, the money was mine and I was to just "move in." It was surreal.

SASHA

If I drove along the back lanes I could park my car and cut through the woods to the boundary of '*Dreams*', from there it was easy access, the fence was just a marker of the edge of the property, it was not designed to keep people out. Sometimes I spent the whole day up there in the woods. I got so cosy I even used to take a flask of coffee and tuck in. Through my binoculars I could see the house and catch glimpses of Simon as he went about his business. My vantage point gave me a clear view of his study; he sat for hours in front of the computer not doing anything at all, just staring into the screen, or out of the window. I wanted to go and fire his imagination, give him all the ideas he needed for the book he always wanted to write. I could have done that. *That* woman just seemed to revel in cleaning the kitchen, she was so common, fancy not even hiring a cleaner, but as far as I was concerned it kept her out of the way. When they did seem to come together I detected Simon's weary resignation toward her. There wasn't any hand holding going on now. I couldn't have been more pleased, her days were surely numbered and I would be there to pick up the pieces and get my beloved Simon back on his feet. We would be happy; I would make sure he was happy. I stood and stretched, I reached my arms above my head easing my muscles, rubbing my back on the rough bark of the tree as I rotated my head on my shoulders to ease the tension.

I heard the dog barking. Simon was gone from his study window, he must be about to take that hound for it's exercise, he spent too long with that dog, when I was mistress of '*Dreams*' I wouldn't want that thing - so smelly and horrible! Simon was far too fond of it as far as I could see. For now though if they were coming into the woods I needed to disappear. I gathered up my belongings and scrambled back to the lane and my car.

SIMON

I couldn't shake off the feeling of being watched. Part of me wondered in all this madness whether the house had been wired with cameras – would she be so crazy. Who knew? Anything now seemed possible.

Donna had settled into the house in no time, she seemed to thrill just wiping down the kitchen units, to see the vast, gleaming expanse of black marble as shiny and bright as the day we had moved in. The cupboards were packed with food in her determination we would never go hungry and do without again. All day long she cleaned and polished and admired, her enthusiasm pushing as much of a wedge between us as my disinterest in the whole ghastly set-up.

The kids were in seventh heaven too, each with their own room and with the swimming pool to play in whenever they chose. When she was home from 'Uni' even Suki seemed to lose her aggressive edge as she floated on a lilo in the water, drifting lazily until one of her brothers would 'bomb' her, drenching her with water which rose in a fountain and sprayed everywhere. Peta stayed where she was as it was her 'A' level year, but the boys settled into their new school with ease. Donna now had her own car to ferry them back and forth. I held on to my old beaten up Escort, clinging on to my modicum of normality. I could not bring myself to touch the money, although Donna was doing a pretty good job for both of us.

It was eerie, the feeling of eyes on me. I looked everywhere but saw nothing. Day after day I sat in 'my' study. For years I had nurtured the dream of writing a best seller, or even a minor seller, now I had the time not a single word would form. So I sat and looked through the window into the woods with blank eyes. Only occasionally noticing the green woodpeckers flitting from bough to bough, barely registering the rabbits which braved the edge of the lawn to nibble on the grass, or the grey squirrels which scampered in and out of the branches with sharp clicking noises, all sights which would have held me enthralled previously. It was all there and I suppose some small portion penetrated my sub-conscience but nothing made any real impression on me.

Then I saw it! A flash of something bright! It was there and gone in a fraction of a second. It was so quick I questioned myself as to whether it had been real. I ran from the study.

"Where are you going?" called Donna from the hallway. I didn't answer. Rosa came running from her basket as I flung open the front door and ran for the trees, she ran with me excited at this unexpected jaunt. I raced up the slope into the woods, scrambling through the bracken, through the trees to where I thought I had detected the glint of light. My breath was ragged, my heart beating so hard in my chest that I thought I might burst and I didn't care. I ran, looking this way and that, looking for what could have made the sudden reflection of light. Nothing! There was nothing there. By the time I reached the top of the rise I had slowed to an exhausted, grappling, climb, bent almost double as I fought for air. The only sound was my pumping breath as I held onto a young oak tree for support. But no, not the only sound, there in the distance the roar of a car's engine being started and being driven at speed. The throbbing, pulsating roar of a high performance sports car, the roar of a red Lotus perhaps? I sat down on the ground my head in my arms. Rosa came and nuzzled into me, pushing me with her nose, checking I was all right. I put my arms around her neck and burrowed into her soft golden fur, feeling I had all the misery in the world pressing down on me.

It was a catalyst, the glint of light had been real, the car engine had been real, and it shook me from my tauper. I couldn't sit around and do nothing, something was happening, had happened, I had to find Sasha and deal with it. Where did I start? When I began to recall everything from our time together I realised just how little I knew. I didn't know where she lived; I didn't even know her surname. She had told me just what she had wanted me to know and at the time I hadn't noticed, I had been so wrapped up in the sensations she had invoked in me that it was as if my mind had worked on another parallel and all the mundane, trivial things which one normally exchanges in a new relationship just hadn't happened. We had just fallen into lust and fed each other honeyed words as we brought each other to unconsummated, rapturous euphoria, it had been mad. I had thought it had been me who had been the instigator but the more I thought about it the more I felt like a fly trapped in a spider's web, a beautiful, poisonous spider that had done one thing and made me believe another. I could still feel inside the way she had inspired me to breathe my fantasies into her ears, how her lips had parted as I slow dripped and teased my thoughts around her silken skin. I could still sit back now and close my eyes and smell her soft scent which seemed mixed with a desire so powerful that it intoxicated me. I could feel the remembrance of a hundred throbbing erections as she told me how, deep beneath the sheets, her fingers sought the place I most longed to go, how she whispered my name as she touched and teased her body and she desired me so strongly she could not wait a moment longer but found her release in a writhing, glistening climax where at that moment she wanted me and had given herself to me.

But of course she never had. She never had given herself to me either physically, or it seemed now, in any way which would provide me with clues to lead me to her. My only clue was Mr Markham and he gave nothing away either, he was, when I tried to probe him for help, "not at liberty to say."

SASHA

"Pull the sheets up Sasha." So I pulled the sheets up to my chin, as tight as tight could be as he burrowed in from the side, like some grey whiskered old hog seeking truffles, snuffling and grunting and fiddling about. Fiddling and fumbling about down there. The sheets rose and fell as he fiddled but I kept my eyes tight shut, blocking out the sight of the mound of his body as his work-rough hands fiddled about, fiddled about down there. I opened my eyes once; 'she' was standing in the doorway. I didn't know for a long time what the look on her face was. Years later I saw the look again on another woman's face. I recognised it then. It was resignation. In the morning I took my sheets to the bathroom and scrubbed them and tried to get them dry before putting them back on the bed. I couldn't always; I often slept on damp sheets. "Pull the sheets up Sasha, pull them up tight."

I awoke trembling, sweating, the nightmare was back. It was back as often now as when I was a small child. I turned on the light and threw the bedcovers back to my calves then kicked them down with my feet until they were an untidy heap at the bottom of the bed, it felt safer with no covers, even though I was cold and shivering it still felt safer.

I didn't go back to the woods for a few weeks.

SIMON

I was jumpy all the time. Whenever Donna or one of the children asked me something I snapped my answers back at them until they only spoke to me as if they were treading on egg shells or not at all.

When I looked in the mirror I didn't recognise the man looking back at me. The man in the mirror was grey faced and hollow eyed. When I looked at Donna I didn't recognise her, the money had changed her. Her hair was chic, her clothes better quality, but more than anything she seemed to be under a spell from the house, it's magic had her trapped into this madness with it's size, it's pristine finish, it's beauty. But it wasn't beautiful to me, it was a living nightmare. My dream house had become a prison.

"Donna," I begged, "let's just go, let's just find somewhere else and leave all this."

"Are you mad? Go where?" she snapped back at me.

"Anywhere, out of here, away," I finished lamely.

"Simon, we have no where to go, no money to go with. Remember the terms of the agreement, five years minimum."

"Five years," I yelled at her, "it's a bloody jail sentence."

"Simon, you're being ridiculous. Jail sentence!" Her words were scornful. "What's the matter with you? You're given the gift of a lifetime, this beautiful house, all the money you could spend, for the first time in our lives we're not struggling and you want us to throw all that away and go where?" her words came out laced with a torrent of accusation.

"But we could be happy somewhere else," my voice was small, pleading, desperate.

"We're happy here," she snapped at me.

What was the use? The house had her in its spell.

SASHA

I was shocked when I saw him.

I so nearly walked into him. I had wandered back into the woods, I was getting a bit more sleep, the nightmare seemed to have faded again and for the last couple of nights I had slept through. On that particular morning I was feeling springy again. I drove out to my hidden lay-by and wandered idly up through the trees, scaling the fence and meandering through the woods to a different vantage point, I liked to vary my position a bit. Straight ahead of me there he was. He appeared to be on his own and there was no sight or sound of the dog. He was sitting on the ground with his arms wrapped around his knees staring down toward '*Dreams*'. My heart gave a leap.

He was so lost in his thoughts he didn't notice me. I backed away and watched him quietly. He looked ill. My whole being longed to go and cuddle him close and make things better but I resisted the urge, this wasn't the right time. It was *that* woman, I knew it was her, I'd seen them arguing before, but that was all to the good, soon he would kick her out and then I would go to him and make it all well.

Very quietly I tip-toed away.

It was some weeks later when I saw from the woods a minibus pull into the drive. It had a yellow square on the back, a taxi. *She* came out of the house, followed by her brood of children. They were all laughing and joking. They loaded up suitcases and holdalls and one by one climbed into their seats.

"Simon, we're off," I heard her call, her common voice carrying on the crisp air.

Simon was at the threshold, he kissed her on the cheek, a perfunctory kiss and with a half hearted wave he saw them off.

This was perfect.

He didn't seem sorry to see them go. This was my time. I gave them an hour to be well clear of the area so there would be no danger they had forgotten anything and would turn back. Brushing the leaves and twigs from my jeans I made my way down the hill, keeping to the edge of the wood, not wanting him to see me too soon. I wanted to surprise him. As I neared the house the dog barked and I heard Simon snap at it to be quiet. That was good; he didn't even seem to care for the dog anymore. The dog could go too. Perfect.

"Hello Simon," I said to his back. He was standing in the kitchen, his hand froze midway through the action of stirring his coffee, his back tensed, he didn't turn round, not at first. When he did I was really shocked, up close he looked even worse than he had from afar. He stood there looking at me as if he had seen a ghost. The minutes ticked past, I could hear the clock on the wall beside me echoing loudly in the room and still we just stood facing each other. Slowly he reached to the counter and put down the spoon which he was still clutching tightly between his fingers, never taking his eyes off me.

"Why Sasha?" he asked. "Why?"

I wasn't quite sure what he meant, I moved my head in a motion of enquiry.

"This," he gestured with his arm, sweeping it around to indicate his surroundings. "All this," the tone of his voice was full of something I couldn't identify, perhaps exasperation, disgust even.

"I did it for you Simon," I said simply.

"For me?" he gave a hollow mocking laugh. I was puzzled, I hadn't expected this reaction. "For me," he said again, scornfully.

"It's your house, your dream house, I built it for you." I told him.

"My dream house," he was shouting now, taking a step toward me as I took a step back. "My dream house? It's a fucking nightmare!"

"No," I rushed to his side grabbing at his arm. "Simon, can't you see, I built it for you. For us."

"For us? What the hell are you talking about? There is no us." I flinched at his words.

"But there could be," I tried to explain so he could understand. "There could be, just tell *her* to go and then you and I could be together."

"*Her*? Donna you mean? Donna is my wife Sasha. There is no us. There was never any us. You and me it was just some ...... some cheap thrill, it was nothing, nothing at all." He shook me from his arm and paced across the kitchen.

"You said you loved me."

"It was madness Sasha," his voice was calmer now. "It was a few months of madness, which somehow has escalated into this," once more he indicated his surroundings.

"Not madness Simon," I said levelly. "It was never madness. I love you. I have never loved anyone, but I love you and you love me, you said so. You said it the day you went away I heard you. I know why you went. I know you went back to *her* because that's the sort of person you are, good and kind and you thought you had to do the right thing but now it's different. Now you have money and you can pay *her* off and we can be together. It's right. It's our time now."

"*Her*?" he spat the word at me. "Her name is Donna! DONNA, you hear me and she is my wife, she is the woman I love, the woman I chose to spend my life with, the mother of my children. We were so happy before you came along, we were so happy after you went, then this happened," once more the gesture.

"Happy? You weren't happy. You had a crap job, you lived in that pokey little house and you were going to lose that. I've given you all this, I've made you rich. I can make you happy too. Simon we can be together."

"How could you possibly make me happy Sasha?" he asked wearily. "How could you make me happy? With your whispering and your stories, your fantastic fantasies, could you make me happy by taking me to the secret places in your head but never letting me touch you or having you touch me," he was sneering as he spoke.

"SEX!" I yelled at him. "Men - that's all they think about!"

"No Sasha, no it's not." He walked over to the table and sat down. "I can't be with you Sasha. I don't want to be with you. This house is not my dream house..." I made to interrupt but he stilled me. "Oh! I know we talked about it, it was a fine dream then, but the reality is it's a nightmare."

I too went to the table and sat down. "You just need a little time to adjust to the idea of us being able to be together. They've gone now, I saw them go, I ...." He didn't let me finish.

"You've been spying on me. I knew it. I saw you, that day, up in the wood. I heard your car. I saw you, even back then in Fallgrove, I saw you in that fancy car. It was you." He was looking at me with a look of horror on his face.

I didn't know what to say. "I love you Simon," I tried.

"Love! You don't know the meaning of the word. That's not love Sasha. Spying on someone, watching them, giving all this isn't love, it's warped. Can't you see how wrong it is?"

What was wrong with him? He didn't seem to be able to understand.

"I'm leaving this Sasha. I don't want it. It's wrecking my life."

"You can't leave it, it's yours."

"Yes, yes I can leave it. I don't want it!" His voice was rising, getting angry, but I was getting pretty angry too.

"You can't, it said five years in the terms."

"Well fuck the terms," he spat at me, "you can have it back, you can come and live here, you can have it all."

"You'll have to pay back the money you've spent, how can you do that?" I tried a different approach.

"I don't know how, but if that's what you want I'll do it, even if it takes until my dying day."

"Right," I sneered, I didn't mean to sneer but he was making me really angry now. "Right you will, what are you going to do, drive a minicab?"

"I'll do whatever it takes," he said quietly, so quietly I hardly heard the words. In the same flat tone he continued, "Can't you see Sasha how wrong this is? Can't you see how unhappy I am? If you love me as you say you do then you will want me to be happy and this isn't making me happy. If you really love me Sasha you'll let go." He reached out as if to take my hand and then seemed to change his mind.

"I do love you Simon." I stood and walked away. I didn't want him to see me cry.

SIMON

I wanted that to be an end to it. She had come, we had talked, she had gone. I thought for one horrible moment she was going to cry, but she had risen quietly and just walked away.

I sat at the table for a very long time, hours in fact. I felt I had been in the ring with Mike Tyson for about ten rounds. My emotions were battered and bruised. For months I had wanted to find her, to sort out this whole miserable mess and then she had been there, as calm as anything, just there in the kitchen.

She was mad.

She was mad and I was scared. I hardly wanted to admit it to myself but she was so far beyond the edge of reason that I feared for my own safety and more particularly my family. Thank goodness they had gone away for a fortnight to Florida. I called Rosa to me and patting her head told her she was a good dog.

Donna had been excited about the holiday, thrilled to bits the day the passports arrived in the post. None of us had ever been abroad. Donna had asked if I would go but I said no, I wasn't going to use *that* money for a pleasure trip.

"What's the difference, you eat the food I buy with it," she had thrown at me. The difference was I had to eat. Donna went ahead and booked the trip anyway, she booked me a place but I wouldn't go.

"Why not, it's paid for now, you might as well," she said. I couldn't, so they went without me. That would never have happened before, but I was glad they'd gone, there would be time now without them there to sort things out. I knew what I had to do and there was no time like the present.

I stumbled out to the shed where the garden tools and lawn mower were kept. Picking up a can of petrol I carried it back to the house. I left it by the front door while I went upstairs. Over the banister I threw quilts and books and toys anything that would burn. It fluttered or flew down the well of the stairs forming a huge pile, forming a funeral pyre for the death of '*Dreams*'. From the bedroom I gathered up the few photographs we had of the children and me and Donna before all this – we were so young, so happy in the pictures. I paused for a moment to recall the family we had been, before my anger flared again. I put them to one side; they would be the one thing I took with me. The rich embroidered cushions, the fucking awful silver quilt, they all went over the banisters – I was a man possessed.

Then down the stairs and into the study – books flew, papers, bank accounts with lines of black ink figures (lots of zeros), I threw them into the pile. I was exhausted, I stood panting surveying the heap of meaningless, material things, all the bits and pieces which had contributed to the downfall of my family life, tolling out the death knell of my descent into loathsome self pity as I had let the house and the money come between me and Donna. Tolling out the end of my marriage, because when Donna came back I would have to tell her everything, I would have to confess all to her and she would never forgive me, not now. Not the initial betrayal I don't mean, stupidly enough I think if I had explained at the start I might have been able to make her understand, but now she had become used to a different life, living the rich life, I don't think she would forgive me now for taking that away from her. I have nothing to offer except love and I don't think love is enough.

I loaded a few old clothes and the children's photographs onto the backseat of my old Escort then returned to the house. The petrol can stood where I had left it beside the door. I walked to the heap of belongings and slowly began to unscrew the cap. Before I had it half way loose the impact of force hitting my back sent me sprawling onto the pile, the softness of the quilts and cushions breaking my fall. She was a wild cat, scratching and biting and screeching at me.

No –oooo!" over and over she screamed it at me. I couldn't fight her off of my back, her legs were wrapt around me as she pummelled at my head and scratched at my eyes. We rolled, grappling on the pile, the corner of books stabbing at me, the glass in a picture frame shattering as over and over we turned as she clung on like a giant limpet with the strength of a tiger. I staggered to my knees and slammed her hard back against the banister and her grip loosened. In that instance I pushed away free and fell on my hands and knees trying to catch my breath, in that moment of delay she pounced again, only this time I turned in time to be facing her. Her face was glistening with sweat, her eyes blazing with fury.

The sudden impact sent me toppling backwards causing the damn silver quilt to billow up around me and she fell with me. It seemed to take the wind out of her sails; she lay sprawled on top of me panting as hard as I was. Looking into my eyes her anger dissipated and was replaced by something totally different, something I remembered from another time and which had stirred my insides then and made them ache as they did again. She felt me, felt me harden against her pelvis and she looked deep into my eyes with something like triumph.

Her face moved down toward mine, in a slow, controlled movement, savouring her power over me, the curtain of her hair falling either side of my face as the curtain falls on the final act. Only this wasn't the final act, she placed her lips on mine and I heard a groan and I knew it was me. I knew I was too weak to resist but not too weak to respond. She released the grip she had on my wrists, kissing me deeply as she did so. My arms went around her my fingers combed into her hair as I ground her face down on mine, my tongue probing deep in her mouth, the well remembered taste of sweetness like honey. All those months I had spent wanting her and loving her and all the months I had spent in anger and hate spilled out of me. In a sudden movement I flipped her onto her back and ripped her shirt open. She had on no bra, her breasts were heavy, her nipples pink and erect. I kneaded her breast, squeezing her nipples until it couldn't help but be hurting her. I ripped at her belt, tugging her jeans, undoing each button in a frantic, desperate assault as she slapped at my hands, twisting beneath me, but I was strong now. I had the strength of ten men. I had the strength of extreme love and extreme hate. I had some driving force urging me on. I undid my own jeans and forcing her legs apart I plunged into her, riding her for all I was worth, hating her and wanting her – she couldn't stop it, she was powerless, after all these months it was her who was powerless. I felt the first waves of her orgasm, I pushed deeper, with brutal force I thrust myself as hard into her as I could go and she came, her muscles tightening around me, screaming out my name as I flooded into her, filling her with hot sticky liquid, the months of frustration pouring out of me and leaving me drained and exhausted.

SASHA

'Pull the sheets up Sasha'. But there were no sheets to pull up.

He had done that thing to me; that thing that men like to do. It had not been the soft and gentle act we had talked of so often. We had not floated and twirled. There was no ethereal splendour. No tenderness, no gentle stroking, teasing, no whispering touch. He had done it as men do it - as animals do it – base, primitively. After all his sweet words, all our dreams and spoken journeys into exquisite lovemaking, he had been nothing more than an animal, a man grunting and rutting. He had invaded me, taken me, and in doing so, he was now mine.

The weight of his body on top of mine was comforting in a way, but already I could feel the sticky mess oozing from me and I had to press down the feeling of nausea. Simon couldn't look at me; I was holding the trump card now. I gently pushed at his shoulder so he had to raise himself a little and I placed a hand either side of his face.

"You're mine now." I told him.

He sunk back down, it was as if he had lost all power of movement, he was just dead weight. I was getting incredibly uncomfortable but I didn't want to break the spell, the longer I kept him held close to me the stronger the bond became. I put my arms around him and made soothing noises like a mother to a baby. "There, there," I whispered, "it's all right, there, there."

We laid there so long I thought he had fallen asleep but finally he moved, raising himself, doing up his jeans. I looked away, didn't want to see *that.* He moved like a zombie, slowly and painfully walking toward the kitchen. I heard the click of the kettle. I got up myself, I could understand why Simon was walking slowly, I was pretty stiff myself, I went to the cloakroom and cleaned up the mess, flushing away the wads of tissue I used, it was the best I could do for the moment, later I would get the nail brush and clean myself properly.

I went to the kitchen, Simon was making two mugs of coffee. He carried them slowly to the table and sat down in front of one. I went over and sat in front of the other. I reached out a hand to touch him; he withdrew as if I were going to scald him. I took charge of the situation.

"After this Simon I'll help you clear up, get everything back in its place." He just looked at me, staring blankly. In the end I did most of the work, Simon sat in his study chair and hardly moved a muscle. I remade all the beds; put the luxurious silver quilt back on the bed, smoothing it level. I found the petrol can buried beneath the pile, it had seeped a little so I scrubbed the floor to get rid of the smell and I returned the can to the shed. The paperwork I piled into the study, there would be time later to sort through it. I cleared up the broken glass and the picture frame, I threw away the picture, it was a picture of *her* and all the children; he wouldn't need that.

I needed to get home, to get clean and to collect some clothes.

"I'll be back later," I told Simon, who was back in the kitchen sitting at the table.

In my own house I collected a black bin liner from the kitchen and made my way to my bathroom. I took my clothes off and threw them in the bag; I would dispose of them later. I ran a bath, so hot the steam rose in billows of clouds and I could hardly see across the room. Cautiously I stepped into the water, the rush of heat caused me to sweat and feel faint but I forced myself to sit down, it was scalding hot. My skin turned scarlet, I gritted my teeth against the force of the heat; it had always been like this. Inch by painful inch I lowered myself into the water as the line of bright red rose on my body as I sunk into the fiercely hot water. It was the only way to get clean. I lathered up the soap and taking the nail brush I scrubbed. I scrubbed hard all over but particularly in that place where I was still sticky and dirty. I scrubbed so hard I was bleeding and the pain was excruciating, only then was it time to stop. I emptied out the water and went and stood in the shower cubicle, where I turned the jet to cold. I stood under it feeling disorientated and shaky from the sudden contrast, gripping the walls to steady myself. When it was over I stepped shivering from the cubicle and wrapped myself in a large fluffy towel. I took some toilet tissue and used it to pick up the soap and the nail brush from the side of the bath and drop them in the bin liner, then I took a new bar of soap and washed my hands again.

I was so sore I could barely walk, gingerly I made my way to the bed and lay down, and still wrapped in the towel I climbed under the covers. *"Pull the sheets up Sasha, pull the sheets up, there's a good girl."*

I slept.

SIMON

I was not someone who knew violence. It was true I had grown up on the Blackbird Leys estate where it was hard to walk from one place to another without someone taking pot shots at you with an air rifle but this had been a different kind of violence. This had been my violence, from deep inside, that I hadn't known I possessed. The fact I had been capable of it shocked me more than the actual act. I had been fighting for my life as Sasha, like a wild tiger, had clung onto my back with her sharp nails and her sharp teeth. I had been gripped in her madness. Suddenly, forcefully, what had been a desperate scramble to get her off of me had turned into something else. I had wanted to possess her. I had wanted her to suffer something of what I had been through in the last few months. Fighting had turned to power, the power of the physical strength of a man over a woman – an assault - rape! It had been little more than rape and when it was over I didn't understand it but I had sensed triumph in her. She had me trapped even further in her web than I had been before.

I think it got dark. I think it got light again. I don't know how many times. I made coffee, lots of coffee and I sat drinking it slowly, sleep never came. I wanted to lapse into a deep sleep, to wake and find it hadn't happened, that somehow, magically, it had all gone away. I don't know how long I sat there.

SASHA

I didn't go back that night or the next day. Too sore to walk I lay in my bed or tip-toed cautiously to the bathroom or downstairs to fetch food and drink. I hadn't seen Mrs Bobbitt in days and days, I didn't know if she still came. Finally, I couldn't leave it any longer. I had to get back to Simon before *that* woman and her brood returned to him or he did something silly. He was sure to have cleared up and we could set about making our plans.

When I returned to '*Dreams*' the front door was on the latch. I peeped into the study; all the papers were exactly as I had left them two days previously. I moved cautiously towards the kitchen, sitting at the table was a shadow of a man. He raised his head wearily as I entered. His eyes were bloodshot, his whiskers a stubble, he looked like one of the dirty old winos under Waterloo Bridge. I could smell him from the threshold of the room.

"Oh Simon," I murmured sadly, "what have you done?" He looked back at me blankly; there was no expression in his face, no flicker of recognition or acknowledgement. I went to him and urged him to rise. Staggering a bit under his weight and repulsed by the smell of him I lead him from the room and up the stairs. In his bedroom I slipped off his shoes, loosened his trousers and took away his belt. I pushed him gently back on the bed and lifted his legs under the covers. He lay back on the pillow with his eyes wide open but unseeing.

I didn't want to involve a doctor, I rummaged in the medicine cabinet, there was some Nitrazepam in a bottle which I knew were sleeping tablets, I was shocked to see they had been prescribed to Simon. Returning to the bedroom I lifted his head, forced one tablet, as prescribed, into his mouth and held a glass of water to his lips. The water trickled from the side of his mouth. I pinched his nose and he swallowed. I sat on the chair beside the bed and watched as in time his eyes closed and he slept.

"What have you done Simon?" I asked his sleeping form. "Where's the man I fell in love with?" I would have to nurse him better. I would get back the old Simon and then he would love me more for having saved him.

SIMON

I think I was tired but sleep wouldn't come, whenever I closed my eyes I saw Sasha lying beneath me, brutalised, violated, so I snapped my eyes open to stare at the wall and extinguish the image. The wall began to move, at first it gently swayed, then it began to have swirling patterns, then pictures formed, beautiful pictures, sunshine yellow pictures, it got so I didn't want to leave the pictures, so I just sat on the chair in the kitchen.

Then Sasha came back.

She looked bright and fresh, she didn't look violated at all. She prised me from my chair, her sweet smell was obliterated by a foul odour when I stood up, the smell wouldn't go away, I think it was me; it was the smell of despair.

She laid me in my bed, she fed me tablets. I didn't know what they were. I didn't care. I was frightened of sleep and scared to stay awake. Sleep did come, total oblivion, as I feel into the black abyss I hoped I might never wake up again. But I did - eventually. When I did it was dark, only the light from the landing shone though the doorway. Sasha was sitting in the chair beside the bed, a book fallen onto her lap as she dozed. Even in sleep she was beautiful, her mouth hadn't lolled open, no dribble oozed from the corner of her lips, no snores rent the air, she was ghostly in the half light, her golden hair a halo around her perfect face, a picture of innocence. But my God she wasn't innocent, she was bad and I had to get away. I tried to move my legs but they didn't want to go anywhere, I felt as weak as a baby. Sasha stirred, opening her eyes and looking straight at me, a shiver ran down my spine.

"Hello Sleepyhead," she said to me as if everything was normal. "You've been asleep a whole day and part of the night. Can I get you anything?" I shook my head. "Don't be silly, you need building up, I'll go and fix you something," and in saying so she rose, stretching gracefully before heading for the door. At the doorway she turned, "I like to watch you sleep," she said. I was gripped with fear. I heard her descend the stairs, I made a desperate effort to sit up and move. It must have taken me longer than I knew for I was only just on my feet when she returned to the bedroom with a tray set with what looked like chicken noodle soup and some bread.

"And where do you think you're going?" she asked, as if addressing a small recalcitrant child.

"Bathroom," my voice came out hoarse, like a man who has lost the habit of speaking.

"Just wait, I'll help you." She put the bread plate on top of the soup to keep the heat in, then coming to me she put her arm around my waist in order to support me, my body recoiled from her touch, but I had no choice. In that manner we shuffled to the bathroom.

"I'd like a bath," I told her. I had a feeling a hot soak may revive me a little. She looked doubtful but ran the water for me, then leaving me to undress she went back to the bedroom.

"Leave the door open, Simon," she instructed, "just in case."

I pushed it shut but didn't lock it, she was probably right and instinct told me that the sight of my naked body would not be one she would be rushing in to see. Cautiously I climbed over the side of the bath, I smelt foul, sweat, piss and worse of all stale sex and my breath could have blistered paint. My body was bruised and battered, long scratches from Sasha's nails criss-crossed like the claw marks of a wildcat. I lay in the hot water soaking and it was having a reviving effect. I slipped beneath the surface, my face an inch below the water level as my hair floated out like seaweed drifting on the edge of the shore. I could have drowned, I could have stayed under the water and drowned, let Sasha come and find me, let her pull me from the cooling water and try to revive me, let her drag my naked slippery body over the edge of the bath and bang on my chest and breath into my foul mouth – but would she? Would she willingly touch my body, my naked body – I doubted it.

I DOUBTED IT!

That was her weakness.

I pushed myself up along the back of the bath, the water rocked back and forth, splashing onto the floor, it drained down my face, it gave me life and it gave me strength. She had held me a prisoner of my mind for two years. She had had such a grip over me. I had been shackled by my guilt, but not any more, she had exposed her underbelly and her weakness was my key to escape. I was not physically strong yet, but I would be, strong enough to deal with Sasha. Strong enough to get her out of our lives before Donna returned with the children. I rose from the bath, dried myself, brushed my teeth and walked naked from the bathroom. It took all my courage to do so. I felt vulnerable and yet powerful. Sasha was just putting the finishing touches to making the bed, she turned and I heard her sharp intake of breath.

"That feels better," I told her in a would-be jolly voice.

"Here, let me get you something to put on," she said, averting her eyes.

"No, don't be silly, I never sleep in anything and I think I should go back to bed for a while, that bath has quite taken it out of me. Come and lay down with me Sasha." I walked to the bed and lay on top of the covers, hoping with just a touch of male pride that in my mock bravado state my manhood had not shrunk to the size of a pickled walnut. I held out my arms. "Come on Sasha, slip off your clothes and lay with me, we've talked about it so often, let's do it. Come on."

"I have things to do, no you slip under the covers before you catch your death," she instructed, "I'll go and reheat your soup," and picking up the tray she left the room. It was all I could do to keep from chuckling. I did climb beneath the covers, it was cold. I waited for the soup and ate it gratefully, afterwards I slept again.

For two days we played the patient and nurse, me taking every opportunity to goad her with my nakedness and my suggestive invitations, her avoiding eye contact and even more particularly physical contact. When I felt well enough I ventured downstairs.

Her temper was short, but then so was mine now, although I was keeping mine in check. Even so we ended up exchanging words and soon it had erupted into a full scale row.

SASHA

Noooooo! No, I didn't want to hear this. I felt as though I had been kicked very, very hard in my stomach. I felt the colour drain from my face. I stood as if I were a statue and looked at him across the expanse of black, gleaming kitchen unit. In front of me was the knife rack and for a fleeting moment I wanted to grab the carving knife from its wooden block and plunge it into him, to slash wildly at the lips that had dropped such cruel and dramatic words at my feet. My fury was as red as fire, as dangerous as molten lava spewing from the mountain top, but my pain was white. A flash of brilliant white blinding pain as intense as any I have ever known and it superseded the anger and knocked me off my axis.

"It's true," he said.

I rushed at him scratching and kicking, storming at him. If he could have found any weapon to hurt me, any blade honed to sharpness, any bullet designed to explode and shatter on impact it could not have wounded me more. I covered my ears. I didn't want to hear it again. My knees gave way and I sank to the ground and I could hear the room fill with uncontrollable sobbing. My face was awash with tears but my throat felt dry, it ached, I was racked with primeval crying and all the time he stood quite still, not coming to me, not comforting me, not reassuring me it was a mistake. He never came to me and said it was a lie. He did not pretend he had made it up to frighten me. I tried to look at him, tried to plead with him, I struggled to my knees and went to him, grasping onto his arm, telling him it didn't matter, telling him we could get through this, he looked at me with ... what? Disgust? Pity? It wasn't love. I saw it in his face that there wasn't any love.

He shook my hands free of his arm and he turned away.

SIMON

I hadn't wanted to tell her, hadn't meant to tell her, but she had been going on and on. She had made herself quite at home and was acting like it was her and I who were married. She seemed to have settled into the house and Donna counted for nothing. I tried to explain, tried to tell her this was not what I wanted but I was still weak and I had so little fight left in me.

We were rowing, shouting across the kitchen, I was pleading with her to go, to give me back my life, to just walk away and set me free. I was a man trapped and however much I begged for my release I could see in her eyes she had no concept of my anguish. She was my gaoler and was not going to throw me the keys.

"Donna needs me," I had screamed at her.

"I need you!"

"Yes, but you're not pregnant." The words were out, unintentionally I had spurted them out and they had flown across the room and with pin-point precision they had hit their target. Her face had drained white and had frozen in a rigid mask of disbelief. We stood like that for what seemed an eternity. A flicker of her eyes told me she was aware of the knife block in front of her and my breathing deepened as I anticipated her thoughts. But she didn't reach for the knives, instead she came across the kitchen with the speed of a tornado, a wild animal, scratching and biting. I couldn't defend myself against her onslaught, but it was of short duration, she fell in a crumpled heap to the floor and dry, heaving sobbing filled the room.

"How could you do that to me?" she asked, "how could you?"

"Do what?" I spat back at her, "Donna is my wife." I tried to make my tone gentle, "Sasha, there is no 'us', there can never be any 'us'. I love Donna. I don't want any of this," I indicated the room, the house, "I need to be left to get on with my life." She was looking up at me, her face blotched with crying, for a moment I almost felt pity for her and then I hardened my resolve as I remembered the torture I had felt over the past months.

"You told me you loved me," she whispered in a pathetic, little girl voice coming to me on her knees, grabbing at my arm, clinging with desperation.

"I was wrong." I shook her free, her touch an anathema to me. I turned and walked across the room. I wanted distance now. I wanted to be as far away from this sorry looking creature as I could. I wanted her gone so I could close up this monstrous house and when Donna returned we could start again somewhere else, where I could re-establish myself as the breadwinner, a proper husband and a father to the children and the expected baby. I could regain my pride, my dignity. I could be poor and happy instead of living under this heavy cloud of guilt and oppression.

SASHA

He walked from the room and I was sunk into blackness.

I don't know how long I stayed there but I knew it was over. I knew whatever I did now, however much I pleaded, begged, cajoled it was over. I was distraught. I knew I could not keep him through love or fear or desperation. She had won. That frightful woman had won. She had used the oldest trick in the book and my blood ran cold at the thought that he had been with her, had done with her the things he had talked of doing with me. He had planted his seed in her body when it should have been mine, when he should have been loyal and true to me. That awful, tatty, cheap-looking woman had won. My nails made half moons in the palm of my hands.

Simon came back into the room. "I'm going out" he said. "I expect when I get back you'll be gone."

I picked myself up and made my way to the table as if I were walking in heavy space man boots. I sat rocking in the chair, the pain was unbearable. I had given it all to him, and he was throwing it back in my face. I had let him see inside my head; let him lead me down alleys of fantasy. I had thrown away my chances of staying married to Nigel. I had lost my daughter. I had used my escape fund to give him his dream. The months of planning, the months of excitement and anticipation when finally he saw what I had done for him had all meant nothing.

"You can't buy me!" He had flung those words at me. I hadn't wanted to buy him; it was in my gift to provide this for him. I had worked tirelessly for months because I thought he wanted this.

I sat on the chair and rocked.

It was cold, so cold. My heart ached. The light faded and I sat and rocked. There was the sound of humming. A tiny remnant of a tune remembered from childhood. I sat rocking and humming, slowly, tonelessly, rocking and humming as the evening drew in around me.

Rocking and humming and holding in my pain, with my arms wrapped around my stomach.

It was cold. So cold.

I felt so lost that not even God could have found me.

SIMON

I drove away. I didn't want to stay, couldn't stay.

The last I saw of Sasha she was a pathetic bag-wash on the kitchen floor. I breathed a sigh of relief as I left the house for I felt that finally I had broken her and I was free. I called Rosa to me. I wouldn't go back that night. I would wait until daylight and then I would go and collect my personal belongings and find somewhere else for me and my family when they returned from The States. After that I would never go back to that place I thought of as Hell.

SASHA

Rocking back and forth in the cold.

My mind was numb. I think in my rocking I may even have drifted into sleep. Sitting in the kitchen rocking on the chair, lulling myself into a comfort zone, trying to escape the feeling inside that I had been ripped wide open and my heart exposed to the elements, which buffeted it against the rocks, and with each tiny shard of a memory of Simon that invaded my thoughts, the pain cut knife-deep once again. So I hummed my little tune and rocked away the hurting until dawn broke.

My body felt bruised and battered both inside and out, but it still functioned in some ways and I was forced to get up from my chair to use the cloakroom. In the mirror I saw a very old woman looking back at me. I saw an echo of a time long past, a resemblance in my face, a shadow of that old be-whiskered man who had fiddled and fumbled about in the darkness of the night. He was in the mirror staring out through my eyes, all the badness and the dirty probing stared back at me. All the years he had whispered at me *'pull the sheets up Sasha, pull the sheets up',* all the years he had crept into my bed and tortured me, and all these long years afterwards he still invaded my head, even long after I had ... long after he had *gone*. Now Simon had made what we had dirty, just like that old man looking back out from my eyes in the mirror. I had thought what we had had been perfect - pure, untainted, beautiful. All the time he had been talking to me, and I had been thinking of him, he had been with her, doing that thing with *her*. All the rage I had inside me wanted to obliterate that face in the mirror. I clenched my fist and with vehemence and an almighty effort the mirror shattered into a star of a thousand fractures. Splinters of glass imbedded themselves into the side of my fist, I almost welcomed the pain, but the sight of the oozing blood was ugly, I retched. My stomach was almost empty but foul green bile splattered into the wash hand basin, acid-pungent it burned my throat into rawness. When I looked into the cracked mirror again the old man had gone and all that was left was just a hollow eyed woman in a thousand pieces. I turned on the tap and watched the foul liquid circle the plughole and swish away. I splashed cold water on my face and washed my hands, easing out the fragments of silver.

I had done it all for him.

I had given him everything.

I had given him a gift. People cannot go around returning gifts, it just wasn't right. The red anger was rising in me again but it felt better than the white pain. I saw then, with sudden clarity, my mistake. He was just a man; just a common working class man. He was not some hero, not the man I had put on a pedestal. He was nothing. He had no finesse, no manners; he didn't know that it was not polite to return a gift. The scales fell from my eyes. I would teach him.

I would teach him that a gift is not just for Christmas it's for life.

I laughed in the distorted pieces of broken mirror. My fractured image laughed back at me, laughed at my joke, "Not just for Christmas," I laughed that lovely, bubbling, gurgling laugh which doesn't know how to stop, but that was okay, there was only me, I didn't have to behave in front of a site foremen or a decrepit old solicitor or even Simon. If I wanted to laugh I could laugh, I could laugh until I went bang if I wanted to.

I would teach him.

This would take some thinking about, even as I was laughing I was thinking.

SIMON

It looked as though she were still there. It was ten in the morning; I had slept in my car and woken stiff and cold. I walked over the rise to the house, cutting thought the woods, there were still signs of life, her car still in the drive, so I walked away again. I had left my car down the road a little and walked across the ridge. I didn't want to see her again so thought it better to check that she had cleared out. She hadn't. I would drive away and return later in the day or maybe tomorrow. I couldn't face another scene.

SASHA

I knew what I had to do.

A plan formulated in my mind. Love had turned to hate and I would not let him get away with that. Love and hate, which is the stronger? I think I now know.

The telephone bell shattered the silence. My hands gripped the door handle as it trilled into the otherwise silent house, loud and penetrating cutting through the air. It stopped abruptly and I heard the answer phone pick up the call, it clicked into life and I heard a female voice.

"Simon, Simon, it's me, are you there? Pick up if you're there ..... well I guess not ...."

It was HER! I ran across the hallway to his study and picked up the answering machine with every intention of hurling it against the wall. If she had walked in the room at that moment I would have hurled her against the wall, spreading her bulk against the book-lined walls, splattering her silly insipid face into a squashy pulp.

Her voice was tinny down the line and on the verge of venting my fury I caught her words.

"Simon, we haven't seen everything yet ... we want to stay another week ... is that okay? I'll call you again later to check, bye Honey, kids send their love, miss you." A slow smile spread across my face as I heard kisses down the line. Her and her brats were staying in America ... time for me to put my plan into action ... it was forming nicely ... it was time for revenge. Simon would keep appreciating my gift forever.

A gift is not just for Christmas.

The machine clicked and I replaced it.

I had a feeling that Simon and *'Dreams'* were destined for each other but that bitch, that tinny voiced bitch might find her man a changed man when she came home.

I went to Simon's computer and interrupted the bing-bong ball. I typed four letters. Taking envelopes from the drawer I folded one letter into each. Two I addressed to Mr Markham. I placed one envelope inside the other to my solicitor. The third I simply wrote Simon on the envelope and I put it in the desk drawer. The fourth I put into my handbag to be dealt with later.

I had a few things to do, things to sort out before this day was finished. All the loose ends had to be tied off. I had everything covered. It was all coming together very neatly. Simon would play his part I was certain. I drove my car away from the house, left it deep in the woods where I threw a few branches and handfuls of leaves over it, no point in it being found too soon. Then I doubled back on foot. On the way back to '*Dreams*' I dropped the letter to Mr Markham in the post box at the end of the lane, and as luck would have it the opportunity to sort out the final part of my plan presented itself. Luck was definitely on my side, I saw that as a good omen.

Now Simon would think I had gone, I reasoned to myself. He would come back if he thought I was gone.

On my return I collected together all the things I needed. A strong length of rope, a crisp, white, brand new sheet from the linen cupboard, a stepladder from the shed: I gathered them together in readiness. I put them in the hall cupboard lest he should return too soon, although I had a feeling, some instinct, which told me he wouldn't be back for some hours, or more likely not until the morning.

I went and took a bath; I felt a strong need to be clean and pure. I soaked in the hot water, it was burning hot and my body tingled as though it were being blistered. I washed my face again, washing away the tears which sprung into my eyes without warning, washing away the longing that I had felt for Simon. He meant nothing to me now. Or at least he was loved and hated and surely that meant the two things cancelled each other out. I reflected on what a difference a few little hours could make, just a few little hours.

In a few little hours what a difference to Simon's life I would make. I saw it all. I looked inside my head and I saw it all. He may not want me, he may not need me, he may not even love me, or have ever loved me, but I had loved him. Oh Yes! I had loved him with every fibre in me. I would have walked barefoot over burning coals for him. I gave him everything, not only '*Dreams*' but everything I could give of myself. I had allowed myself to let go of that part of my being which I had kept locked away deep inside and he had taken it, used it, and returned it broken. I rested my head against the back of the bath as the smell of lavender rose on the steam. The last thing he would remember about me would be the smell of lavender.

SIMON

I felt dirty and bedraggled; a night in the car was no fun, certainly no fun at my age. Rosa was bored and hungry and so I drove into the nearest town and looking like a tramp I checked into '*The George*', a small hotel, more like just a few rooms over a pub really. I had a feeling Sasha might not be in a hurry to leave '*Dreams*'. I would give it another day, then she would have to go, Donna would be back and I wanted this mess sorted before she was. In the meantime I could play the waiting game.

I was still weak. I took a bath and rinsed my clothes, hanging them over the towel rail to dry. Wrapped in only the big bath sheet I climbed beneath the covers of the bed, where I ate the meal the landlady had provided. Steak and kidney pudding and a dish of apple crumble. I fell asleep warm and full, the food and the heat had the effect of numbing my brain, or maybe it was just the extreme tiredness, but I fell to sleep with empty thoughts. Rosa jumped on the end of the bed and circled a few times before settling down to make a warming weight at my feet.

SASHA

The steam rose and I couldn't help but smile as I remembered happier days. His hand in the small of my back which had sent shock waves of longing through my body, when he had come back to The Ashmolean for the second time and it had all started. I remembered the way he had held me close, the feelings which had flowed between us. Then later, our dates in Maidenhead, walking hand in hand, talking and laughing like any lovers might. Sitting on 'our' bench, cuddled up as the days turned colder and the autumn had clothed the trees in fiery rich, tapestry hues and scattered leaves like jewels upon the ground. We had kicked through the leaves, like children, gathering handfuls and throwing them over each other before he chased me, grabbed me and in a pool of russets and gold he had pulled me to him and we had become suddenly serious, the smiles slid from our faces and we had kissed, our tongues dancing together, probing deep, bodies pressed tight, as any lovers might.

Then autumn had turned to winter. The icy wind had cut the air and the rain turned the autumn leaves to mush. We had sat huddled away in the coffee shop, still laughing and joking, still whispering our love, as any lovers might. We had twined our hands around each others and told our deepest secrets, desires and thoughts. We had whispered our love making in husky voices which throbbed with yearning. We had talked our way to rainbow coloured orgasms and the slippery wetness of our dreams. The cold wind blew and it blew no good. Summer was over. Our summer was over. He left me in the winter on 'our' bench bereft.

That was the first time he walked away, he wasn't going to walk away from me again, not this time. Oh No! This time I would bind him to me forever, irrevocably, I would never leave him. I would be in his every waking moment and his troubled sleep. I had given him everything.

I had done it all for him.

It is not right to refuse a gift.

He would see it my way in the end.

The thing was I knew Simon. I knew him better than he knew himself. He would stay. I knew he would stay. I would make sure he stayed.

The water was starting to chill around me. I rose up dripping. I towelled myself vigorously. Wrapped in the towel I took Simon's toothbrush and cleaned my teeth. I ran a brush through my hair, his brush. I noticed some of my long golden hairs tangled in the bristles, I left them there.

My skin felt soft to the touch. I let the towel fall to the floor, I looked good, a little thinner perhaps but that was understandable, but still good. This would be the first time Simon would have seen me naked. I hoped he would appreciate the wait. I was ready for him. I was ready to tie him to me and '*Dreams*' forever.

I knew Simon better than he knew himself.

I was ready.

SIMON

My clothes dried stiff on the towel rail, I pulled them on, creased as they were. The day was new and it was with a heavy feeling of dread I faced it. It was too early to check out of *'The George'* I waited for the light to break through the windows. I hoped and prayed Sasha had left and I could just collect my things, shut up the house and leave. I couldn't face another row, another battle trying to introduce some reason into her manic, twisted thoughts. I felt like a very sick man. I felt I was close to breaking and I didn't think I could take much more, I really didn't.

SASHA

I don't know what other people feel when they are in this position. I don't know if they have fear, despair or regrets? I don't know if they have doubts. All I know is I have no doubts, no fear, no regrets. I am absolutely certain that I am doing the right thing. I am standing on a ladder, the sheet crossed around me and tied at the nape of my neck, like a Grecian robe. I can feel the scratch of the rough loop of rope around my neck, the knot digging slightly behind my left ear. I had to look up on the Internet how to make the knot. I practised it several times over. The other end of the rope is secured to the banister rail upstairs. Standing on the top of the set of steps I feel all the power of my revenge surging like electricity through my body. I am all powerful, for I know Simon better than he knows himself.

There is no other way for me.

I have lost everything. I can't go back to being poor, working in some deadbeat job where men maul and leer. I can't go crawling back to Nigel and admit I took his money. I can't go back to the looks of distain from my daughter. I can't live a life with no love from Simon. I hate him. I hate him and love him all at once. I tried to turn off the love, I wanted to turn off the hate, but I can't. I want revenge and this is it.

I know Simon better than he knows himself.

My life hasn't flashed before me as I stand upon these steps. No heavenly choir is singing me on my way. I have no urge to confess my sins and ask for forgiveness, no need of a priest, or God or even the Devil. Standing on the ladder, draped in my Grecian folds, with my violent necklace of hemp what I feel most of all is power – exciting, exhilarating, all consuming power.

I know Simon better than he knows himself.

The night will soon be over and he hasn't returned, but he will.

I suppose the end will not be as romantically smooth as I would like. I will have to jump and kick the steps away at the same time, I'm glad no-one will see that, not terribly dignified, but after I have danced in the air and became still I will swing with elegance and grace, draped in my white sheet, a princess ready for the ball . I will dance for all eternity as light as air. I will dance in Simon's mind and bind him to me. I will dance my slow, spinning waltz of death. I will be Simon's dance partner forever because he will see me every time he walks into this house (and he cannot escape now, I have seen to that). He will see me when he closes his eyes to sleep. I will float before him, a phantom of love and hate and sweet revenge. I know what Simon will do, you see. I know him so well. There is no escape for him this time. He cannot walk away from me – I will be in his head forever.

It is time. The clock has long since struck past four, I have not tracked time.

As I stand in an elegant pose on my stepladder plinth, words float into my head and I smile at the irony of them:-

I take upon myself the burden of all suffering. I am resolved to do so, I will endure it. I do not turn or run away, do not tremble, am not terrified, nor afraid, do not turn back or despond.

I smile at the irony that I had read these words at The Ashmolean the day I had waited for him, the day when it had all started.

I raise my arms into the air and scream Simon's name.

"I'm doing all this for you Simon, I did it for you and you shall have my dream forever," I scream out the words, I jump, I kick, and then ... ...

SIMON - 7.40am

I couldn't be certain but I thought she had gone. The house was silent and locked tight, her car had gone. Rosa was asleep on the back seat of my car, lazy old hound. I left her there. I didn't intend to be long, just long enough to pick up a few bits and pieces and then go. It was certainly cutting it fine with Donna due home later. I would collect her and the kids from the airport when it was time and we would never, never ever, return to this place. I had to tell Donna the truth, I realised that now. If she never forgave me I didn't know what I would do, but it was a risk I would have to take. She would be hurt and angry, I know she would, but perhaps when she calmed down she would understand that Sasha, in all her madness, had lured me into her dangerous game and once captured there had been no escape.

I would make Donna see and I would beg for her forgiveness. I was full of new resolve.

I put my key into the lock and it turned smoothly.

It was early; the hall was in half light, all the doors to the adjoining rooms closed with the exception of the kitchen, where the electric glare filtered into the hall. My nose was assailed by the acrid smell of pee. I cursed Rosa under my breath assuming she had left a puddle on the floor. I pushed the door open wider and a shaft of light illuminated the hall and in the triangle of mote speckled early morning sun, swinging in a slow circle, above the ground, I saw her.

I stood rooted to the spot, she turned in the autumn wind which was buffeting through the doorway, leaves scattering across the floor, making small scratching sounds as if dozens of tiny brown mice were scrambling over the black and white marble. It was as if time had ceased to exist. She was draped in a sheet which hung almost to the ground, her feet lost higher in the column of fabric. Her head rested at almost a right angle to her body and as her face turned toward me I saw it was contorted, her eyes staring like opaque glass. A puddle of liquid caught the reflection of the light. A short distance away a ladder lay on its side. The grotesque marionette hung limp and heavy, like a sandbag. I turned from the threshold and regurgitated last night's dinner on the front step.

Stumbling like a drunkard I bumped and scurried my way back to the car, grappling for the handle to get inside. Rosa started to bark. The bloody door wouldn't open, I tugged and pulled in my desperation until finally it gave way and jerked wildly wide on its hinges, cracking me on my shin, but I hardly felt it. I flung myself into the seat and slammed the door shut behind me, thumping down the lock. Keys? Where were the fucking keys? I fumbled at the ignition, in my pockets, around on the seat .... Oh God! They were with the front door key. They were on the same ring. They were still in the house lock!

I grabbed the steering wheel and crashed my head down on my rigid hands and sobbed.

I don't know how long I stayed like that. Rosa was whining, nuzzling at me, my eyes burned in my head. The police, I had to tell the police. I had to get the keys and tell the police.

I raised my head and took a deep breath. The sour taste of vomit scorched my throat. Slowly lifting the lock I then pulled on the handle and the door gently opened. I felt that all the demons of hell were lurking outside my car. I felt I must tread gently so as not to stir the shadows of this nightmare, for they would surely rise up and encompass me in all their evil blackness if they were disturbed.

I swiped my hand across my mouth, aware of the stubble on my face, the dry flecks of puke, the gauntness of my skin. With slow, reluctant steps I walked with fear and horror back toward the house. A few metres from it I stopped. I stood swaying, trying to find the courage to move forward, my hands were clasped together in something resembling a motion of prayer. My breath was deep and laboured. My ears were filled with a void of silence. It was as if no birds sung, no wind blew and no squirrels clicked their gripping claws up the sides of the trees. The world was silent, ominously silent, the silence of threat - the silence of death. I swallowed hard and forced myself forward. I tried not to breathe so deeply, I didn't want to inhale the tainted air; I pressed a hand in front of my mouth lest the putrid contamination should invade my body. Then I was level with the open door, I had only to reach out and take the keys, which hung motionlessness in the lock.

I willed myself to reach out and just pull out the keys, to not look inside, to not let my eyes be drawn to the ghost like form which floated above the ground in spectral suspense. But I couldn't. Against my will as if my head were being tugged at with invisible threads I turned to look once more upon that gallows corpse, and having looked, I could not look away.

"Sasha! Oh! Sasha, what have you done?" I whispered. The black-death shadows crept reluctantly away as pity and sorrow washed over me. Tears sprung to my eyes and clouded my vision; I sunk slowly to the ground, gripping the door stanchion, never taking my gaze from her strangely elongated body in its ghostly shroud.

It was cold, so cold.

The wind was blowing fiercely and it blew through the doorway, scattering seasonal debris in the hall. It blew the edges of the cotton sheet and swung the body, I watched its lazy movement as it twirled in a slow dance of death. Where were those happy summer days? Where had they gone? I cried for Sasha and I cried for myself. I cried for love which had been false and for the grotesque face which had felt driven to do this thing. I cried for Donna and the children and my unborn baby, but most of all ... I cried for me.

Time passed.

I forced myself to my feet, raised my hand to take the keys from the lock with the intention of closing up the house and driving to the nearest police station to report Sasha's death. It never occurred to me to telephone; I just wanted to be away from her. I pulled the door closed; it clicked, obscenely loudly and it was as if someone had flicked a giant switch and all around me the clattering din of wind and tossed leaves vibrated through my head. Suddenly all the world was noise, the keys jangled in my hand with as little subtlety as the organ music of a fairground ride. The robins in the naked cherry tree shrieked and squawked like kookaburras while the squirrels ran from tree to tree with the metallic clanging of a factory floor. So much noise did not seem respectful with a body so close. It rang and jangled through my head accompanied by pictures vivid with blood. A vast lake of ink-black blood spreading out through the bottom of the door and down the steps, over the grass, over the shrubs, spreading over the whole area and beyond and out of the melee rose Sasha. Her sheet was flimsy and tattered, spider web fine, it wafted and floated in the air. She came at me with her beautiful smiling face, the face I had known so long ago; it was framed with gold, fine spun hair which glowed with an otherworldly aura. She came at me on white wings of love, gently, serenely, beckoning me to her and I wanted to go. I was tempted, as she had tempted me before. At that moment I wanted to follow her, take her outstretched hand and fly with her to a happy land where forgiveness ran free. Down she fluttered and I raised my arm to catch her.

With shrieking, wailing speed her face distorted, contorted, the blackened rotten teeth stood like tombstones in her gaping mouth, the green haze which issued from it smelt of sulphur and lime rotted corpses. Her robes were now cobwebs of thunder-clouds. She shrieked at me, came bearing down on me with the Devil's kiss on her lips.

In frantic panic I ran to escape the horrible vision. I made it to my car and with trembling hands I revved the engine into life and crunched it into gear, it jumped and jerked as I pulled out of the drive displacing a shower of gravel and with my foot flat to the floor I ascended the hill.

She didn't give chase.

Once clear of the house I pulled my car to the side of the lane. My hands were shaking uncontrollably, my whole body shook. I was going to go to the police to report Sasha's death and then what? They would come to the house, see her, and want to know all the details, maybe arrest me.

Donna would have to be told, the children, everyone would know me for the adulterous bastard I was. Donna would go. She would take the children and leave me and I could be residing in a damp prison cell somewhere. It wasn't a pretty picture.

Unless ......

Unless no-one need ever know.

The thought whammed into me. I tried to shake it away, tried to dislodge it from my brain but it wouldn't go. What if no one knew? No-one seemed to know where Sasha was, or even less care. Only I knew. What if I took her body and ... what? Buried it, burned it, threw it over a quarry edge? The thought of going back to the house was repulsive ... but ... the thought of prison, or even just questions, endless questions which I could hardly explain the answers to myself much less a police officer, how could I explain? The thought was unbearable.

Could I get away with it?

I could - no-one knew - I could!

* * *

And so I returned.

With furtive footsteps I once again ascended the steps. I inserted the keys into the lock and I pushed the door open. I walked into the hall and with my back against the door I pushed it closed. I couldn't look at her, but even so the picture was vivid in my minds eye. Taking a deep breath I raised my eyes from the doormat and forced myself to see her. I would have to be quick, Donna was due back with the kids that same evening and I was to collect them. With fear and dread in my heart I went to her. I tried to lift the dead weight of her body but there was no way I was going to release her that way, my feet slipped in the pee which was puddled on the floor beneath her. I recoiled, slipping onto my back, whacking my elbow on the fallen step ladder, which I realised she must have used and kicked aside. I was frantically crab walking my way back from the awfulness of it, my prone angle making her elongated form even scarier. I needed scissors. I went to my study to get some. The answer phone light was flicking its little red message indicator.

Automatically I pressed the button, praying Donna wasn't calling to say she would be home sooner. Her voice was unusually loud in these grisly walls. She was staying another week ... Oh God! My breath puffed out from my chest in a gasp of relief. I think I was laughing and crying all at once. Time was on my side suddenly.

I took the scissors from the pot on my desk and climbed the stairs. At the banister at the top I tried to cut the rope, but it hung too tight and the scissors made no impression whatsoever. With a growl of impotent impatience, down I went again, keeping as great a distance as I could manage as I edged past the hanging form to the kitchen. I took a serrated knife from the block. Was it yesterday, or the day before, that Sasha's eyes had drifted to those knives and I had feared for my life? It could have been years ago so distorted had time become. Taking a wide berth once more past her body in the hall I climbed the stairs, my feet dragged like lead weights and each step was a mountain to climb. My breath was traction engine loud as clinging to the rail I edged my way across the landing until I was once more level with the rope looped around the handrail. I took the knife in both my shaking fists and began to saw, back and forth, back and forth, the sweat ran from my face, back and forth as little by little the rope frayed, then snapped in sections. My t-shirt clung to my damp back, I did not stop; my whole body was moving back and forth with the rhythm of my sawing, back and forth - half way through. Down below I tried to avoid the fact that the motion of my cutting was causing Sasha to kink and jerk in tiny movements. Back and forth, three quarters of the way through, small chunks of paint were being cut from the banister, a gouge in the wood as I changed the angle and altered my hands to alleviate the pressure from one to the other, hardly noticing the blister which had sprung up.

Back and forth and then ... snap! There was a horrible, weighty crunching, the thump of a body cut down, the sound of bone on marble as her skull connected with the floor. I peered over the banister and the crumpled heap of Sasha was like a broken doll. The sheet had fallen open exposing her lean body, I thought ironically about how this was the first time I had ever seen her naked, but the blue white of her flesh was repulsive and I recoiled from the thought I must touch her to move her. I moved from the upper landing to the top of the stairs and I sat down, I was exhausted. I sat with my elbows resting on my knees as I stared through the bars of the banister at her limbs, now at unnatural angles. I seemed to be in another place, in a void, disconnected. I tried to keep that feeling as wearily I rose to descend the stairs. I pulled her straight, trying to give her back a little dignity. To see her now, after all this time was wrong. Her pubic hair was shaved; she was as naked as a young girl. It was an obscenity beneath my gaze. I flicked the sheet to cover her modesty and my nostrils were assailed by a strong waft of something familiar, something powerful. Lavender, it came to me, she smelt of lavender, like old ladies sometimes do.

Only Sasha would never be an old lady.

Suddenly I was galvanised into action. I rolled her reluctant body over and un-looped the rope from around her neck, a red welt raised in an upward grin on her bruised neck. I untied the sheet, which was knotted beneath her hair, almost apologising as I pulled a strand too hard, causing her scalp to rise in small white peaks. As I rolled her onto her back again a deep groan issued from her gargoyle mouth, I leapt back in horror. Oh! God, she wasn't dead! She wasn't dead! She didn't move. She was blue-grey, her skin was cold, and her eyes were lifeless. Of course she was dead. Then I remembered something I had read in a life I had seemed to live a thousand years ago, that bodies did make a noise if there was air left inside them. I told myself off, mentally admonishing myself for being so stupid. I wrapped the sheet around her tightly, covering her distorted face with relief, wrapping my grisly parcel as the smell of lavender and urine hung in the air. In the kitchen I took twine from the drawer and I wrapped it round and around Sasha so there was no chance the sheet could flap open.

When she was secured, an abhorrent parcel of lumps and bumps, I sat back on my heels. The sweat was running freely down my face, my body was soaked, my t-shirt had changed colour, from a mid blue to a more forbidding darker shade. My own smell of perspiration blended with the taint of Sasha's body. I didn't know much about dead bodies but I knew I didn't have too much time to play with before rigor mortis kicked in, I felt even as I had been binding her she was less pliable. I didn't know how long she had been dead - hours? - I had no time to waste.

I had to pull my car right up to the front of the house.

I felt weary in body and soul as I stepped outside. The sun was bright in the sky now, a crisp, brilliant morning that under other circumstances would have caused me to smile as I beckoned Rosa to her morning walk and we tramped across fields, the wind biting my cheeks and Rosa finding that she could not run as fast as a rabbit. Only not this morning, this morning I kept my head bowed against the elements and the wind chilled my sweat-damp t-shirt.

I nearly died. I jumped so violently that the postman must have wondered what he had said to scare me so.

"Sorry about that Mr Koweski," he called out jovially, "didn't mean to startle you," his voice a rich, slow, Oxfordshire burr.

I felt myself staring at him as if I were looking at an alien life form.

"You all right?" he asked, sounding concerned.

"What, yes, sorry," I stuttered out.

"You sure, only you don't look so good, if you don't mind me saying", he was looking at me with curious concern.

"I'm fine," I reassured him, "bit of a sleepless night, that's all".

"Well, if you're sure," he didn't sound convinced. "Been working out have you?" he asked nodding toward my sweat marked clothes.

"Yeah!" I agreed. "Did a bit too much I think".

"Here's your post anyway." He handed me a bundle of junk mail and envelopes. I took them automatically and almost dropped them again as a bang caused me to whip round in time to see the front door, which had been caught by the wind swing open, right back on itself.

"That's a fierce wind blowing up the day," he remarked, "aye, right fierce, but bright, we can't complain when the sun's still shining." I tried to smile in polite agreement with his summary of the weather.

Through the opening I could see the very end of Sasha's bundled feet. The postman was standing to the left of me, he couldn't see, I prayed he couldn't see, but I took his arm and gently led him back toward his van, making blithe small talk as I tried to appear normal and distract him from the swinging door. I wished him a good day, and stood and saw him drive off back down the lane, as I waved, in what I hoped was a normal fashion. Swallowing hard I held on to my stomach as I forced myself to not retch again.

I sprang across to my car; Rosa was going mad inside, leaping across the seats and barking loudly. I gunned the engine into life and eased it the twenty yards or so to the front steps, I couldn't get any closer. As I opened the door the stupid dog leapt out of the gap and hurtled toward the house. I charged after her and both of us came to a sliding halt on the marble floor. A deep growl grumbled in Rosa's throat as she surveyed the grizzly package. Her neck hair rose in hackles, her black nose twitching at the pungent reek. I soothed her with calm words.

"Its okay, come on girl, come on old thing, let's takes you in the kitchen then shall we?" I reached for her collar and she jumped, startled, not expecting contact, her growl more menacing. "Come on," I persuaded, "come on Rosa," and half dragging her, we made it to the kitchen. I poured dried food into her bowl and exited as quickly as I could, pulling the door tight shut behind me. From the other side I could hear her whining and scratching at the woodwork. I didn't have time to do more, I ran back outside and opened the boot of my car and then back in the hall, I drew in a deep breath as I prepared myself to hoist Sasha up to take her outside. I was repulsed; the thought of touching her was a complete abhorrence. Beneath the tight bound wrapping I could still visualise the contorted mask of her face, the blue tinged skin, the waxy, yellowing hands, her nails gone death white at the ends of her toes and fingers. I squatted down and heaved the gruesome bundle with the intention of slinging her over my shoulder but her dead weight was heavier than I had imagined and I got her no further than the height of my knees. Rethinking my strategy I hauled her unceremoniously across the floor, leaving a clean trail the width of her body in the dust which had blown through. I dragged her out of the house, checking before I did that the coast was clear. This was a lonely spot but even so I scanned left and right and raked my eyes across the horizon of woodland. Her head bumped with a sickening crack over the doorstep. Once I had her at the top of the steps and could stand lower than her prostrated form I was able to lever her up higher, cradling her in my arms like a giant baby in swaddling robes. I lifted her and laid her with as much care and respect as I could into the boot of the car, taking pains not to bump her poor head again. Rigor mortis was, I felt, definitely settling now, her legs were stiff and I could not easily bend them into the car. I was sobbing as I tried again and again to re-angle her body, pulling her this way and that, until finally I bent her legs at the knees and rammed them with all my might into the confined space and with a crack as loud as gunfire I heard a bone break in the torment which was my morning.

I slammed shut the boot.

I drove: drove deeper and deeper into the countryside, through sleepy villages, where pensioners gathered in shouted conversations against the swirling wind. Through long stretches of winding roads, where gnarled tree roots groped out of the eroded earth, snatching at my mind like witches fingers. I drove with white knuckles, and my body bent forward toward the steering wheel as I pushed my foot down as hard as I dared on the accelerator. I drove up into the chalky mounds of the

Cotswold Hills, to the most isolated spot I could find and there I stopped my car. Stupidly I had put the shovel and the pick in the boot, beneath Sasha's body, I cursed at my mistake. I tugged at her body, but I could not reach them without taking her out first. She was definitely stiffer. Her head and feet tucked beneath the curve of the shape of the boot. I pulled and tugged at her.

"Come out of the car," I pleaded through gritted teeth as my frustration mounted. "Come out of the fucking car!" I pulled so hard I loosened the sheet and the twine bit into my fingers as I looped under it to get more grip. "Please Sasha, please ..." I bent her legs further up and that way managed to finally prise her out. She fell heavily at my feet. I was exhausted but there was no time to rest. I grabbed the pick and the shovel and started to dig. The chalk soil was hard but as I plunged the pick into it, it came loose in huge chunks. I dug a hole, a square hole, because there was no way now I was going to be able to uncurl her legs. I dug as far as I could in my exhaustion, not nearly far enough, but I couldn't go on, and I didn't want to be there any longer than was necessary. I half rolled, half dragged the body, the sheet coming unravelled as I did so, and dumped her callously in the shallow grave. Her hair streamed out like golden whispers of light in the gaping hole. Her eyes stared through me, past me, void of life, of pain, of pleasure. Void of feeling and accusation. Void of the hopes and dreams and fantasies we had shared. Void of the glint of madness as she had tipped over the edge. They stared blankly into the distance, as if glazed with cataracts, and they took my reason with them, stripping me of any vestige of civilisation for this barbaric act I was committing.

I pulled the sheet over her face, over her broken body, and shovelled the earth, stamping it down when there was no more to shovel and kicking leaves and twigs over the area until I felt there was no sign of any digging, no sign of the hideous grave. I threw the tools back into the boot of my car. I felt maybe I should say a prayer or something, but no prayer came, only the groan of words, "Oh Sasha, what have I done?"

SIMON – 1.00pm

The wind dropped and the sun dazzled out of the sky as I drove away. That clear, extraordinarily brilliant light which is angled low, as autumn chases on to become winter. It blinded my eyes as I wended my way through pretty Oxfordshire lanes, it flick-flacked through the trees, now you see it, now you don't; a brilliant dance of disco lights dangerously strobing. I squinted against the brightness. I closed my eyes against the light. I pressed my foot hard down and I drove blind down a straight stretch of narrow lane, straddled either side by crop-empty fields, where the last of the summer swallows looped and swooped in frantic flight. Through my closed lids all went dark. I opened my eyes. The sun had gone behind the one and only cloud in the sky. I stopped my car. I watched a hawk as it circled overhead, then hovered, then dove. I watched as it soared up and away with its lunch between its talons. The swallows had disappeared. At all four points of the compass there was not a living soul, not a house, not a car, just me, sitting in my little metal box as it softly spluttered and guzzled its petrol and hummed its monotonous tune.

I held my hands out in front of me and looked at them fronts and backs. The palms were blistered and had been bleeding. The nails were ragged and encrusted with mud. But more than that they had the shadows of evil engrained in each line and crack. I thought I would never be able to look at my hands again without seeing evil.

A hare raised its head, I saw it sniff the air; it scented danger. I wondered if it scented me, scented evil. Its ears twitched, lay flat and it was off, leaping and bounding across the ruts of the uneven field into the safety of the copse beyond. I never saw what it was running from.

I pushed the gear stick into first, slipped off the handbrake and drove back toward *'Dreams'*.

It was after two o'clock when I reached the house. If I were to maintain my cold-blooded act of having disposed of Sasha's body I would need to do some clearing up. I started with sharp, frantic movements to first sweep and then scrub the hallway floor. The disinfectant I had poured into the water stung the open wounds on my hands, but I cared not. I scrubbed all over the floor and went back to the spot where she had fallen again and again and again. I scrubbed it so many times I lost count and still above the antiseptic scent of the fluid came the putrid odour of lavender and piss combined. I changed the water three or four times, every time pouring in a liberal dose of disinfectant but it made no difference, I couldn't get rid of the smell beneath.

I went over the house with a fine toothcomb looking for traces of Sasha. I picked out long blond hairs from my hairbrush in the bathroom; I found mascara I didn't think was Donna's. I collected them up with her pile of clothes neatly folded on the silver dressed bed. I put them into the Aga and they burned away. I scrubbed the floor again. Rosa was repulsed by the smell of disinfectant and stayed in the kitchen, tail tucked between her legs. When I could find nothing else left to clean I cleaned myself. I stood beneath the shower and ran the water as hot as I could stand and I took the nailbrush and scrubbed my hands. The bristles of the nailbrush caught beneath the bubble of my blister and ripped the skin, the white flap of it bouncing back and forth under the water jets, the pink beneath a small area of intense pain in a body that was totally racked with pain and fatigue. I brushed my teeth until my gums bled and spat out the vile taste of puke and the taste of the smell I could not shift from my senses. I scrubbed and washed, I brushed and scraped and still I felt dirty. I dressed in clothes which suddenly seemed to hang loose on my body. I burned my clothes from earlier in the day, prodding them into the fiery heart of the Aga with the poker and slamming the door shut as the smoke billowed.

SIMON – 5.00pm

I couldn't cross the hall, couldn't walk across the patch where Sasha had smashed so unceremoniously to the ground, I took a circuitous route around the edge of the wall. I drank a glass of orange juice and the citric acid caused my stomach to bubble and growl as I fought to keep the juice down. When I was certain the fire had burned my clothes, my shoes, my belt and all Sasha's clothes I made my preparations to leave. I gathered a little food and a litre bottle of water. I didn't know where I was going, but I knew at that moment I would never come back. I would figure out later what I would tell Donna.

I walked around the edge of the walls to the study to collect the few bits and pieces I would need. I opened the drawer of the desk and lying on top of pens, papers and odds and ends was an envelope with my name. I recognised Sasha's artistic sweep of letters, the elaborate 'S', the long tail she had given the 'n' and the hard, determined underline in a sharp diagonal. I sat and looked for a very long time at the envelope. I was aware it had become dark outside, but still the white letter seemed to glow from the drawer in ghostly brightness. Eventually I forced myself to pick it up. I thought it would weigh heavy in my hand but it was as normal as any other letter. The same weight as a water bill or a party invitation, it ought to have weighed heavy.

I flicked on the desk lamp and the sudden brightness made me blink. I angled the lamp-head away from my face, lessening the impact. I took my letter opener, a gift from Donna, and I slit the flap of the envelope. Inside was a single sheet of paper, it was printed from a computer, probably from my computer. My hand shook and the paper rustled between my fingers. Laying it flat on the desk I smoothed out the folds and started to read.

My Darling Simon,
If you are reading this, I am dead.

I have loved you Simon, I have loved you more than you will ever know. It has hurt me to love you and it hurt me even more when I came to realise that you could not love me in the same way. What we had for a while was pure and beautiful. We didn't need the grunting, thrusting physical love which men inflict on women, we were above that, better than that. You took me to places in my head which made me soar; you made me feel safe, protected and cherished.

I loved you so much. I was always grateful for that day we met. Even now I am still grateful, for you made me so very happy. I wanted to make you happy. I wanted to help you, to save you from a life of drudgery and struggle. The day we sat in 'our' steamy little coffee shop with the rain trickling down the window pane and we chatted all afternoon was one of the happiest of my life. Our fingers entwined on the table top, our legs wrapped around each others beneath. I loved the way you kissed my finger tips, I loved the way you brushed your thumb over the inside of my wrist, so sensual, but so uncomplicated.

I wasn't trying to buy your love. I truly wanted you to have happiness with 'Dreams', it was your house, mostly as you had described it that afternoon. Your dream house - it was my gift to you. I can't pretend I didn't have visions of us being there together, of course I did, and now we can, for although you will not see me I will always be with you. I have nowhere left to go now, and you will not let me stay.

My former life no longer exists and because you do not love me my present life no longer exists. But I have a future life, I truly believe that. I know you Simon, and I am gambling on the fact you will do just as I anticipate. I have watched you these last few days; you are a man on the edge. I am certain of that, as certain as I possibly can be.

I do know you Simon.

I have written to Sylvester, Markham and Tweed advising them that if you try to sell 'Dreams' or if anything should happen to it, an unexplained fire for example, then they are to open a second letter which I enclosed. In that I have explained that I feared for my life and I feared you. There will no doubt be an enquiry to find my body. By that time Simon what will you have done? I'm sorry, don't think me cruel, but you must stay at 'Dreams'.

We can be happy here Simon, you have a beautiful house, you have all the money you need, and I will be near.

My crime was only that I loved you too much.

Look for me, for I am always near.

With all my love my Darling,

Sasha x

I sat for a very long time, the letter trembling slightly between my fingers. I sat and stared into the past and into the future and wondered how the hell I had gone so wrong. The clock in the library chimed, waking me from my trance. I had never drunk in my life, never felt the need, never wanted to lose control, but I felt the need now. I went into the library, to the dark mahogany cabinet on the far wall and opened the doors. There was an array of bottles, all untouched; they had come with the house. I didn't know what to drink but I wasn't sure it mattered. In films people always seemed to grab whiskey, so I grabbed whiskey and poured a large tumbler full. I threw the liquid down my throat, coughing and spluttering at the awfulness of it. 'People actually drank this for pleasure,' I thought wryly – 'how?' I poured another, and another, warmth was creeping through my body. The taste was no less repulsive but the anesthetising effect was welcome. I drank straight from the bottle, weaving back to the cabinet to pick it up and on wobbly legs carry it to the kitchen. I flung open cupboards and the fridge to find food, I was suddenly violently hungry. I found cheese and crackers and ate them straight from the packets, washed down with more of the disgusting brown liquid. I think I rammed into the units a couple of times, they seemed to keep looming out in front of me, I remember no more.

SIMON - 10.00pm

I awoke cold and stiff. I had no idea where I was, or how I had got there. I tried to move but my head throbbed as though a thousand soldiers were yomping inside. It felt as though it was a lead balloon, I could hardly lift it. The effort was too much; I let it lie again and drifted away.

SIMON – Midnight

If ever I felt ill enough to want to die this was the moment. I lay still, trying to work out where I was and what had happened. The floor beneath me was hard. I was cold. The side of my face was crusted and the smell of sick was strong. I tried to move but I just couldn't. I drifted away. As I closed my eyes again the thumping in my head it echoed in amplified boom-beats around my temples. I shifted very slightly and my stomach leapt somersaults of nausea. Better just to close my eyes and not wake up. I shivered violently.

SIMON – DAY 2 - 5am

It surely must be easier to be dead. My eyes felt crusted shut and I had no idea of the day, the time, the place, all I knew was, I was too cold to move, too sick to care and my head hurt too much to endure.

I needed to pee.

I dragged myself to my knees, still unable to open my eyes. The room was spinning wildly, bucking and revolving in a mad fashion as my arms, too weak to support me, cause me to pitch forward onto the crown of my head. My limbs felt as though they were made of rubber, squishy and uncontrollable. I tried again to prise open my lids, one just about made it, the other appeared glued down. The light was spilling from the kitchen, too bright.

I was on all fours, my right arm coated with dried sick, and my hands resting flat in the half digested pool of cheese, crackers and whiskey. I was in the hall, lying on the very spot where Sasha had laid. I raised my one open eye and saw her naked body swinging above my head. There was no winding sheet, just the soft blush of her skin, the mound of her bare pubic bone, the flat, taut stomach, the full breasts, the smiling, kindly face, looking down on me with the sort of look a tolerant mother gives an errant child.

'*Come*,' she whispered to me as she held out her arms, but her voice was a rasp of rope tightened hoarseness. The fibrous rope held her caught, stretched tight like a Mexican finger trick. Trickling from beneath the brown noose a globule of blood seeped, her face began to loose its smile as she felt the passage of the single drop as it ran over her collar bone. A ruby bright bead trickling down her chest, between her voluptuous, pink tipped breasts, I watched its steady progress as it passed her ribs, detoured around her belly-button, veered slowly toward her hip and traced down the long, smooth golden brown of her leg. I watched as it passed her ankle and ran slowly to her ballet dancer poised toe, where it hung suspended. I watched it, and I waited, and it hung, and she hung, and suddenly it was too heavy and it splashed to the floor, exploding as if a whole tin of pillar box red paint had hit the spot. I leapt back to avoid the cascade of heavy droplets. My body recoiled from the sight of her.

But she was not there.

SIMON – DAY 3 – 8.00am

The previous day passed - passed with me doing nothing more than sink into bed and sleep and suffer. Drinking had not been the answer.

On this Wednesday, this new day I woke with a different perspective. I lay looking at the ceiling going over the events of the last year and particularly the last few days. For reasons I did not recognise I felt unshackled from my hell of the last days. Maybe drink had been the answer?

Sasha was dead and I was set free. I preferred not to think of my foray into the woods with her still body, I pushed that to a recess of my mind where it would not come tip toeing out to disturb me. She was dead; she could not come creeping from her resting place to hurt me now. As I lay still I knew I had a chance to rebuild. I showered then stripped the bed. I took a piping hot cup of coffee to my study in my Bart Simpson mug, and I pulled out Sasha's letter. I read it again and again searching for a line, a word, which would suggest suicide and not implicate me as a murderer. There wasn't one; she had thought her words out very carefully. I raked my fingers through my hair again and again until it stood on end. I scanned through the computer looking for clues, anything which would help, there was nothing; she had deleted any documents she might have made. I considered the possibilities of what would happen if I now went to the police. I wasn't sure I could even lead them to Sasha's grave; it had been a very isolated spot. The thought kept coming back, she was gone and I was the only one who knew. So long as I stayed at '*Dreams'* and Mr Markham were not given any opportunity to open that damning letter I was okay. It was an axe hanging on a thin thread over my head, but whilst it continued to hang and did not fall I was safe – I hoped.

If I said nothing, did nothing, just carried on with Donna and the kids as normal, all could be well. If I picked them up from the airport, brought them back to this house and we faced each day as it happened, if I faced each day as it happened, it might be all right. Was there any other way? I didn't think so. She had entrapped me, had got her way in the end. I could not leave '*Dreams*'. I had to live her warped fantasy life.

Or I could die as well!

I considered the thought objectively.

I didn't want to die.

I thought of Donna, thought of her soft, round body and the baby growing inside her. I thought of her dark hair with its neat bob swinging on her shoulders. I thought of the smell of her, the soft dusky scent which was so comforting. I thought of her hands, so small, which knew my body so well, knew how to please me. I thought of the contentment I felt in lying in her arms after making love, how she would stroke back my hair and we would chat in low tones so as not to wake the children. I craved her. Suddenly I craved the warm motherly comfort of her. I wanted her to come and wrap her arms around me and whisper into my hair that it would be all right, I had made a mistake, lots of mistakes but it would be all right, she would look after me, protect me, without knowing why or how. I wanted to feel like a child who has lapsed in some small misdemeanour and who finally confides in his mother knowing she will make it all better, will be able to untangle his small mess and repair the damage.

I was in no small mess and the damage was way too serious for simple repairs. I could never tell Donna or anyone else. This was my burden and I would have to bear the guilt of it all on my own. It was my gaol sentence.

I would try to forget, to get on with my life. Surely with Sasha gone I had a chance.

Rosa was being neglected – I would start as I meant to go on and first thing first was to take Rosa for a long walk. I pulled her lead from the door and she leapt to her feet excited, looking like she had previously and not the sad, mopping, nervous creature she had been since encountering Sasha's parcelled body. I walked around the edge of the re-cleaned hallway; Rosa did too, funny how she would not pass over that spot either.

Her tail wagged slowly at first and then more eagerly, she understood 'walkies'. I carried her lead, I only took it from force of habit;

I hardly ever needed to use it. She came out of the house leaping and bounding in expectation, running fast and elatedly ahead before veering back to my feet, whatever game was going on in her head she was enjoying it immensely. We walked up the incline to the woods. The crisp air felt good on my face, clean, brisk air which was blowing away all the cobwebs of guilt and awfulness I had experienced. I felt it was blowing colour into my face and washing away the grey tautness of my nerves. I looked to the sky and sucked in the blue canopy and the fluffy white clouds scudding across the vastness of it. The weak sunrays shone through my closed eyelids purging my soul. I breathed in the clean wind that blew, I breathed deeply, sighing at the rejuvenating effect and for that moment I really believed it could all be behind me.

Rosa was ferreting around in the undergrowth, smelling out all kinds of doggy delights, I followed her through the woods, the ground had the softness of a thick, spongy mattress of rain squashed autumn leaves; they dipped below my feet as I tramped through the trees. I stopped to untangle a bramble which had hooked my jumper pulling a long brown tread loose. When I turned to continue on my way, Rosa had disappeared. I called her, but got no answering bark. I looked thought the trees, shaking her lead, that normally brought her running - but nothing. As I sought her left and right the hairs on the back of my neck rose, my nerves were not as settled as I had hoped. Finally I spotted her blond body ahead of me through a thicket. She was crouched on the ground. I called her and saw her ears twitch, but she did not turn to me, her focus was on something directly ahead of her. Her body was a twitching electric current of terrified expectancy, as I approached I heard her growling, deep and low. She jumped as I stood on a twig and it cracked like a whiplash but still her eyes did not move. I edged closer, I didn't know what to expect. My legs felt heavy and my mind was once again in turmoil as I thought of one possibility after another and the small, still rational part of me eliminated them. We were near the stream; it was bubbling and gurgling over smooth pebbles, swollen as it had been by recent rains. It sounded cold, the very rushing of the usually tiny trickle of water sounded icy. Rosa was crouched down looking toward the stream and as I rounded the final tree I saw a beautifully carved wooden plaque. It was mounted on a post. It gleamed in its newly polished finish. Rosa was growling at the plaque. I drew closer.

"It's okay girl, it's nothing," I whispered, trying as much to convince her as myself. I drew close enough to read the words: *'In the cloud shrouded cottage, set before the flowing water one can forget the troubles of the world'.* I stood transfixed. I had walked this way a hundred times and the sign had never been there before. I stood and I wanted to cry. My face screwed up in an effort to hold back the sting of warm, salty water at the back of my eyes and the swelling in my throat. In my anger and despair I rushed at the sign. "Leave me alone," I cried, as I tore it from it's post, tore it with both my bare hands and flung it to the ground. I jumped on it, my heavy hiking boots skidding on the polished surface so I nearly lost my balance. I stamped one foot hard and harder onto the shiny face of the sign, hard and harder until it cracked, cracked clean in half. Then I picked up the two pieces and flung them, one west and one east, flung them as far as my angry outburst could project them. I karate kicked out at the post, kicked it again and again until it leaned in a drunken fashion and with one final heel kick was felled to the ground. I pulled it up, pulled it from the hole in which it had stood and the heavy javelin of wood flew, went splashing into the stream and the icy water eddied around the pointed spike and washed away the mud which clung to it.

"Leave me alone," I screamed into the golden-brown autumn woods. "Leave me alone."

The trees whispered back in sinister tones.

I looked for Rosa, she was gone.

I ran stumbling back to the house, whistling and calling on the way.

As I ran pell mell over the ridge I was greeted by a sight which made my heart leap. The house was all activity, for there in the drive was a maroon seven seater Volkswagen disgorging children and luggage all over the gravel and amid the throng was Donna, calm, organised, barely recognisable as the wife who had left Fallgrove all those months ago, but still Donna, my Donna. I ran forward, the hill propelling me at speed.

The children spotted me and began pointing and shouting, Rosa was in the midst of them, tail wagging joyously at the petting she was being given. They came at me as one, and I hugged and kissed tanned brown faces, and ruffled hair lightened by the Florida sun. All except Donna who stood statue still behind the taxi, staring at me, when I could disentangle myself from the throng I walked toward her, stopping a few steps in front of her. I felt suddenly shy with her.

"I wasn't expecting you just yet," I told her.

"We were worried about you, I never heard anything back from you so we got an earlier flight." Her voice was slightly hesitant as if she didn't know me either.

"Oh God Donna, I've missed you," there was a throb in my voice as I moved to take her in my arms. She melted into me, soft and yielding. My sweet, sweet Donna, my wife, my life, I smelled her hair, her skin, pressed her to my body with the intention of never letting her go, kissed her just above her ear and her arms around my back were all comforting.

It was her who moved first to pull away; she held me at arms length and put her head to one side quizzically. "Have you been ill? You look dreadful."

"I've been fighting off some flu bug," I lied.

"You look like you've been on the Atkins diet, you've lost so much weight," her eyes were all concern. "I'll have to feed you up now I'm back," she smiled at me and the love and the trust in her eyes tore at my guts.

"Come on, I said let's get you inside, I bet you could do with a cup of tea."

"I'd murder for one," she laughed. I tried to laugh too, but the word *murder* reverberated in the air, I almost felt I could see it written in smoke between us. "Come on," she encouraged linking her arm through mine, "we've so much to tell you." We all headed for the house, a noisy, chattering mass, clutching suitcases and holdalls as the taxi pulled away.

We dumped the bags just inside the front door and the children scattered to their rooms. Donna was fiddling with one of the bags as I headed to the kitchen to put on the kettle.

"What are you doing?" she asked.

"Going to put on the kettle, why?"

"I know that, but why are you walking around the edge of the hall?" the expression on her face was one of puzzlement.

"Was I?" I tried to sound perplexed. "I hadn't realised." She raised her eyebrows and shook her head in that way which implies no understanding.

We drank tea and Donna rattled on about sun and sea and sand. About Disney, the rides, the thrills, about shopping and the children trying all the water sports and how glad she was to be home. I only half listened, I watched her face, so animated, so innocent and more than ever at that moment I wanted to turn back the clock and eradicate the bitter past. I had a new steely determination to only look forward and although I was tied to this monstrosity of a house at least I still had Donna and the kids and a tenuous hope sprung up that I could move forward and not look back again. Then I remembered the plaque by the stream and I shivered involuntarily.

"What's the matter, someone walk over your grave?" Donna quipped lightly.

"Don't say that!" I almost shouted it at her, banging down my mug and spilling my tea on the counter.

She looked alarmed. "What's the matter? I didn't mean anything. What's the matter Simon?" She reached out her hand and touched my forearm.

"Nothing. Sorry." I mumbled. "I'll take the bags upstairs." I left the kitchen, skirted the hall and picked up two of the suitcases. I felt

Donna watching me from the threshold and I turned to give her a smile. Hovering above the ground between Donna and me was a shadow of a figure. I saw Donna through the misty silhouette, still standing looking puzzled as my eyes focused first on the nearness of the shape and then at Donna in the background. She came forward; she walked right through the shape of the other woman.

"Noooo!" I shouted out a warning, but it was too late, she didn't heed my hand outstretched as a signal to stop until she was right there, right in the middle of the luminous haze. Then she stopped, her face a frown of bewilderment which softened even as I entreated her with silent gestures to move, it softened to a smile framed in a cloud of corn-blond hair as Sasha nodded at me. Her hands were crossed over at her throat. She lowered them, first one, then the other and the wicked smile left by the hangman's rope glistened purple and red from her eerie light.

Donna was pulling at my arm, "Simon, Simon, what's wrong? Simon." I looked past her to the empty hall. Slowly turning my head toward her I raised my hand to touch her face, her face - Donna's face, soft skinned and real. I touched her hair, silky smooth, dark and shiny - Donna's hair. "Come on, I'll help you take these up," she said. She picked up a couple of the smaller bags and we made our way up the stairs.

Music was thumping out of Peta's room and the boys sounded as though they were using their beds as trampolines. We dumped the cases on our bed and Donna unlocked them and began to sort out the contents for washing or putting away accordingly. I went cautiously back down the stairs to collect more cases, I looked around me warily but the hall was empty – she was gone.

That night when the children were all asleep in bed or at least in their rooms being quiet, Donna and I sat in the playroom, off the kitchen, sunk deep into the squishy sofa sipping our coffee and snuggling close. The television was on but we weren't really watching. It just felt so nice to have her in the circle of my arm. She smelled different, not the baby powder softness I was used to but a new, more womanly smell. It was intoxicating. I felt desire stir in me as I held her close, but I also longed not to break the spell. Every now and then I dropped kisses on the top of her head or she would turn to kiss my cheek. The moment was building and I knew she was anticipating it as much as I was. Our coffee was drunk and I didn't want to wait any longer. I took her empty mug from her hand and put it on the table. I pressed the button on the remote and the glare from the television faded to blackness. We rose as one, flicking light switches as we went, moving to the stairs, still hand in hand.

"I need to brush my teeth," she told me, so we separated to our own bathrooms and prepared for bed. I was lying between the cold sheets when she came back into the room. She stood at the foot of the bed and in the small light from my bedside lamp she slowly and seductively began to undress. Teasing me with her eyes I watched as she undid the buttons of her shirt, slowly, from the bottom, one by one, then slid it from her shoulders. Her skin was bronzed and gleaming with good health. My breath caught in my throat as I took in the sight of her tanned stomach, swelling with the new life inside her, the ripeness of her breasts above her cream coloured lacy bra. She reached her hands behind her and pulled the zip of her skirt, it fell in a swirling pool to her feet. The side strings of her thong arched snugly over her hips holding a cream triangle of matching lace, showing dark pubic hair beneath. She stepped out of the puddle of skirt and walked to the bed. Sitting down with her back to me, she looked coyly back over her shoulder. "Unhook me," she whispered. I was all fingers and thumbs as I fiddled with the fastening of her bra and I could feel her smile, it was as if this were our first time. Her bra fell open and she crossed one arm over her breasts to stop it from falling. One strap slipped down her shoulder and I leaned up on my elbow to kiss her skin, she shivered in delicious anticipation beneath my lips. Standing again she paused for a moment as I took in the curve of her bottom in her lacy thong, a triangle of white missing from her tan, bikini shaped. She turned slowly, seductively, peeling the other strap of her bra with her free hand and then letting it fall. She was a goddess standing before me in her lush, warm, sexuality. I was aroused, deeply aroused, my erection pushing up against the bed sheets. She was enjoying her display, enjoying my gaze upon her. This was a new Donna, exciting, passionate, boldly sensual, she exuded confidence and sexuality and I wondered if she had always been this way and I had just forgotten. She came across the bed on all fours, a predator, her mane of hair swinging back and forth, her breasts jiggling, her eyes gleaming with passion. She came at me and sunk her moistened lips upon mine and consumed me. I went to embrace her but she pinned my wrists to the bed, climbing astride me, I could feel the dampness of her as she brushed the skin of my stomach. Holding me prisoner in her grasp, lost beneath the tangle of her hair she kissed me deeply, tongues probing, exploring, learning all over again what we knew so well. I hungered for her. She released my arms and straightening her body upwards she pushed the soft fabric of her thong aside, she lifted my hardness, guided my swollen head along the length of her, grazing her clitoris before sinking slowly down on me and I sighed a sigh of deep satisfaction as she began to slowly rise and fall as she impaled herself on me, her eyes locked on mine.

Donna's deep brown eyes seemed almost glazed with blue, her rich chestnut hair swung blond in the half light, her smile increased from love to predatory, my stomach recoiled, my erection shrank as I wriggled beneath her, fighting to be free, pushing her roughly off of me as the misty vapour of her legs and arms floated around my body and I thrashed wildly to disperse them.

Donna moved with speed away from me. Her face was a mixture of hurt and puzzlement; she grabbed a corner of the quilt and held it protectively in front of her nakedness. "What happened?" she asked in wounded tones.

"Donna, I'm sorry, I ..." I didn't know what to say. "Come here, please come here."

"You looked at me as if you ... I don't know ... were scared of me ... hated me even," she was looking to me for an explanation. I held out my hand and with some reluctance, it seemed, she lay down beside me and I held her tight. In time I felt her relax.

"I'm sorry." I whispered to her.

"It doesn't matter," she tried to reassure me, but it did matter, she had been so ripe, so ready, and I had been unable to satisfy her and I could feel her undercurrent of frustration. I held her even closer and eventually we drifted to sleep.

SIMON - DAY 4

I awoke late the next morning; it had been a refreshing sleep. The smell of bacon and coffee drifted up the stairs. I checked the clock and unbelievably it read 10.50. I lay gazing into nothing and felt more like me than I had felt for a very long time.

The bedroom door opened and Donna was walking in backwards, bumping the door open with her bottom, a tray in her hands. She smiled when she saw I was awake. I smiled back at her.

"Donna," I started tentatively, "I'm sorry, last night, you know ..." I left the sentence unfinished.

"It doesn't matter, really it doesn't," she smiled at me and sounded like she really meant it. "Now sit up and eat this whilst it's hot," she ordered.

"You're spoiling me."

"You look like you need spoiling. That flu must have really taken it out of you, you look awful."

"Thanks," I responded with mock sarcasm.

"S'okay," she was smiling at me, "I'm back. I shouldn't have left you for so long. I'll look after you."

"I love you Donna, you know that don't you?" There was a note of desperation in my voice, I heard it myself.

"'Course I know it. I love you too." She balanced the breakfast tray on the bedside table and sat down on the side of the bed. "You're okay aren't you?" she asked trying to mask the concern in her voice. "I mean, well, while I was away, I know you were ill but you and me ... we're okay?"

I reached for her and drew her close. "We're okay," I reassured her. "I am so glad you're home."

She rose to get the tray and place it across my lap. "Well, for someone who was ill you did a fine job of keeping the house clean, I could eat my dinner off the floor downstairs." The china rattled on the tray balanced on my knees as I forced a smile.

"Well, you do what you can, don't you," I quipped, hoping my voice sounded lighter than I felt.

"You enjoy your breakfast, I'll be up shortly for the tray, I just need to clear up the kids breakfast things, Suki said she would take the boys to the cinema in Oxford this afternoon before she goes back to college, they're dying to see some machines fighting against the world thing," she rose.

"Don't go," I entreated, "sit with me while I eat." She dutifully sat back down. I polished off the bacon and eggs and mopped my plate with the hunk of bread on the side. Donna must have been out early to the local farm shop. It was all delicious. When it was done and washed down with hot coffee I lay back and gave a sigh of satisfaction. Donna moved the tray and came back to the side of the bed and perched on the edge. I took her hand, kissed her fingers and lay it down on my bare chest. Her small palm radiated warmth through me, I pulled her closer, she kissed my forehead. I raised my face for more. Her kisses landed light as butterflies down my face, my cheeks, my nose and finally her soft lips brushed mine. I pulled her down, rolling her over my body until she was flat on the other side of the bed and I was above her. Her eyes danced as she looked into mine. She could feel me pressing hard against her, gently thrusting against her jeans. Her small hand came down to stroke my throbbing cock and I closed my eyes and moaned with pleasure. I grappled with her belt, her button, her zipper. I pushed her jeans from one side then the other over her hips, feeling my hand brush against her soft, warm skin. She thrust her bottom in the air and wriggled her trousers down her legs, kicking them with one foot and then the other until they were off. She was wearing nothing underneath and the very thought of it made me feel even more horny. I moved between her legs, spreading her wide open ready to take me inside her and become one.

Golden hair spread out on the pillow beneath me, I saw it and I smelt it, the cloying scent of lavender. I shook my head and told myself she was not there, this was Donna, Donna my wife, I could feel her spread around me, waiting for me. I looked and Sasha had pain in her eyes, *"Don't make me do it, please don't make me,"* her voice was pleading, her eyes begging for me to stop. I sprung from the bed, all arousal diminished. I ran for the bathroom and gripping the edge of the sink I stared into the mirror and looked at the gaunt man staring back.

'I'm going mad,' a voice in my head reasoned. I jumped as Donna stood at my back, fastened back into her jeans a look on her face which belied understanding.

"Get showered Simon," she told me gently, "get showered and dressed and come downstairs, we should talk."

The hot water pouring over me did nothing to ease my turbulent mind, but I stood under it for a long time, too weary to move. The rejuvenating effect of a good nights sleep was eliminated by the ghost of Sasha stealing into my reason. I dried, dressed and made my way downstairs. Donna must have heard me for she popped her head round the kitchen door in time to see me inching around the edge of the hall.

She said nothing.

"How long have we been married Simon?" she asked as soon as I walked into the kitchen. She continued to stir milk into two cups of coffee as she spoke.

"Twenty years, near as damn it," I responded in what I hoped was a jovial fashion.

"Twenty years? Do you think I don't know you?"

"What do you mean?" I asked, taking a proffered coffee and turning away to sit at the table.

""Twenty years! I know you inside out."

Stop a voice inside my head screamed, stop those words, *'I know you Simon better than you know yourself,'* I pushed them away and looked back at Donna with wide eyed innocence. "Well if you don't who does?" I tried to stay calm, stay light, but fear was licking at my conscience.

"What's wrong? Something is wrong? Can you tell me?" her voice was anxious. She came to the table and putting down her coffee she rested her hand over mine, her eyes were misty with concern.

Between us on the table was the morning's post, a small stack of envelopes unopened. My eyes were drawn to it, angled below the top one was a white envelope, I could just see a corner of the writing, spirals of tails and swirls. It was writing I recognised instantly, like when one opens a book and your own name leaps out from a page of print. I released Donna's hand and grabbed at the post. The envelope was one of my own; I recognised it as being the same as the type Sasha had left in my desk drawer. This one was addressed to Donna. 'How can it be?' A voice screamed inside my head. 'She's dead, I saw her. I buried her!'

"Simon. Simon, will you listen to me, I'm trying to understand here. Will you put down the post and talk to me," her voice sounded exasperated. I tried but the envelope in my hand would not let me go. Donna snatched it from me, saw it was addressed to her and ripped it open.

"No!" I cried out, making a grab for it, "No!"

But she was too quick. She jumped up from her seat and put some distance between us. Unfolding the single sheet her eyes scanned the page. There must have been few words for it took seconds. She looked from the letter to me and back again. I couldn't meet her eyes. "What does it mean Simon?" she asked, flinging the sheet of paper toward me.

It skidded across the table; I didn't touch it but read the single line of printed words. *Your husband knows who gave him the house – ask him.* That was all it said.

Donna's voice was low. "Well?" she asked. I didn't answer, I sat slouch shouldered, my head hung low. "Well!" she screamed at me, "what does it mean, what do you know?"

"Shhh!" I tried to calm her.

"Don't Shhh! me, what does it mean? Do you know?"

It was time.

I nodded almost imperceptibly. "Let's go in the library," I suggested, "before the children hear." I rose and led the way before she had time to object. The library was set out with two deep cushioned sofas at right angles to each other. Huge comfortable pieces of furniture with dusty pink damask roses printed on a cream background. The children loved to curl up on these sofas with their books, or more especially their Gameboys, lost in the vastness of them. Donna sat on one. I pushed the door behind me until it clicked shut then made my way to sit beside her. She held up her hand indicating I should sit on the other sofa, rebuffed before I had even started I took my place. She looked at me, her eyes enquiring.

"So who gave you the house?" she asked in a would-be calm voice.

"Donna, I ..." the words didn't seem to want to form.

"No, go on," she urged, with a hint of sarcasm, "I'm all ears."

"Look, I need to tell you this story, but please don't interrupt me, hear what I have to say." She lifted an eyebrow but refrained from comment.

My mouth was suddenly dry. The day had come when I must confess my guilt, must confess my adultery, for although apart from the frenzied attack in the hall, which hardly counted as the same thing, I had not been physically adulterous. It had all been mind games; my whole mind had committed adultery a thousand times with Sasha. I wondered if Donna would notice the distinction between thought and action.

I told her in stilted words about the meeting at the Ashmolean. I did not spare myself any shame as I confessed to being attracted to Sasha and wanting to meet her again. I told her about our walks by the river, our chatting over coffee, the hand holding, the kisses; I told her of our whispered passions, the need and the longing without ever consummating our relationship. It sounded disgusting. To my own ears it sounded sordid and sleazy, making me appear like a furtive pervert in a dirty raincoat as I wanked myself to satisfaction. I did not spare myself. I confessed how I had dropped Sasha because I knew I loved Donna, I heard her "Huh!" although she did not interrupt further. I told how I had seen the red Lotus but had not connected it to Sasha, how I had even pointed it out to Donna in the village, she gave a small nod of acknowledgement. I explained that I did not realise I was being stalked and when the house had been presented to me I had felt trapped, unable to explain my suspicions.

"You were so enthusiastic for it," I said.

"So now it's my fault," she threw at me bitterly.

"No, no, I didn't mean that, but you loved it so much and I couldn't tell you the truth," my words sounded lame.

"You could have turned it down."

"I tried Donna, if you remember I did try,"

For a moment she looked as though she was going to concede that point, but the words she spat back at me told me pain had won over reason in her mind, "you should have tried harder."

"Yes, I should," I agreed.

Then came the question I had been dreading. "So where is she now?"

"I haven't seen her in weeks," I answered carefully.

"So you have seen her since we've lived here?" There was pained accusation in Donna's voice.

"I didn't seek her out Donna. She came here, came to find me."

"Well she didn't have to look very far did she? You were in a bloody house she'd bought for you ... what is she this woman ... desperate!"

I couldn't tell Donna any more of the truth; I was now floundering in lies and deception once more. I couldn't confess to finding Sasha hanging in the hall, to being so scared and so certain no-one would miss her? How could I make my dirty secret even more disgusting by confessing to burying her body? I was a criminal.

"Did you ever sleep with her?" Donna asked.

"No." My answer was emphatic, but I don't think she believed me.

"So you're telling me, you met a woman, a very stinking rich woman, and she fell for *you*, a bloke with nothing, not two h'pennies to rub together? You meet ... what weekly? A couple of times a week? You meet, you talk, you exchange sexual fantasies, you never once jump into bed together and she gives you a million quid and a house? I have got that right haven't I?" Distain was dripping from her lips.

"Look, I know it sounds improbable ..."

"Improbable? Improbable! It sounds like your little world of fantasy has gone into overdrive. Don't take me for a fool Simon, I feel foolish enough already. What is she mad?"

"Yes. Yes," I agreed eagerly, she's mad. Donna. I've been scared, frightened, for myself and for you and the children. I was glad you went away I thought I could sort it all out. She was mad, Donna, she would never listen to me."

"Was mad? Is she suddenly cured? What makes you think she'd listen now?"

"She's gone ... I ... I made her see sense in the end ... she went away." I tripped and stumbled through my web of deceit.

"So you can leave all this?" she swept her arm around, taking in the whole room and so much more.

I suppose I had anticipated this but I didn't have a ready prepared answer. "We can stay here now," I said feebly, "it doesn't matter, she won't bother us again. She's gone away."

"So let me get this right," Donna spoke carefully, her voice keeping pace as she formulated her thoughts, ticking the points off on her fingers one by one she continued. "A mad woman gives you a house, then this demented creature very conveniently goes away, then you, who according to you never wanted to accept it in the first place, want us all to live here now, happy ever after. That is what you're saying is it?"

I shrugged. "Sort of, I suppose."

"You want *me*, to live in a house, given to you, by another woman?"

"It's not like that ..."

"It's exactly like that," Donna's voice was rising again. "You can make a whore of yourself Simon, but I will not be a whore with you."

"I never thought that."

"Well what exactly did you think? Or didn't you think at all? Who's really mad Simon, this strange delusional woman or you? I don't think I know you any more."

"Donna, I am so sorry, I didn't mean ..."

"Don't!" She screamed at me. "Don't you dare do that!" I shook my head not understanding. She leapt from the sofa and came at me, hanging over me; her lip curled back, her face screwed up in fury. "Don't you dare apologise." Her fists were clenched, I felt she was ready to strike me, I was prepared for it; I almost wanted her too, to punish me. Then, like a punctured balloon, the anger went out of her and she sank onto the coffee table and tears poured down her face. I reached out a hand to her shoulder, but in a swift flick she deflected my touch. "Don't you dare touch me," she hissed through her teeth. "Don't you dare ever touch me." She rose, walked across the room, stood with her back to the drinks cabinet.

'She hates you Simon.' Sitting perched on the top of the cabinet sat Sasha, her long legs crossed, her hands curled over the edge of the polished wood. She sat smiling her beautiful, supercilious smile, looking down at Donna. I stared at her open mouthed, wide eyed, she just smiled serenely back at me.

"I'm going. Did you hear me Simon?" Donna's raised voice brought me back to our situation. "I'm leaving, today. I'll take the kids; we'll find a hotel for now. I need to think."

"Donna, can't you think here? We should talk more," my voice was whining, pleading.

"No Simon." I had never seen Donna so in command of herself. "No, I don't think so. I can't stay under this roof another minute."

'But she can use the money for an hotel,' Sasha threw out sardonically.

"But you can use the money for a hotel room," I heard myself say.

"You bastard!" Donna spoke contemptuously. "You complete and utter bastard. Yes, I'll use the money for a hotel, for me and the children until I know what I'm going to do, you owe me that much, *she* owes me that much." Donna made '*she'* sound like a dirty word.

'Don't worry Simon; we're better off without her.'

"No!" I screamed at Sasha's cloudy form.

"Yes!" Yelled back Donna. "Yes, I think you do."

I heard Donna go upstairs, heard her call the children, I heard her hurried commands, broaching no arguments. There were footsteps above as they scurried to their rooms, gathered a few things together and as a group they descended the stairs, Donna leading the way, a ship in full and magnificent sail, head held high as she took her troops. I leaned defeated against the door jamb at the entrance to the library. The children looked at me but made no move toward me. I didn't know what Donna had told them but they stayed close together. I had seen their faces since they had been back, seen they were now scared of me, uncertain, noticed how after the initial enthusiastic greeting they had been avoiding me. They didn't understand the dangers which I could see for them. As I hovered in the doorway I hoped somehow Donna could read my mind, I hoped she could know it all, without me having to put anything into words. I hoped she could see pictures, see Sasha dead, and my guilt, see my sorrow, my remorse. I hoped she could take my dirty, tumbling thoughts and wash them clean, absolve me, comfort me and finally forgive me. I willed so hard that she could see the truth from me just as it was, but she just commanded the children to stop and wait as she went to the kitchen to collect her handbag.

* * *

The jangling of the doorbell shook my nerves. Peta rushed to open it.

"Good Afternoon," a deep, confident voice greeted her. "Are your parents' home?" Peta looked over her shoulder at me. I walked slowly to the front door, leaning for support against it as I drew up.

"Good Afternoon Sir." A policeman stood on the threshold. My hands shook. I crossed my arms, pressing my hands under my armpits. "My name's P.C. Duncan, Peter Duncan, we're making house to house enquiries in the area, I wonder if you might spare me a minute of your time?"

"Well," I suggested, "this isn't a very good time."

"I'm sorry Sir; it really won't take very long." His manner was firm, broaching no argument. By this time Donna had joined me and the children, who were all wide eyed with ghoulish anticipation.

Donna was the one to answer him. "You had better come in Constable," then over her shoulder, "kids, to your rooms; I'll call you in a minute." There were moans and groans.

I heard one of the boys kicking at the floor. "It's not fair we never get to hear anything fun."

I saw the policeman smile at him. "Not really fun son, just routine."

"Does that mean we can listen?" Ryan responded excitedly.

"No!" shouted Donna, "now go." Turning back to the policeman she ushered him into the library, the room where only a short time ago my life had fallen on the rocks, now here we were playing cosy-cosy, by silent agreement setting aside our differences in front of this stranger. "How can we help you?" Donna asked.

"The policeman took out his notepad, I had the feeling he didn't really need it, it was a prop, something to do with his hands. Looking casually at the page he intoned in his deep baritone voice, "We are trying to seek the owner of a car abandoned near here."

Donna looked puzzled, my heart bounced around in my chest. I knew what was coming.

The constable continued. "A red Lotus was found near here and on making enquiries the owner has not been seen for some considerable time, we are asking if anyone has seen, or has knowledge, of such a car. It's a pretty flash car, we feel someone must have noticed it in the district," he finished on a laugh, "Not your regular farmers type vehicle."

Donna was looking at me. "No," I told him, "no, I haven't seen it." I didn't dare look at Donna.

"Madam?" he enquired, looking toward her.

"The children and I have been on holiday for almost three weeks."

I silently blessed her.

"Oh well, Sir, Madam, if anything comes to you please don't hesitate to contact us, no matter how unimportant it may seem." He took his leave, shaking our hands. I saw him out. As I closed the front door Donna was standing at the entrance to the library, she turned into the room, her body language telling me to follow her.

She stood in the centre of the room and watched me as I made my way across the floor. She cocked an enquiring eyebrow. I shrugged.

"Coincidence?" I suggested.

"I don't think so Simon," she was still staring at me, unnerving me. "Remember I know you Simon."

'Go on Simon, tell her.' Sasha was standing behind her, peering over her shoulder, then in a mimicking voice she spoke, *'She knows you Simon, not as well as me of course, but she knows you.'* Sasha was laughing, her head bobbing, the room echoed with her laughter. *'She doesn't know you at all, does she Simon?'*

I put my hands to my ears trying to block her out, I swung round away from the sight of her, but not before I was aware of the vision of her open mouth, her pearly white teeth, her pink tongue and as she threw back her head with hysterical laughter the red welt on her neck which stood out as a crimson, violent slash.

I ran from the room, round the hall and up the stairs two or three at a time. The girls and Ryan were at the top, obviously eavesdropping. Ronnie was standing back a way from the others.

"Don't touch that!" I yelled at him. Ronnie jumped with guilt clearly written across his face as he was caught in his transgression. He stood staring at me, looking at me as if he didn't know me. I thought for a moment he was going to cry. Slowly he removed his hand from the banister, from the gouge in the wood that he had been picking at ... the gouge I had made as I had cut Sasha free.

I looked from his stricken face to the slit in the banister. It was leaking. Oozing from the gash in the otherwise smooth rail was thick cloying blood. It slimed out from between the chipped flakes of paint.

"Get out of the way!" I screamed at Ronnie. I lunged at him, pulling him clear of the flood of crimson tide which was unleashed and was now gushing down the spindles. I watched in horrified fascination as it erupted in a gurgling, bubbling spew of red corpuscles, pouring through the banisters and down to the hall below, cascading like a waterfall to the spot where Sasha had fallen.

I pushed Ronnie aside. He slammed more fiercely than I had intended against the wall. As I leaned from the landing to look with trepidation over the edge, I expected the hall to be filling like a swimming pool, but as the bloody fall seeped through the rail and down into the hall it vanished into the marble floor.

I turned to attend to Ronnie but Donna was already with him, I hadn't heard her, hadn't seen her, she was checking his eyes, feeling for the bump on his head, she looked over at me and slowly shook her head.

"I'm taking the children. I'll come back when they're settled, you had better do some serious thinking Simon; there are things which need answering. For now I think the kids will be better away," turning from me as she ushered them down the stairs, assisting Ronnie to his feet and lending him a supporting shoulder as they walked away.

The gouge had stopped bleeding; the uprights were clean white again. It was as if it had never been.

The front door slammed shut and Donna's car revved into life, the gravel sprayed out beneath her wheels and landed with a scattering like heavy rain on a glass roof. She was gone, the house was quiet around me, but it was only resting. I sat down with my back to the wall and watched the banister lest it should start to bleed again. I didn't want to touch it but thought perhaps I should at least bandage it in case it happened again. I would - later.

* * *

Time slipped by, a haze of nights and days until I hardly knew which was which. I didn't see Sasha but I heard her. She would hum a little tune, not very melodic, the sort one might hum if concentrating on a tricky piece of embroidery or rocking in a chair, a tuneless little piece of something I thought I knew but couldn't place. I tried to catch her out, swinging round suddenly to see her, but she was never visible.

"I know you're there," I said into the empty room.

The tune came again, low pitched, so low I wondered if it was only in my head, when I stopped any movement the tune stopped. I walked cautiously forward but it did not restart, I think she knew I had sussed her.

SIMON – DAY 7

I walked into the kitchen, it stank. I had forgotten to let Rosa out for a day or two and the poor dog had made several piles in the corner of the kitchen. Breakfast cereal was scatted on the floor and the box chewed open. Her dirty paw marks were on the counter around the sink, she must have been trying to get to water. I couldn't be angry at her, it was my fault. I led her round the hall to the front door and opened it to let her out to run a bit. On the doorstep was a package. On the package was my name and address written in that beautiful, flowing hand, all tails and swirls. My heart gave a massive jump, beads of sweat broke out on my upper lip, my breath came shallow and rapid, and my hands shook. I stared at the small brown paper wrapped parcel with my name and address but no stamps or postage marks, and anyway it was too early for the postman.

It was a hand delivered package.

I poked my head out, looked all around but there was no sign of human life. Rosa was straining away from my grip on her collar so I let her loose. She sniffed at the package and whined miserably, backing away from it with her tail between her legs, she backed nervously back into the house and ran toward the study. It was not going to go away, I stooped to pick it up, it weighed next to nothing. I tentatively shook it close to my ear, a small rustle of noise was all that issued.

I closed the study door to keep Rosa out of the way whilst I cleared up her mess. She whined pitifully.

"I'll see to you in a minute," I reassured her.

I set the parcel down on the unit in the kitchen. The smell in there made me gag, I threw open the windows, dealt with it, and then I washed my hands, twice. I put on the kettle as a further delaying tactic, barely taking my eyes from the parcel, watching it suspiciously, as if it might do something, escape, turn somersaults, self-destruct, I didn't know what. Finally when my coffee was made I could put it off no longer. I carefully peeled the sticky tape from the neatly folded ends and peeled back the outside wrapping. I checked the inside of the paper, nothing, no clues there. My fingers felt like sausages, so clumsy had they suddenly become. Inside was a box, a plain fuchsia pink cardboard box with a lid. Swallowing hard, I dislodged the lid; I held it in one hand and the main part of the box in the other, inside was tissue paper, pale pink. I dropped the lid on the counter and pulled out the contents. Perfume wafted up to greet me - Sasha's perfume. I closed my eyes and swayed a little, it was heady, evocative. I felt as if I might faint and through my head a thousand memories trampled. Not bad memories. No, on the contrary, the sweetness of her scent conjured good memories, reawakened recollections of gloriously happy days, when I had thought I loved her, had desired her, had wanted to make her mine and yet never did. I could almost feel us back by the river, the dark water of the Thames fast flowing, carrying along stately swans in its drift, and supposedly salmon beneath its murky surface. I could all but hear the splashing and tumbling near the weir gates where we had stood and leaned on the old thick timber fence, standing so close together that even through thick layers of winter clothes we had been aware of the intensity of our feelings. I remembered her gloved hand in mine, remembered pulling off the glove so I could touch the soft skin of her palm as I tucked her hand into my pocket with mine and we proceeded on our walk. I recalled I had flicked at her nose with her own glove as I teased her about being work shy, so soft was her skin. The smell of her perfume was alluring, tormenting and captivating, I felt drunk on it. I opened the tissue paper so carefully, like separating the moist petals of a folded flower, peeling back the layers of womanhood, seeking the very core, revealing the mystery.

Beneath the flimsy paper my fingers connected with something fine, something sheer and feminine. I pulled out a small bundle. It appeared to be a pair of stockings and some sort of panties; they were wrapped around with a pink ribbon with hearts dotted along. I rubbed the small bundle between my fingers and the stockings slid easily against themselves. I held the soft silk to my face, taking care not to damage it against my whiskers, closing my eyes as the essential sensation of Sasha was there beside me. I buried my nose into the bundle, breathing in her quintessence, the embodiment of all that had been good about her, all that had attracted me and everything about her that had made me love her, however much I might try to deny it now. What came after had been wrong, so wrong. This was Sasha, this soft silk, this powerful aroma of flowers which breathed life and exuded goodness. I held her in the palm of my hand, pressed her scent to my face and drunk in all that was good. Looking into the box I saw a flatter second tissue-wrapped parcel, I pulled it free, this one was slightly heavier. Opening the paper I revealed a pair of silver handcuffs. I remembered the imaginary games we had played, my knight in shining armour to her distressed damsel, arms bound behind a tree as I deflowered her before I rescued her. I placed the handcuffs back in the box.

'Go get cleaned up Simon,' I couldn't see her, but I heard her request, *'Take me with you.'* We went upstairs together. I ran the shower and stepped under the jets, using copious amounts of soap until I felt cleaner than I had in weeks. Sasha watched me from the chair in the corner, I couldn't see her but I knew she was there, a small secret smile on her lips. Still under the shower I pulled my razor from the rack and

shaved my face, wiping the steam off the mirror occasionally as the hot water fogged it.

'Don't stop,' Sasha whispered as I went to replace the razor in the rack. I raised an enquiring eyebrow, but I knew what she meant. I soaped my leg and taking the blade back down I pulled it slowly from my ankle to my knee, gathering up a thick cloying pillow of foam, speckled with black hairs. I repeated the action, again and again until I was smooth legged, smooth armed, my armpits devoid of any hair, my pubic hair washed away, clogging the plughole. I stood under the water baby-bare, feeling strangely vulnerable, the water caressingly different against totally naked skin.

When I stepped from the shower I wrapped into a warm towel, hiding my body, I wasn't certain it felt quite right. Sasha came over and helped to pat me dry. She stood me in front of the long mirror and eased the towel away from my body. She stood behind me holding the wet towel, I couldn't see her but I knew she was there. I knew she was smiling at me and tentatively I smiled back.

'You are beautiful Simon.' We both smiled more. She dropped the towel and took up the hairbrush, running it though my hair, I moved my head with the pull of her strokes, closing my eyes to savour her confident handling of the hairbrush, letting my head be pulled this way and that, it seemed as though each brushstroke were causing my hair to grow longer.

'Do you have any cream?' she asked.

"No, but ...." She didn't let me finish, she knew what I was going to say.

'Go and fetch it then.' we looked at each through the mirror, seductively from under our lashes.

I went across to Donna's bathroom; there were bottles and tubes of all sorts of creams. I took a bottle of body moisturising lotion, it was brand new - it wouldn't smell of Donna. On my way to leave I saw a bottle of pearly pink nail varnish on the side along with some bits and pieces of make up. I scooped them up and took them with me across to my own bathroom. The sight of my naked body, reflected in the mirror as I re-entered, still surprised me, smooth and hairless as it was.

'Shall I do it or will you?' Sasha asked.

"We'll do it together," I said. She picked up the bottle of moisturiser and poured some into her hands. Starting at my feet she smoothed it up over my ankles, up my calves, across my thighs. She refilled her hands and brushed a white streak of cream down each arm before rubbing it in, massaging it across my shoulders, spreading the surplus over my chest. She rubbed my stomach; she even smoothed it over my bottom, rubbing right into the crescent moon creases beneath my cheeks. She struggled with my back, I helped her, twisting and straining to get to the hard to reach places. Finally she took a little more and made five dots on my face, forehead, nose, chin and cheeks, we giggled. She rubbed it in. We stood back and surveyed our handiwork and nodded satisfied as my skin gleamed in the harsh bathroom light. I picked up some of the make-up and looked to Sasha for guidance. Some we dismissed straight away as being too tarty. She wore very little make-up herself. We selected a pink powder and I brushed a little onto my lids, instantly the effect was gratifying. Gaining in confidence I smudged some dark blue around the very edges of my eyes. As my eyes were already dark shadowed the result was strangely effective, it reminded me of the model pictures I had seen a couple of years before in the Sunday supplements, where the catwalks had been criticised for 'heroin chic'. I brushed blusher onto my cheeks, instantly I looked more sculpted. Then mascara, blackening and thickening my lashes, lastly I found a double ended tube of lip stuff, one end colour, the other end gloss, I painted the shape of my lips pink, pouting at the effect, then I glossed them. *We* looked totally stunning. I tousled my hair, hanging my head upside down then throwing it wildly back to get a messy effect. I swear it looked lighter than it had previously, lighter and longer.

'Put them on Simon.'

The steam from the bathroom seemed to intensify the smell from Sasha's small gift, it filled the whole room, was totally intoxicating. I pulled the end of the pink, heart-dotted ribbon which held the bundle together. The slippery stockings slithered apart; I caught them before they hit the floor. Sitting on the closed lid of the toilet I concertinaed one stocking, then pushing my toes into the small ball I had made of it I slid the silky fabric over my foot, and carefully up my leg. I repeated the process with the other. As I stood they slipped down slightly, I had no suspender to hold them in place. We pondered. Pulling out drawers I looked for inspiration. A packet of headache tables were in the third drawer down, I had seen this done in the movies, I popped two from their bubble packaged sterility, I slipped one into the top of our stocking and twisted the fabric round and around until it pulled tight on my thigh, then I tucked the end back in on itself. It felt very secure. I repeated it with the other leg.

The other item was a small lace thong. It was transparent black, it had the tiniest side straps, and a tiny pink bow at the front for decoration. The back was shoe-string thin, with a little triangular lacy patch of pink at the 'T' where it joined together. I slipped in one foot, then the other, clutching the wall to balance with my free hand. I pulled up the scrap of lace and adjusted myself comfortable.

Sasha hummed her little tune, sounding less melancholy now than she had for days; in fact I found I was feeling better myself.

* * *

It had been worth the wait. I was glad we had not rushed in, glad that Sasha had made us wait until now.

"That time Sasha ..." I started, "You know, in the hall, when we, when I ..." I hung my head in shame at the memory.

'Simon, Simon, it's okay. I know you didn't mean it.'

"No, I didn't, but it happened and I ... it wasn't supposed to be like that."

She took my face between her hands and I covered them with my own. *'Can you feel me Simon? Can you feel that I forgive you? Do you know that it is all right?'* I almost cried. I had to stop the tears falling from my eyes and running over her fingers and over my own. *'There, you see, I know now you really are sorry.'*

"I don't deserve you Sasha," I told her.

'Yes you do. I always told you we would be together and it would be perfect, didn't I? Now we are. This is our time Simon.' Her voice was soft and caressing as she led me through to the bedroom. Led me right up to the edge of the bed, I pulled back the covers and climbed beneath the duvet and she was with me.

I closed my eyes underneath the warmth of the covers. It felt strangely erotic to be laying with her our legs both stocking clad as they entwined around each others. I could hear the soft swish muffled beneath the duvet. Without putting it into words I knew that we would be mirrors, whatever I did to her she would do back to me, and visa versa. I had waited so long for this moment and I was overwhelmed at how much tenderness I felt toward her, tenderness mingled with a desire born of waiting.

She ran her hand down the side of my face, her fingertips tracing the line of my cheekbone, tracing my blusher line. Her little finger ran across my lips, so lightly it tickled and I had to draw them in between my teeth to stop the sensation. Down my chin she moved, admiring the satiny smoothness of my shaved and moisturised face. I raised my chin back, my hair fanning out on the dark blue pillowcase beneath my head and her fingers continued to trace down over my neck. She was in no hurry and I had no wish to hurry her. Beneath the covers I could feel my erection pressing into the confines of the small lacy thong. With the touch of her fingers on my skin I was feeling wilder and more wanton than I could ever remember. I desired her so much - wanted her. This wasn't just a quick fling, this was two years of waiting for this moment, this perfect moment in time, and I wanted to savour every second of it.

Her hand had moved beneath the covers, drawing small circles on my chest. As she leaned over me I drew circles on her back. I could feel her ripe full breasts pressing onto my naked skin, made so much more sensitive for being stripped of all my body hair. She had been right; it had been the thing to do. I kept my eyes closed as her hand slid down to my stomach and my breath came shorter and deeper, I could hear myself breathing. Her hands fanned out on my hips as she moved down over the thin side straps of our thong, along the naked flesh of my leg and over the stocking tops. She revelled in the feel of her silk against my legs. She gasped at the sheer eroticism of my legs encased in her stockings. We writhed and wrested together as our bodies grew more frantic with longing. Her hands were all over me, grasping my bottom, pulling me toward her, over my chest they ran, brushing across my hardened nipples, up my neck and down my throat. They massaged hard around my shoulders down my arms, drawing me to her. They pressed hard against my skin as they skimmed my hips and legs again and again, the stockings becoming the ultimate turn on for us. Beneath our smidgen of lace I pressed hard, the confines of that thong both exciting and restricting, finally I could stand it no longer. "Touch me," I entreated her. "Please touch me."

Her hand came to that place and I felt the elastic pulled away from me, felt her hand peal inside, felt her grasp me in her confident fist. Her thumb brushed my head, a small trickle of creamy liquid escaping from me as she massaged it around my tight skin. I felt her move down my shaft, the pressure perfect as it rose again and circled my tip. Up and down our hand rose and I strained up toward her. Every need and desire in me was rushing to a single place. The very core of me was on fire with my need, it grew and grew, the sensations snaking through me like electric currents and joining together, building and building until I knew that I could take no more, could wait not one moment longer, "now," I whispered between ragged breaths, "now," and so I came. I came hard and furiously, shooting hot liquid between us, spilling down the length of me, spilling over her thong, over our stockings, spilling over our hands. I came and I screamed into the air. "Sasha," I cried out again as she eased the need in me. "Sasha," I called out to her as we joined together in such exquisite ecstasy. "Sasha," I whispered as the tremors subsided and I came back down to earth.

I lay back ready to sleep. As I drifted away I heard her gentle voice. *'Pull the sheets up Simon, pull the sheets up.'*

I slept. I woke, and each time I woke Sasha was there, her hands working over me, driving me again and again to higher and higher pleasures. I felt weak as she wove her magic round me all night long. The sheets clung wetly to my skin as she drove me relentlessly to come time after time until I was sapped of all energy and aching and sore and still she would not stop. *'Just one more time,'* she would whisper and her hands would massage my, by now fragile cock and a small trickle of semen would escape as I longed to sleep. *'Just one more time.'*

SIMON – DAY 8

The next morning I awoke gasping for a drink. I rose from the bed on shaky legs. I walked carefully, my calf muscles sore from so much stretching in the night. I made my way to the kitchen, Rosa whined from behind the study door as I descended into the hall, "I'll be there in a moment," I called to her. I was feeling too fragile to face her exuberant bounding. I drank orange straight from the carton and as I lowered it from my lips I saw the remnants of the package still scattered on the counter. I went once more to pick up the handcuffs. I held them from one bracelet up in front of me, level with my face, and remembered how one time Sasha had talked, once long ago of something she would love to do. How she had confessed at that time that she should have loved to have found me waiting for her handcuffed to the banisters. Blindfolded. Having to trust completely that she would come to free me but not before she had driven me to the extremes of ecstasy first. For a while it had been one of our favourite fantasies, we had fine tuned it, improved it, and been so turned on by it. Even sitting now, exhausted as I was, by our night of lovemaking I was still aroused by the memory of those whispered dreams. I took the handcuffs and held them out in the palm of my hand, jiggling them slightly, weighing them, and remembering.

I walked into the hall, right across it, no need to skirt it now, not now the good Sasha was with me again. Rosa whined.

"I told you I'll be there in a minute," I shouted at her impatiently.

I rubbed my hand along the turned upright at the end of the banister, the wood smooth beneath my fingers, slightly cold to my touch. I caressed the acorn shaped finial, its polished sheen sliding easily beneath my palm. I moved closer, putting my back to the end post, remembering how it had been when we talked, remembering the urgency of my drive home afterwards as I had headed to the shower to relieve the intensity of the feelings we had provoked in each other. I could feel my erection once more rising. I was still wearing Sasha's stockings and her thong, a sweatshirt thrown on as I had come downstairs. I stood with my back to the post and closed my eyes. I pressed myself against the post and grasped my fingers together, the handcuffs dangling down in my hand. It felt so damn good, so damn sensual. Almost without knowing what I was doing I clicked the bracelet of one cuff onto my left wrist, the noise of the ratchet exciting me further. I looped the other link around my right wrist and clicked it closed and I stood and waited for Sasha to come downstairs.

From behind the study door Rosa whined weakly.

And come she did!

Not the woman who had shared my dreams the past twenty four hours, not my beautiful Sasha with her golden hair with her warm love. I waited for that Sasha but what rose up before me was the other one.

I don't know how long I stood waiting for her, but it grew cold and Rosa's whining was irritating me. It was then I realised I had no keys. My wrists were bound behind my back to the banister post and I was waiting in vain. With realisation came a low rumbling noise. I heard it increasing in volume, as one might hear an express train approaching. I felt helpless, tied to the tracks as it bore down on me. The low sinister rumbling became louder, clearer, more manic, the sound of laughter, but not friendly laughter, not the laughter of children at Christmas or the joy that friends bring, not that sort of laughter. This was a mad sound, which just like an express train became a screaming crescendo of noise as Sasha ascended out of the floor, her arms waving wildly, her nails long and pointed as any witches, her skin stretched taut, her mouth gaping wide. She rose as if on a platform, elevating her effortlessly from beneath a stage; indeed she rose making an entrance. I struggled against my shackles, cursing my stupidity, fearing her revenge. Higher she soared, her long white robe billowing around her as she was disgorged from the ground, and as she rose I saw the hem of her makeshift dress was red and whipping wetly round her ankles. I saw the outline of her feet, her toes pointed within her mantle as with arms stretched to the ceiling she left the ground and floated above it. She was white. Her face, her arms, her gown were white but for the blood soaked hem, the hangman's mark, and her eyes. Her eyes stared out red rimmed: red as burning coals, red as two brimming cupfuls of blood, red with incandescent rage, red with hatred as she swung her face to mine. I cringed beneath her look of complete vengeance. I fought and struggled to break free as she hovered above the gap in the floor she had opened up. I heard the gurgling before I saw what was happening. I heard it building as Sasha's laugh had built, fast approaching, I saw the bubbles of red come bursting and popping through the floor, disgorging from between the black and white tiles. Spreading over the marble as oil spreads, with a clean, bulbous, unbroken edge. It puddled out in a thick, cloying, scarlet blanket. The room was silent now as I watched its steady progress, and Sasha hung suspended in the air with a look of malicious glee on her face. I scrambled up a step or two to avoid it covering my feet. I was frantic. I needed to get away but I was trapped, held captive by my own doing, lulled into a false sense of security by believing Sasha could ever have been good again. She wasn't. She was evil and I was trapped. I watched as the crimson tide washed around the bottom step, as it gained speed and momentum reaching across the floor, as it seeped beneath the doors of the cupboards, the library and the study - the study with Rosa trapped inside - now silent.

And then I heard it - a slow drip. Like a slow dripping tap I heard the sound of a single splash of liquid. My head spun toward the noise. Then as if sound and movement were in slow motion there was another one. From my uncomfortable perch my head twisted round to see where the noise was coming from, but I already knew. Sasha had drifted a little to the side and from above where she had been hanging, the banister bled. I had not had time to bandage it, or I had forgotten, and the gouge was again leaking. I saw another red bead hit the floor, already puddled in deep blood and I saw the indent as it hit the surface, saw the drops rise around it and the ripples fan out. Faster they came and faster until there was no time to see ripples, no time to see the pattern of the drops, the drips became a flow and the flow a cascade, the same waterfall force as before, only this time it did not disappear into the floor it joined with the gush from the hole in the ground and it grew deeper and deeper. I cowered on the step as it rose so high it began to creep over.

I screamed at Sasha to make it stop, I begged her to make it stop, I pleaded for my life and for escape from this horror.

She smiled malevolently.

PART THREE

Meanwhile

"How's tricks Gerald?" P.C. Duncan asked.

Duncan was a man happy with his lot. He had been a policeman for twenty-eight years and considered that his life was comfortable. He had his outlying district of Oxford to look after and usually the worse he had to deal with was a few teenage rabble rousers on a Saturday night, who's high jinx involved kicking over dustbins and shouting too loudly. He knew them all by name, he spoke to them next time they attended the youth club and on the odd occasion he would have a word with their parents.

The red Lotus was a pain. It had been reported a week back by a walker who had noticed it tucked back among the trees. He had tracked it to a woman living in Marlow. The housekeeper had given him the husbands London number, he had seemed singularly unconcerned even though the woman had not been seen for some time, but apparently that was not unusual. The man seemed concerned neither for his wife nor the car. The car worried at Peter Duncan, like a child worries at a scab until it festers. He had conducted his house to house and no-one had known anything, except perhaps the new people in the big house, '*Dreams*' it was called. There was something there that hadn't seemed quite right. The husband had been odd, to say the least, jumpy, nervous.

Duncan had made notes and continued to investigate, in his quiet manner, digging around, chatting with people, asking questions in a way that belied his intentions. So it was, on a wintry late December evening, as off duty propped against the bar in *The White Mare* enjoying a quiet pint, Gerald had cautiously pushed open the door.

Gerald was a simple soul. He had appeared one day, thirty years earlier, at Cockcroft Farm, when he was a boy, maybe aged fourteen or fifteen, no-one knew for certain. The old farmer, Mr Pickett, had given him food and shelter, in the form of a couple of rooms over the stables, and work. Gerald had been there ever since. The current owners, the Buckley's, had taken him as part of the fixtures and fittings. Cockcroft

Farm was a chicken farm and Gerald was seeped in the overpowering stench of guano. He was known locally as Chickenshit Gerald, or just Chickenshit, except by the Buckley's, who were kind enough to still call him Gerald, as was P.C. Duncan.

In the mellowness of the bar, warmed by a blazing fire in the hearth and the landlord's best brew Gerald, whilst not completely losing his nervousness of authority, became pliant to Duncan's unobtrusive enquiries.

"Got a bit of a problem Gerald," Duncan confided.

"Oh Aye?" Gerald looked over the rim of his glass, warily.

"Oh nothing to do with you," Duncan laughed easily, "no, nothing to do with you." He continued in his rich, round, country accent, "But you gets out and about, goes places and sees things other people don't see."

"I don't know about that Mr Duncan," Gerald spoke defensively.

"No, but you're astute, you take things in Gerald," Duncan flattered. "This is a problem that's been nagging at me for a while and I just can't get to the bottom of it." He drained his drink and indicated to Mike, the barman, that he needed a refill. "You'll have another won't you?" he asked, turning back to Gerald.

Gerald hesitated for a moment,

"Go on then," he responded reluctantly, more afraid of saying no to a policeman than saying yes.

"The thing is Gerald, someone dumped a car in the woods. Damn thing is causing me no end of an headache," he picked up the new pint and sipped off the frothy head.

Gerald said nothing. He drank long and deep, watchfully.

"Course it's been towed away now but I'm having problems locating the owner. It was a fine car, not the sort you see round here too often, it hasn't been reported stolen or anything. I just wondered if you might have seen something?"

"No," replied Gerald slowly, his eyebrow twitching. "No, can't say I have."

"Right," Duncan knew he was lying, but he kept his voice level and his manner light as he reeled Gerald in, like an angler with a disinclined fish. "Damn fine car, wouldn't mind one of those myself, but not sure I'd even fit in it, not with this," and he indicated his round stomach, laughing at himself.

"What sort of car is it then?" Gerald asked.

"A Lotus. One of those long, low, sleek looking things, a dream car Gerald, that's what it is, a dream car."

"Not much call for dream cars around here I don't think," Gerald chuckled.

"Had the Devil's own job getting the thing out of the mud without damaging it, I can tell you," Duncan complained.

"Yeah, well the ground gets pretty boggy up on Tyler's Mound," Gerald answered incautiously, realising his slip as soon as the words fell from his lips.

"Yes, it does," replied Duncan. "You want to tell me what you know Gerald?" His words had taken on a slightly more commanding tone.

"I don't know nothing," Gerald answered defensively, looking fretfully around, feeling cornered.

"You know it was on Tyler's Mound, what else do you know? Did you see who left it there?"

"No, no I never saw." Gerald was trapped and looked agitatedly around for escape.

Duncan cocked an eyebrow at Gerald, who retracted tortoise-like into his heavy overcoat.

"I never saw who left it there. I swear," Gerald reaffirmed as he saw Duncan's look of disbelief. "I just saw it there. I saw it there and I knew a car like that didn't ought to be up there in the woods like that."

"Go on," Duncan encouraged.

"That's all. I never saw who put it there."

"But you'd seen it before?"

Gerald nodded reluctantly.

"Mike," Duncan called, "get Gerald another pint will you." Mike picked up the empty glass and looked wryly at Gerald.

"Right, go on," ordered Duncan. "You'd seen the car before?"

"Aye, I'd seen it afore, a few times."

"Did you see who was driving it?" Duncan kept his voice level.

"It's got them dark windows, them ones you can't see into," Gerald replied sulkily.

"But you might have seen someone getting in and out o' the car?"

"Yes Mr Duncan," agreed Gerald, realising there was no point in denying it further.

Duncan knew the rules of the game, he didn't betray his impatience. He reeled a little and let the line play out again.

Gerald drank from his glass and wiped his dirty sleeve across his mouth, he burped quietly, the air between them filled with the smell of regurgitated beer and Duncan leaned back a little way. "It were an angel, Mr Duncan, that's what," Gerald's eyes had misted over as he remembered the vision. He spoke in whispered awe.

"An angel Gerald?" queried Duncan gently.

"Aye, she were an angel. I saw her. She had hair like gold. I never saw such beautiful hair in all my life, it was like ... like ... some of my girls." Gerald spoke dreamily, referring to his chickens. "Some of my rare girls, my Pyle Leghorns when they're little chicks Mr. Duncan, they got feathers so fine and lemony, they is just the same colour as the angels hair."

"How many times did you see her?" Duncan asked.

"Oh, a couple, three maybe," Gerald turned back from his reverie.

"Where?" Duncan asked leaning forward again to catch the answer.

"I saw her up by that new house. That big one built into the hillside. See her there a couple of times I did." Gerald sunk further into his coat.

"Anywhere else?" Duncan asked, watching Gerald carefully.

"No." Gerald asserted. "Nowhere else," Duncan could see he was not telling all he knew, but he was not going to get any more from Gerald this evening.

"I'm a patient man Gerald, but if I find you haven't told me the whole truth I can get very cross."

"I've told you all I know Mr Duncan," responded Gerald nervously, sliding back down into the collar of his coat. "I don't know no more." His sweaty palm in his pocket held on tight to a roll of banknotes and his lips remained tight shut as he peered from under his brow at Duncan.

The next morning, once more in uniform, P.C. Duncan set off in his car toward '*Dreams*'. He had a number of questions he wanted to put to Mr and Mrs Koweski, his tongue twisted around the unfamiliar name. This business was looking more and more suspicious the deeper he probed. He liked to keep a tidy patch and he wasn't going to let this little problem spoil his clean sheet.

There was only one car in the drive when he arrived, an old escort, not the sort of car one would associate with a property of this sort. He wandered over to it trying the doors, it was locked. He automatically checked the tax disc, which was in order.

He wandered toward the house, scanning around him as he approached. All was quiet, no sign of the children or the dog, even as he rang the bell the dog did not bark. He assumed they were all away from the property. Standing with his back to the door he looked around. He sucked in a deep breath of cold morning air, so cold it made his chest hurt and his tooth ache, a reminder that he was due a dental appointment. It wouldn't do any harm to wander around a bit he considered. His thick soled shoes scrunched on the icy ground, leaving size ten footprints in the hoar frost and his breath formed clouds which hung in the air behind him as he descended the steps and made his way to the rear of the property. He looked through the doors to the swimming pool and without envy admired the expanse of still blue water.

His brows knitted in puzzlement as he wondered what Mr Koweski did for a living that earned him enough for this sort of opulence. He would dig further on that one. He climbed the steps to the terrace above the pool, which led off from the kitchen, rattling the handle of the locked door, not expecting it to be open. He looked through the glass panes and was greeted by the sight of unexpected mess. Strewn across the units were mugs, spoons, and an open jar of coffee. Food wrappers were discarded; the sink looked piled with a higgledy-piggledy jumble of dishes and milk cartons. To the end of the counter was a cloud of tissue paper and brown paper, open like a giant clam shell on its back, carelessly thrown aside. The impression was one of neglect; it was one more surprise to P.C. Duncan. He made his way back down the steps, taking extra care not to slip on their icy surface, and round to the front of the house again. He trod carefully across the flower boarders, his feet sinking in the soil as he leaned across a prickly berberis to peer into the window of the library, balancing his hand on the cold Portland stone sill to lean further forward and get a better view. He remembered this room, it was a warm, welcoming room the way it was decorated, but on the day he had visited he had detected a distinct chill between Mr and Mrs Koweski. He crossed the drive past the front door to the next window at ground level and once again stepped cautiously across the flowerbed. The weak winter sunlight gleamed off the glass making it impossible to see through until his face was pressed right up against it, freezing cold on his forehead as he clasped his hat in one hand and shielded his eyes with the other against the back-glare.

The room was a mess of papers; they were flung with no regard across the desk beneath the window. Once again P.C. Duncan felt surprise at the unexpected mess. Then he saw it - a head. The dog's golden fur but with its eyes open and glazed and its black lips looking dry and lifeless as its tongue lolled onto the rug. Duncan was too long in the tooth to be too shocked, he blew out his cheeks as he contemplated this development. Hurriedly backtracking to the front door he uselessly rattled the handle once more, then stepping to the small window at the side he looked through that. It took a moment for his eyes to adjust to the darkness and scan the hallway, but he was pulled up short when he spotted a body slumped on the bottom stairs, showing no signs of life.

He ran down the front steps, faster than he had moved in years, round to the back of the house and scaled the steps to the rear terrace three at a time. Taking his baton from its holster he turned his face away as he gave a sharp blow to the glass in the kitchen door, it shattered and fell tinkling to the ground. He pushed his baton through the hole, clearing away sharp shards in the frame and pulling his arm up into the sleeve of his coat he pushed it through and fumbled for the key in the lock. It was there, he turned it and the door swung open. Stepping over the broken glass he made his way to the hall, looking left and right as he went, checking for signs of movement up the stairs. Half registering the putrid smell which he recognised as decomposing flesh, he stooped down to check the body on the stairs.

Mr Koweski, dressed in stockings and women's underwear, handcuffed to the banister. His wrists rubbed red raw, with blood dried around the wounds. Duncan felt for a pulse in his neck and was relieved to find a small flutter. He did not dare move him. Although the heating was working Simon's body was icy cold. Duncan ran up the stairs and pulled a duvet from the first bedroom he found, and rushed back down to wrap it around Simon, tucking it in all around him. He ran to the kitchen and picking up the phone dialled 999 and asked for an ambulance.

While he waited he went first to the study, on opening the door he was assailed by the most appalling stink. The dog lay half under the desk, it must have been dead for at least two days. Duncan pulled the door quickly shut again, it was impossible to ever get used to the smell of dead bodies. He looked in the kitchen for some sort of implement to release Simon from his handcuffs but found none and he didn't want to leave him alone while he went searching further afield so he waited until the ambulance arrived. He stood on the stairs next to Simon's prone body, checking him periodically for his pulse until he heard the distant wail of a siren.

* * *

When Simon was on his way to hospital, P.C. Duncan called the main Oxford Police Station and reported his findings to C.I.D. He spoke to Detective Sergeant Malcolm Christie, a man, it seemed he had known forever; a man he admired and respected for his no-nonsense approach and concise delivery of the facts when called for.

"Don't quite know what it's all about Malcolm," Duncan told him, "something's not ringing quite true here."

"What, apart from finding a bloke in women's underwear half dead on the stairs you mean?" Christie laughed ironically.

"Yes, apart from that." Duncan went on to explain about the car and the fact Gerald had spotted the car owner at '*Dreams*'.

"Where's the wife?" asked Christie.

"No sign and from the look of things she hasn't been here a while. The house is a bit of a mess. What do you want me to do about the dog?"

"Don't do anything, I'll get a vet out there, we'll get it examined to establish cause of death," Christie told him.

"Looks like starvation to me, poor creature," Duncan gave a deep sigh of sympathy.

"Does the guy look like it was just some sort of sexual thrill that went wrong?"

"Could be, there's no sign of a break in, nothing forced. With the wife not there ... well ... Maybe that's why she's not here."

"Any sign of any Conservative M.P.'s?" Christie joked.

"Notta one, maybe we'd better look for a different motivation," Duncan jested back.

"Are there any kids?" questioned Christie, once more becoming serious.

"Yes, three or four I think."

"Okay, would you mind waiting at the scene? It must be worth a look in case the guy pegs it. I'll be along within the hour, keep it sealed until I get there."

"Will do," they disconnected.

Duncan walked carefully from room to room, not touching anything, observing. He steered clear of the study, not wishing to disturb that room and not wanting to be subjected to the reek which was permeating out from beneath the closed door.

In the kitchen he took his pen and lifted the brown paper, bending almost in half and twisting his neck until he could see the writing on the other side. No stamps he noticed. He let it drop back to the counter.

Christie arrived with a rookie in tow, D.C. Pennington. "Good God!" thought Duncan, "the police are looking younger all the time, or maybe I'm just getting old." The kid looked as though he was fresh out of the fifth form, his hair hung lank to his shoulders and his skin looked shiny with grease. He was a boy who appeared to live on a diet of kebabs and chips. In contrast Christie stood at the threshold of the front door in his immaculate suit, sharp creased but discreet. His Windsor knot the perfect shape, perfect size, his shirt pressed to perfection. He stood at the doorway and surveyed the scene.

"Hello Peter," he greeted Duncan, extending his arm to shake hands. "Wife well?"

"Fine thanks Malcolm, how's Eileen?"

"Good, worries too much about the boys, but good. This is D.C. Charlie Pennington," he introduced the rookie, inviting the two of them to shake hands. Duncan nodded his head in greeting toward him, and surreptitiously wiped his hands down his trouser leg after they had shaken.

"Nice house," Christie commented.

"Mmm," Duncan responded non-committedly

The three police officers walked around.

"I'm not sure I do think there has been a crime here," Christie asserted.

"I don't know ..." Duncan answered slowly. "There's just something about this whole set-up that doesn't feel right. Call it instinct if you like but the owner of that Lotus was seen here and now is nowhere to be found. We get here and find a bloke half dead in unusual circumstances, the dog is dead in the study and the wife is nowhere to be seen."

"Yes, but what's the crime?" Christie persisted. "Unless the lab report shows up anything suspicious about the dead dog, which I very much doubt, then I fail to see where we come in. The guy may have been tied up but look at what he was wearing. No Peter, as far as I can make out I see no crime, just a bit of an adventure which went wrong."

"Do you mind if I follow a couple of lines of enquiry?" Duncan asked.

"No, I suppose not, but don't waste too much time on it, not to mention money." Their conversation was interrupted by the vet appearing at the door. The police men stood over him whilst he examined Rosa's stiff body.

"What do you think?" asked Duncan.

"Difficult to say without an autopsy," the vet replied, "but first impressions look like the dog was starved, not so much of food but of water. Dog won't last long without water, and this one has been dead at least ... thirty six to forty eight hours I'd say."

"How long will an autopsy take?" Duncan enquired, looking dispassionately down at Rosa's corpse.

"Should have the results back in twenty four hours if I crack on with it today, I'm not exactly run off my feet at the moment. That do you?

"Yes, thank you, that's fine." Turning back to Christie, he spoke directly to him. "Well, if we're all finished up here I think I might just pop along to The John Radcliffe and see how our patient is doing."

Christie nodded. "Might be better to leave it to the morning, time they take to get them through the corridors." Then indicating to Pennington he was ready to leave he shook hands with Duncan. "Got the evidence Pennington?" he asked with a hint of mockery in his voice, as they headed for the door.

"Sir," Pennington answered, raising a hand with several bags containing the packaging from the kitchen counter amongst other things.

"If you hear anything from the wife Peter let me know, just to satisfy my curiosity, you know," Christie spoke back over his shoulder and was gone.

Duncan stood looking at the banister, pondering what might have happened. Old Man Reilly, the local odd-job man, had been to fix the pane of glass in the kitchen door as they had been investigating, there was nothing else Duncan could do, but he couldn't shake off the feeling that things were not quite right. So far there was no crime, but it just didn't add up. And where was the wife? He left the house secure and headed back to his station. Christie was right, probably nothing to be gained from visiting the hospital until the morning.

The John Radcliffe was a huge modern monstrosity, its white edifice visible from miles around. As Duncan drove into Headington, it reminded him of a children's building kit, made up as it was of plastic-looking, shiny slabs. It was one of the most famous teaching hospitals in the country. Duncan, approaching from the A420, was forced to pull over for a fast approaching ambulance, its sirens whining out in impatience for a clear way. Having located the ward that Simon had been taken to Duncan approached the sister in charge for a report.

Sister Walters was brisk and efficient; she led Duncan to her office and wasted no time on small talk. "Mr Koweski is in a pretty bad way," she said, "he appears to be in a condition of semi-starvation and on initial examination I would suggest intestinal problems. We are rehydrating him with a saline drip and the doctor has prescribed little more than rest for the time being. He has not yet woken and I would guess it may be some time before he does. Of course at this stage it is impossible to assess his mental state, but ..." she left the sentence unfinished.

"Thank you Sister. Would it be possible for me to see him?"

"You can see him, but as I say he hasn't woken yet, so I'm not sure what's to be gained." She led him down the ward to a cubicle where there were four beds. Simon lay in the one nearest the window, his face grey against the white linen. His wrists were dressed, his arm exposed above the covers with the drip feeding through his veins. He wore a standard hospital gown, small blue flower print on a white background. For a man who had been so recently found in stockings the garment looked incongruously feminine. Duncan stood looking for a while, his eyebrows knitted as he puzzled over the circumstances which had brought Simon to this.

* * *

Some time later when Duncan approached the main exit, the doors glided apart automatically, a dark haired woman was entering just as they parted. Her head was down but there was a familiarity about her.

"Mrs Koweski?" Duncan queried. The woman looked up, seeing the uniform she recognised him immediately.

"P.C. Duncan, isn't it?" She looked tired. The small smile she gave him in greeting never reached her eyes, which remained dull and dark shadowed.

"Are you here for ...?" Duncan didn't finish the sentence, he didn't see how it was possible that she had heard of her husband's condition from any source other than himself and he hadn't contacted her.

"Scan," said Donna, placing her hand across her stomach.

"Oh Right. I wonder if you have a moment." Without waiting for an answer he guided her toward the seating area and gestured for her to sit down. Taking the seat beside her he took a deep breath. "Mrs Koweski, are you living at home at the moment?"

Donna hung her head low, she shook it in response.

"May I enquire why?"

Donnas head sprung up, with a look of defiance she told him, "My husband and I have had a disagreement." The sentence trailed off insubstantially.

"May I ask what about?"

Donna stared at him puzzled. "Why? Has something happened? Why are you here?" Realisation suddenly seemed to strike her and Donna was becoming agitated. "Has something happened to Simon?"

"Mrs Koweski, we don't know what has happened, but I had reason to visit your house yesterday, your husband was ..." he searched for words, he didn't want to mention the circumstances in which Simon had been found just yet. "He had collapsed. He is here. Would you like me to accompany you?"

Donnas hand flew to her mouth, "Oh God," she whispered, tears sprung into her eyes. "He's ... he'll be all right won't he?"

"I'll take you up; the Sister will be able to explain his condition better than I could."

Donna, was lead to Simons bed, she sat in the hard plastic, functional chair and gripped his hand. Tears poured down her cheeks. "I'm sorry, I'm sorry," she whispered to him over and over. "I'm sorry."

Duncan drank machine manufactured coffee from a plastic cup, in the corridor, whilst he waited for her. Eventually she came toward him, her feet seeming too heavy to lift as she walked wearily to face him. "What happened?" she asked, without preamble.

"Come on, let's go and get a coffee from the canteen, this stuff is vile," and he threw the half finished machine coffee into a nearby bin. They took the lift to Level 3 and Duncan brought drinks to the table in the corner at which Donna had sat down.

"We don't know what happened. Your husband was found collapsed on the stairs; it would appear he had been there for a while. I should tell you that we also found your dog, I'm afraid she was dead."

Donna could not speak in response, but her eyes asked volumes. "At this stage I am not investigating a crime, it would appear the dog was neglected, it was shut in the study and had no food or water for some time, however there is an autopsy and we will know for certain in twenty four hours if that was the case. How long is it since you last saw your husband?"

"Over a week, nine days, I ... the children and I have been staying at The Randolph. Oh God, the children, what time is it, I said I'd only be an hour or two, they'll be worried sick, this has all been very unsettling for them." Donna scanned her watch, leaping to her feet, "I must go and let them know what's happening. The nurse says she's not expecting Simon to come round for a while, I can be back before he does, Oh, and I've missed my scan ..." She sat back down heavily, and burst into tears. "Sorry, sorry, it's hormones ..." she gulped through tears of embarrassment, as she flapped her hands feebly in front of her.

Duncan handed her a clean tissue. "Don't worry; it's a lot to take on board. Look how about I drive you back to the hotel and then bring you back here, your cars in the car park presumably, it might be better if you left it for now."

Donna looked at him thankfully. "Are you sure that would be okay?"

"No problem, come on."

* * *

When Simon awoke he had no idea where he was, he lay back in his bed with his eyes closed as his brain assessed the strange smells and the unfamiliar noises. He wanted to open his eyes, tried desperately hard to do so but however much effort he put in they remained shut. Then he felt movement, someone grabbed his hand and a voice he knew well, loved well, floated to him, "Simon, I'm here, it's okay, I'm here." It was all right, Donna was there. Simon drifted back to oblivion.

For days Simon drifted in and out of consciousness and each time he did so Donna was beside him, holding his hand, looking concerned, reassuring him it would be all right. He did not speak, felt that speaking involved too much effort on his part, and anyway what was there to say, but his eyes told her he was grateful to her for being there.

The saline pumped into his arm and his colour began to return to normal, he began to lose the gaunt, drained look. The nurses began to bully him to get out of bed and sit in the chair, at least whilst they changed his sheets. He obliged, with assistance, but the effort involved left him sleeping for hours afterwards. At the weekend Donna brought the children to see him, they came in two at a time and with shyness they hugged him and stood back from the bed as if looking at a stranger. Simon only half listened as they chatted in staccato sentences, trying to fill the silence with their news; it was hard work for both sides. Donna didn't bring them to visit again.

The ward was empty but for Simon, it wouldn't remain so, but for that evening as Donna sat beside Simon's bed they were alone. The lights were off, but enough of a glow shone in from the corridor to make it cosily intimate.

"I love you Donna." It was the first words Simon had spoken since his admittance and his voice was a croak, sounding strange to them both. She just took his hand in both of hers and held tight, the lump in her throat making it impossible to respond as the tears once more sprung into her eyes. Simon closed his eyes and slept, feeling a sense of peace which had long been absent.

* * *

"Well, well, well," said Duncan into the mouthpiece of the telephone. "Thank you for that Malcolm."

"Still can't see a crime here Peter, but thought you might be interested to hear the results of the fingerprint test."

"Oh I am. I'll let you know what comes of it. Send my regards to Eileen, I'll be in touch." Duncan replaced the receiver and pondered this new piece of information.

Later in the day he was driving along the Sheldon to Matleigh road, close to Tyler's Mound, when he spotted the shambling figure of Gerald. He pulled his car along side him, keeping pace with Gerald's rolling walk. "Afternoon Gerald, how goes things?"

"Fine Mr Duncan, just fine." Gerald kept his eyes ahead and kept on walking.

"What you got there then?" Duncan indicated the bunch of green in Gerald's hand.

"Nothing. Rosemary that's all, just rosemary, I didn't steal it. It was growing wild on the side of the road."

"Get in Gerald," ordered Duncan.

"I'm all right Mr Duncan, I prefers to walk."

"Get in Gerald." Duncan stopped the car, leaned across and pushed the door open in front of Gerald thereby halting his progress.

Gerald reluctantly climbed into the passenger seat, his pungent smell easily overpowering that of the rosemary which he still clasped in his fist.

"Bit of a turn up for the books Gerald," stated Duncan conversationally.

"What's that Mr Duncan?"

"Well, you remember I was asking you about that fine Lotus which was dumped at Tyler's Mound?" he didn't wait for an answer but went on, "I've been doing a bit of digging. Got a sample of the woman's handwriting, the angel, you remember? Well, when I was at the house I found a package with that self same writing on the label, seemed a bit strange to me that a package was delivered with no stamps on but fully addressed, so I wondered if she had delivered it herself, seeing as how you said you'd seen the car up there."

"Well she probably had Mr Duncan." Gerald's voice was nervous.

"Well, I thought about that and I thought if that was so, why would the address be written on the label like that? Do you see what I'm getting at Gerald?"

"I'm not sure I do Mr Duncan."

"Well, try and follow me on this one Gerald, because I have a feeling you might be able to help. I sent the brown paper packaging off to Oxford and the clever bods up there came back to me, and what do you think they found?" he cocked an enquiring eyebrow at Gerald.

"I'm sure I don't know Mr Duncan."

"Oh, I think you do Gerald. I think you know very well that what they found were *your* fingerprints on the package. You see we still have yours on file after that business with the break in at Cockcroft a few months back. Is there something you want to tell me Gerald?"

"That break in weren't nothing to do with me Mr Duncan," responded Gerald alarmed.

"That particular crime is still unsolved Gerald, but the thing is, do we have another one on our hands now?"

"I didn't do nothing wrong."

"I didn't say you did Gerald, but you see how this is a bit of a puzzle to me?"

Gerald took a long breath in then out and Duncan reeled back in his seat as the car was filled with the most appalling smell, but he kept his face straight as he waited for Gerald to explain.

Beads of sweat stood out on Gerald's upper lip. "I saw her," he confessed. "She were floating, like an angel, I saw her through the trees. It were my day off. I was allowed away from the farm, I weren't doing nothing wrong." Gerald was anxious to establish his innocence on that point.

"Go on."

"She sees me an' all and she waves me to come toward her like. I was scared. Then all of a sudden I wasn't scared like. I thought, she's an angel and she's come to take me to heaven. She smiled at me and I knew if that's what she wanted. I was ready to go with her, even though I isn't an old man yet." Gerald was dreamily euphoric at the memory.

"Go on," Duncan urged him.

"She didn't want me to go to heaven. She spoke to me and she sounded just like a real person, 'cepting not like any of the people I knows. Her voice was like music, like a chuckling stream."

"What did she say to you?"

"She said she were heading back to that fancy house. She were coming from the direction of Tyler's Mound. That was how I saw the car, afterwards, later that evening I walked back the direction she come from and I saw it there. She asked my name. I told her, didn't see no harm in telling her. She asked me if I wanted to make a few pounds. That didn't sound too much like an angel thing I thought at the time. I asked her what I'd have to do. She told me to follow her to the big house and when we gets there she says to wait outside. Well she wasn't gone long and she comes out with some boxes. She opens up this flat one and inside is a flat, shiny bit of wood, with writing on. I don't know what it said, I didn't have me glasses with me." Duncan gave a wry smile as he chose to understand Gerald's explanation as to why he couldn't read the words. "She says that she was going away for a few days but as a surprise, to thank the owners for their kindness to her, she wanted to give them a present, and would I put it on a stake in the woods up by the stream in a few days time. I says, I could do that. I says to her, "Is them Gods words?" and she laughs a little bit, not in a nasty way, no, it was a tinkling sort of way, like that there stream what she wanted me to put it next to. She says, "Yes, them is Gods words." Then she gives me a letter and two more boxes and says they are addressed to the people who live in that big house and could I post them for her, one in a week and one the following week as it was for their birthdays. She says she can't post them herself as she's going away. I says I can do that an' all. Then she gives me a hundred pounds."

"A hundred pounds? That's a lot of money for so little Gerald," Duncan queried.

"I know." Gerald looked shamefaced. "I says I would do it for nothing for her but she presses it into my hand and says I must take it and not to say nothing to no-one." Gerald stroked his hand at the memory of the touch. Suddenly his face looked alarmed, as if aware of his broken promise, "But now I've told you Mr Duncan! Do you think I must give it back to her? I've never had a hundred pounds before." Gerald looked searchingly at Duncan, looking for guidance.

"No Gerald, I'm sure she meant you to keep it. Telling me isn't the same thing you know, it's not like you let her down." Gerald looked sceptically grateful, his head on one side and his brows knotted as he digested Duncan's logic.

"Well if you're sure Mr Duncan?"

"What happened to the letter and the packages?"

"Well the letter that had a stamp on, so I posts it that day when I puts up the bit of wood with the words on it, I think."

"And the packages?" prompted Duncan as he watched Gerald searching his memory to get his times right.

"I was passing the house like. I don't like going into the post office. Mrs Myers in there is so fierce and she don't like me, so I just left the first one on the doorstep."

"And the second?"

"Well ...." Gerald shuffled in his seat uncomfortably. "Well what with what's gone on I sort of ... haven't ... I was scared Mr Duncan ... it's still at home..." he finished lamely.

"Perhaps we should just go and collect it then Gerald," Duncan spoke pleasantly and Gerald had no option but to consent.

Gerald's home above the stables was austere. He pulled out an old crate from under a wonky table and from beneath an old hessian feed sack he retrieved the second parcel.

"Thank you Gerald you've been very helpful," said P.C. Duncan.

"I didn't do no wrong did I Mr Duncan?"

"No Gerald, you did everything right, you did good." Duncan reassured him. Back in the car he carefully opened the package, lifting the lid from the fuchsia coloured box he opened the pink tissue to reveal a small hank of golden hair tied with a length of pink ribbon with tiny hearts dotted along it. A small strip of paper bore the words, *'I am always with you.'* Duncan didn't know what to make of it. Time to visit Simon Koweski he felt and ask a few questions.

* * *

"Is Mr Koweski up to answering questions?" Duncan asked Sister Walters.

"Mr Koweski's physical condition is improving daily, there should be no long term effects, however he has suffered a severe trauma and he becomes easily upset."

"But can he answer questions?" Duncan rolled his hat around by the brim between his fingers as he waited for an answer.

"You can have fifteen minutes, no more and if I think Mr Koweski is becoming agitated I will terminate the interview."

"Thank you Sister."

"You'll find him in the reading room down the corridor, he hasn't any visitors yet. Remember P.C. Duncan, I will be keeping an eye on you," her eyes smiled at him belying her severity of tone. Duncan gave her a grin and made his way down the corridor, his rubber soled shoes squeaking on the polished linoleum.

"Mr. Koweski, sorry to disturb you, do you mind?" P.C. Duncan indicated the chair, seeking permission to sit.

Simon looked nervous, but he nodded his consent.

"Mr Koweski, I wonder if you could help, I have a few loose ends and I am not a man who likes loose ends. A car was found abandoned near your home."

"It's not my home," Simon snapped out vehemently.

For a moment Duncan was taken aback, but he showed no signs and continued. "The car was found abandoned in woods, a red Lotus." He watched carefully as Simons fingers began to drum on the arm of his chair. "I believe you may be acquainted with the owner?"

Simon's mouth was clamped rigid, the outline of his jawbone standing out in his now thin face.

"Simon?" Duncan prompted gently, dropping the formality of his surname, easing him lightly to tell what he knew.

"Sasha," whispered Simon. "Her name's Sasha."

"Yes, that's right Sasha. Is she a friend of yours Simon?"

Duncan could not read the myriad of expressions which passed over Simon's face.

"No," he said eventually.

"Was she ever a friend Simon?"

Simon nodded his head, slowly, as if it were painful to admit.

"A good friend?" All the implication of that innocent phrase was there.

"She was evil," Simon spat out. His breathing was deep, laboured and his eyes had glazed as he visited a different time in his head. "She looked so good, she smelled so sweet, but she wasn't, she was evil, she was the most evil person I have ever known." He slumped back in his chair as if the admission had cost him dear.

"When did you last see Sasha, Simon?"

Simon's hands gripped hard on the arms of the chair but it could not disguise the shaking as tears sprung into his eyes, his whole body was shivering violently as he stared through P.C. Duncan into some far off place.

Duncan tried again. "Did she do this to you Simon?"

"Yes," Simon screamed out. "Yes, she did it, yes she did it, she's evil, she did it and she's evil." The words rose on a crescendo, bouncing back off the walls of the small room as his voice rose higher and higher and the sound of footsteps were heard running down the corridor. Simon was screaming, not words, just screaming as Sister Walters came running into the room, with two nurses following her.

"Out," she barked at Duncan. Changing her tone completely she reassured Simon, "It's all right Simon, it's all right, it's okay, really it's okay." An injection of sedative was administered and Simon's thrashing stopped, he was wheeled back to his bed and the nurses made him comfortable, drawing the curtains around the bed; he would sleep for hours.

Sister Walters walked briskly from the room, gunning for P.C. Duncan. "What the hell did you say to him?" she asked furiously. "I told you under no circumstances was he to be upset and you couldn't have done a better job of it if you'd tried. What on earth were you thinking of?"

Duncan had the grace to look shame faced. "He was talking, there were questions I had to ask. I don't know what crime I'm investigating here but you saw the state of him when he was brought in. Something is not right."

"Look," said the Sister, her calm regained, "we all have a job to do, my priority is to look after my patient and I cannot have him upset in this way, it could set him back weeks, months even. I think you had better direct your questions elsewhere for the time being, don't you?"

Duncan nodded at her, "I'm sorry," he said, and replacing his cap on his head he left the ward. Sister Walters watched him go. He was, she thought, a kind man, but she would not have him back causing such an upset again whatever the case might be.

* * *

Simon's agitation bothered Duncan. His face had betrayed fear, terror, and something Duncan couldn't quite get a handle on. Whoever and whatever this woman Sasha was, she had certainly put the fear of

God into Simon Koweski. Back at his small, rural police station Duncan was pleased to see a copy file he had requested had been delivered. Inside was a compliment slip from Malcolm Christie, with a message inscribed in his neat hand. '*Check out the pencil notes in the margins*!' it said. Duncan flicked through the contents. There was nothing relating to Sasha specifically but there was a copy of the coroner reports regarding her parents. He scanned the pages, it seemed they had died in a house fire and that Sasha had been absent at the time. The fire, it was reported, had started from a faulty appliance left plugged into a socket in the hall, and some nearby newspaper and clothing had exacerbated the speed at which the fire had spread. They had stood no chance. Their bedroom windows had been sealed closed. In the court report Sasha had given evidence that her mother suffered from severe neuralgia and any hint of a breeze through the windows could cause her endless pain, therefore the windows were always closed and years of paint had sealed them immovable. A key to the bedroom door had been found on the floor beneath what had been a dressing table and the bedroom door was locked. There was no other key it was reported (by the daughter), and therefore it was ascertained the parents locked the door before retiring for the night. Verdict - accidental death. In the margin someone had scribbled pencil notes, they were difficult to read on the copies but Duncan could just make out the words; '*Daughter – very cool –suspect she knows more than she's telling!!!*' the word 'very' had been heavily underscored.

"Someone had their suspicions," said Duncan aloud to the empty room. What would she have been, seventeen, maybe eighteen at the time? Time to pay the husband a visit I think.

* * *

Donna was furious when she saw how heavily sedated Simon was and was told the reason for it. She did not understand fully why he had been questioned by the police, she had not as yet been apprised of the condition in which Simon had been admitted, she said as much to the Sister. Sister Walters took Donna to her office and made tea for them both from a small kettle she kept on her filing cabinet.

"When is the baby due?" she asked conversationally.

"May. A long way to go yet."

"Donna, may I call you Donna?"

"Yes of course."

"Donna, when your husband was brought in he was in quite a state," Donna nodded her head in acknowledgement of this fact. "It wasn't just the case that he had been neglecting himself."

"What do you mean? I thought you said it was exhaustion and dehydration."

"Yes, I did, and yes it was, but ... forgive me, this is rather awkward and I would have thought P.C. Duncan would have spoken to you by now."

"About what? I know he found him, but ..."

"Your husband was apparently found handcuffed to the banister."

"What!"

"Not only that Donna, but when he was brought in he was dressed rather unconventionally, shall we say."

"What does that mean?"

"He was wearing stockings and women's underwear."

Donna laughed. "What!" but seeing that the Sister was in earnest she flopped back in her chair and stared in disbelief. "He couldn't. Not Simon. Why would he?"

"I'm afraid I don't know the answer to that, I think the police suspect something untoward which is why the Constable has been questioning your husband, but I couldn't say what."

She handed Donna a cup of tea and they sat in silence as Donna digested this new piece of information and tried to assimilate it to the Simon she knew, her Simon.

Later as she sat by his bed the image that Sister Walters had conjured up for her kept invading her thoughts. However hard she tried she could think of no good reason for her husband being found in such a way unless ... unless that woman was back. Was he still seeing her? With his previous description of their tawdry fantasies would this be something she had forced him into or at least encouraged him, and if that was the case why leave him? Had he told her they were finished and she had led him on to one last fling before abandoning him to his fate – what kind of woman was she? What kind of man had she made her husband in to?

* * *

Simon had been assessed by the psychiatrist as being severely depressed, and harbouring extreme and irrational fears regarding his home, although given the circumstances, Donna wasn't quite sure how they could be considered irrational. It was obvious Simon could not return to '*Dreams'* the report said, and as his family were currently residing at The Randolph it was recommended that Simon be admitted to St Judes for a period of convalescence.

St Judes was an old Georgian mansion which had been converted to a hospital in the fifties, the communal area, where Donna found Simon when she visited, was an airy, friendly room, with electric blue chairs scattered in groups around low tables. Simon sat with a book open in his hands but not reading. Donna approached him gently; sudden movement seemed to upset him.

"Hi," she greeted him brightly.

He smiled to see her. "Hi." In one small word he managed to convey a total joy at her being there.

"How's it going? Are you feeling any different today?"

"I'm fine, fed up with bloody doctors asking questions but fine. I feel stronger. Doctors say I might be able to have a day out soon." It was the first time, in the three months that Simon had been a patient at St. Judes that Donna had heard him give any hint of leaving, however briefly; it was heartening to her to know he was getting better. Her mind turned to what might happen if he were discharged; it was a worry where they would go. She and the children were still living at the hotel; she couldn't take Simon back there and they couldn't return to '*Dreams*'. Donna didn't like using Sasha's money for the hotel but she didn't know what else to do. She could see no way of getting any money to buy, or even rent, a place of their own. The days just seemed to drift whilst she sought and never found solutions. She was getting heavy with her child now and was constantly tired from the toing and froing to see Simon.

"I can't go back there Donna, I can't," Simon whispered pitifully.

"No-one is expecting you too Sweetheart," Donna tried to reassure him.

"Yes. Yes they are. I have to go back."

"Of course you don't," Donna kept her voice level as Simon became agitated.

Simon beckoned her closer, whispering his confidence to her, "She's still there."

"Who's still there? You mean ....? Simon, you must tell P.C. Duncan, he's looking for her, wants to interview her. If you know where she is then you must tell him."

He would say no more.

PART FOUR

Donna's Story

One minute we appeared to have it all, the next it was all in tatters.

Even though Simon wouldn't come to Florida with us, I still took the children. I was torn. I didn't want to leave him, we had never been apart before, but the children were so looking forward to it. The boys particularly were thrilled to be going to Disney. They'd never had a proper holiday, and to be honest Simon had been such a misery since we moved into '*Dreams*' that I felt a break from him might do us both good. America was truly amazing. Everything was so big. The people were a delight, so friendly and the chance to escape the dreary British weather and enjoy the sun made us all happy. I enjoyed the luxury of late mornings and no meals to prepare. The food was just fantastic, but goodness the portions, I could never finish anything. It really was very relaxing but I did miss Simon.

I watched the kids turning golden brown under the sunny skies, they looked so well. I lay on a lounger and lazed. This pregnancy was tiring me out more than any of the others had – getting older I guess. It was still early days enough that I could get away with a bikini and loved just lying letting the sun warm every inch of my body, making me sleepy and relaxed.

We wanted to stay an extra week. After a week at Disney I was exhausted. We moved to Tampa, where the calmer sea of the Gulf Stream made it ideal for the boys to be occupied and where the girls found a couple of all-American guys to hang around with. I called Simon but when I didn't get any response I became quite worried, so we came home, earlier than we wanted, but later than we had originally planned. That's one of the bonuses of having money; you're not tied to some package deal, crammed into an aeroplane that you *have* to catch, not that I had any experience of that either, but I'd heard that's how it was.

I loved '*Dreams*'. Who knew then why or how it had come to us but it was a palace. Everyone had their own rooms, and the kitchen was just to die for. The boys were constantly in the pool. Who would have ever thought that people like us, could ever have had a pool, and a beautiful garden, and woods and umpteen bedrooms filled with fine things and well… everything really? The house was very aptly named '*Dreams*'. If only Simon could have been happier. I suppose it was easier for me, men need work, routine to give them some structure, some purpose to their days. I just loved to cook on that Aga and clean down all that glossy marble. I loved opening cupboards full of food and making beds which had thick, luxurious covers and scatter cushions by the dozen. I would walk around the place letting my hand trail from surface to surface, I had never seen such finery, let alone thought to ever own it and live in it. I think I was bewitched by it and for a while I was blinded by it. I never saw it the way Simon saw it.

When we arrived home Rosa came bounding out of the woods at us and jumped all over the children, all over me, she was wild with excitement. Then I saw Simon, he came running helter skelter out of the trees, unable to stop as the slope carried him forward. He arrived among us panting and grinning and hugging the children as if he could squash the life out of them. Then he came to me, slowly and shyly. I felt like I had felt the very first time we met. My stomach gave a leap and my heart began beating faster as I realised just how much I had missed him and how much I loved him. We'd been poor, we were rich; we had struggled as the children had grown and we hadn't always had time for each other but he still managed to make my heart flip-flop when I saw him. I think I had been in danger of forgetting. When he came to me and held me I melted into him and would happily have stayed there forever. He looked dreadful though, so thin, so drawn, I told him I was back to look after him and he needed feeding up.

That night, after the children had all gone to bed we had sat cosied up, like teenagers, and I felt the moment was fast approaching when we would climb the stairs and I could have and hold him properly. There was no rush, the anticipation was thrilling. I was feeling confident of myself, more so than I had in years. Despite the fact the baby was swelling inside of me I felt fitter and more attractive than I had in a very long time. My skin was tanned and I had luxuriated in all kinds of spa treatments whilst we had been away. I went to Simon a self-assured woman, ready to receive his lovemaking. His touch, the feel of him beneath my body was so familiar and somehow unfamiliar, he was tender and yet it stirred my desire into a frenzy, I craved him, wanted him more than I could ever remember. I slid down on him, the feel of him inside me causing me to throw my head back with pleasure. Then suddenly he was frantically thrashing, wildly fighting me off, pushing me fiercely across the bed, I covered my stomach to protect the baby as his arms wind-milled out and made contact with my body, but the worse thing had been his eyes. One minute he had been gazing into mine in the half light, and I had seen a love as deep as my own reflected back, the next it was as if he didn't know me, there had been panic, fear and even hatred, but most of all fear.

I didn't know what had happened or why.

Eventually I crept back into his arms as he apologised over and over but my body remained unsatisfied and my mind was in turmoil as I tried to make some sense of it. In time we slept.

The next morning was no better. After fixing his breakfast and sitting with him whilst he ate we were both ready to try again. Once more it was beautiful and then suddenly it was as if I were lying with a stranger.

It was time to talk.

When he came downstairs there was all the nonsense of him walking around the hallway, even Rosa was following this particular ritual. It was as if he was there but he wasn't there.

Then he told me.

Told me about a woman called Sasha; told me she had given him the house, the money, told me she had been at '*Dreams*' whilst we were away. He denied having slept with her but he surely couldn't really expect me to believe that. Couldn't expect me to believe some nutter had targeted him and in order to keep him had given him luxury beyond his wildest dreams ... there was that word again ... bloody '*Dreams*', and he had never bedded her. I couldn't stay. What could he expect? I felt betrayed. I felt stupid. I felt humiliated. I couldn't wait to get away. I ordered the kids to pack a few things. I would take them into Oxford to a hotel and then think about what happened next.

He had smashed it all to pieces; Simon had taken our lives and smashed them with no more care or concern than crushing an eggshell. Twenty years, four children, five nearly, a life built together, from poorer to richer, in sickness and health, and for what? A fling with some bloody nutter! I just felt so humiliated.

Suki was getting ready to go back to University so was already packed. I told Peta and the boys to throw some things in a bag and to follow me. There must have been something about my tone because for once they didn't argue. I think they already thought their dad was going off his rocker and our clearing out was inevitable. When he attacked Ronnie on the landing, for no apparent reason, well it sort of sealed it. Then the police arrived. That P.C. Duncan questioning us about a red Lotus - that woman, Sasha had a red Lotus. It's funny how the mind immediately springs to the worst possible scenario, but of course I shook that idea out of my head and I didn't say anything to them. When the police left, we left.

* * *

We stayed at The Randolph in Beaumont Street. The hotel was luxurious but I could not value its Gothic splendour. I noticed, but with no sense of appreciation the intricately carved plasterwork and the crystal chandeliers. The boys were thrilled with the staircases which seemed suspended in nothingness and looked as though they had dropped straight out of 'Hogwarts' as if at any moment they might twist and swing and lead somewhere else altogether. It was probably the wrong choice of hotel with the benefit of hindsight for every time I walked in and out of the main entrance my eyes inevitably drifted to the imposing facade of The Ashmolean across the road and my mind was dragged to Simon's confession of meeting Sasha there.

I tried to keep things as normal as possible and encouraged Suki to leave for university as planned. There was no point in her not going back. Peta and the boys were subdued but again I insisted on school and routine, not only because it was good for them to have as much normality as I could possible salvage in their lives but also I needed the time and space that their being at school afforded me. I cried goodness I cried. At night when the kids came back to the hotel we would snuggle down on the sofas in our suite and watch television and I was strong. I kept my tears for when they were not about. After I had dropped them at school in the mornings inevitably as I drove away from them the tears would start, cascading down my face in rivers. More than once I pulled the car into a quiet lay-by and howled uncontrollably. As the howling and wailing turned to sobbing I would rest my hands on my swollen stomach and remember that distress was bad for unborn babies and I should be playing calming music and doing yoga, but life wasn't so kind. Life had unexpectedly thrown at me a whole heap of crap and try as I might I could not always stop the tears.

* * *

It was a cold but bright day, the world was wrapped up in winter still, crisp but not icy. I stood at the window of our rooms on the second floor and looked across the street. Bikes were parked several layers deep beside the gates of the museum. Groups of students gathered in hand-blowing, be-scarfed groups, stamping their feet on the grey pavement as they exchanged news and flirted with each other. Pigeons strutted with unconcerned greed amid legs, scavenging crumbs, and people with heads bent down against the cold, rushed to catch the traffic lights before they changed colour. I looked over the road, beyond the flapping flags, the ropes making a clinking tattoo on the flag poles, and up the stone steps of the museum. Gazing past the pillars supporting the carved stonework with the statue of some sort of God balanced at the apex. I looked at the huge doors and with sudden determination turned, threw on my coat and made my way out of the hotel and across to the museum entrance. I stood hesitating, my hand on the door. An elderly gentleman held it open for me and smiled; he touched the brim of his hat and bowed slightly as I passed. I thanked him and stepped into the square entrance and looked at the signboards for directions.

Straight ahead of me lay the Chinese section. Standing at the entrance I hesitated, a man was coming toward me.

"Excuse me, do you work here?" I asked.

"Yes, how can I help?" he was shorter than me, an obvious academic; everything about him gave an impression that there were more important and interesting things in life than personal presentation. He was a man in muted colours, leather patched elbows and tweed, hair ruffled in a morning bed-head.

"I'm looking for something, it has an inscription. I'm not sure of all the words, something about a cottage, water, clouds, I think," I told him, remembering in patches what Simon had said.

"'*In the cloud shrouded cottage set before the flowing waters one can forget the troubles of the world*', he quoted dreamily, would that be it?"

"Yes, yes I think it is," I answered.

"Well follow me, its right over here."

He led me to a display and I stared at the carved stone of a seal, a little fat Buddha crouched in soapstone pose. Over this seemingly insignificant little piece it had all started. This was the place where it had begun. I was standing on the very spot on which she had stood, touching the glass she had touched, crying on the same spot she had cried.

"Are you all right?" the curator asked, concerned.

"I'm fine, would you mind if I just looked at this a while?"

"No, that's fine," and he left, embarrassed.

I stood crying, but no Simon came to offer to buy me coffee, though I longed and longed for him to do so. No hand offered me a tissue with which to dry my eyes, though I craved his comfort. I knew then that I could not live without him. I knew that if we could leave '*Dreams*', start somewhere new, we would be all right. I didn't know about forgiving and forgetting but I knew that I wasn't ready to let him go. I was suddenly angry. Simon was my man and I would not let that woman come between what we had.

Since that day in the hospital, when I had bumped into P.C. Duncan, I had been visiting Simon as a dutiful wife should. I had been concerned for him, still loved him, but there was a barrier between us of unanswered questions. I didn't understand the stocking thing, I didn't understand how after all he said he had allowed Sasha back in the house and let her get him into that state and then let her secure him to the banister. There were still so many unanswered questions. Despite my misgivings on that score I knew I would fight now for *my* man and *my* marriage. You don't just throw twenty years away, not when you still care.

* * *

I had new determination.

I walked along to Cornmarket Street and entered the first estate agents office that I saw. What appeared to be a twelve year old in a large suit and a red tie rose from behind a desk to greet me. I told him my requirements and he was unable to help, I rather thought he wouldn't. He looked as though he should still be using crayons. I trawled around every agent, becoming bored of my own voice as time and time again I repeated my wishes for a house to rent. By the time I entered Slocombe and Steed I was dropping on my feet. The office was manned by an elderly, military looking man, with yellow stained fingers and an ochre tinted moustache.

"Ah Madam, this could be your lucky day," he spoken in clipped, precise tones.

"Really?"

"Just yesterday we were instructed on a cottage in Norham. The owner would ideally like to sell but they would consider renting if it were for a minimum period of six months, it's still furnished. Belonged to an elderly lady, unfortunately she is no longer able to cope; her family have made other arrangements. The property is small and rather old fashioned, but it has charm."

I left with a set of keys and directions and strolled back to The Randolph to collect my car. Within half an hour I was driving out of the city and along green roads toward Norham. 'Aubrietia Cottage' was set midpoint in a row of what at one time would have been workers cottages, it was one of five. I pushed open the squeaky gate and inserted the key in the lock. The house smelled musty and airless, but that was nothing that couldn't be cured with a few open windows, at least it didn't smell of damp or rot. The door opened straight on to a reasonable sized sitting room. At least it appeared to be the sitting room for there was a sofa, chairs and occasional tables, but in the recess of the chimney was a large cast iron black stove, like the Aga but much older, the real thing, black leaded and reeking of character. The floor was quarry tiled with rugs scattered across it. The furniture was old and in some places patched but there was such a feeling of well being about the room I instantly felt at home. In the far corner a worn smooth, tongue and groove door guarded the entrance to the stairs; it was secured by an old wooden hasp and latch, which was operated with a rope pull. Adjacent to that was the opening to what I assumed must be the kitchen, but it was like no kitchen I had ever used. In one corner was an old fixed stone boiling tub, with a thick stone shelf beneath on which a fire would be laid in order to heat the water in the tub. The cupboards were all freestanding, scrubbed pine, and a pine table was set against the back wall where a large window, which had obviously been added considerably later than the house dated from, overlooked the garden. On the wall, light sconces looked as though they were still gas operated, and on closer inspection I found they were, although there was an electric light as well. It was like stepping back in time. I couldn't help thinking that Simon would be entranced by it all. Off the kitchen in an extension to the original property, was the bathroom, more functional and modern than the rest of the house, immaculately clean although bitterly cold at the moment.

I climbed the steep, narrow stairs, my shoes clomping on the bare boards. Each step dipped in the middle, evidence of years of feet traipsing up and down.

Standing on the top step, which was twice the depth of the others, three doors opened off, one in front and one each to left and right. I stepped into the first room. It was bright and sunny, the ceiling sloped down on one side and dark beams tracked across it. A bed was positioned against the wall, its headboard carved oak; cupids cavorted with woodland creatures and fed each other with plump grapes and wine poured from curved pitchers. The mattress was turned back on itself. Cupboards were built into the room; original pine doors with black hinges lined one entire wall. Two windows side by side allowed light to flood in from beneath the eaves.

The next room was smaller, darker, but with enough room to squeeze two beds with not much room between, it would do perfectly well for Ronnie and Ryan. The third room was lighter again and Peta would be able to manage very well. When Suki came home to visit we would find a way of squeezing her in. We would manage.

The cottage had no mod-cons, it was tiny, quaint and pretty and I fell in love with it. I retraced my steps and took a more practical look at the kitchen. There would be room for a fridge and a washing machine, if the owners agreed to our plumbing one in. The back garden was long and narrow. On the patio was a mangle and I really felt that the old lady must still have boiled her washing in the tub and wrung it through this ancient heavy looking wringer, no wonder she could no longer cope. The back of the garden was a vegetable patch, laid in immaculate lines and well manured. The boarders were full of plants, most of which had been cut down to stumps for the winter, but even now were sprouting back into life, I could see that come the summer this would be a cottage garden of excessive beauty.

I loved it. I loved everything about the place and although it may not be practical, after all I would be cooking in the sitting room and we would be falling over ourselves, I didn't care. This was a real home, a cosy, warm home which felt like the people who had lived here had been happy.

The deal was done. The owners agreed I could have a washing machine installed and they accepted six months rent in advance. The children and I moved out of the luxury of The Randolph and into the chaos of '*Aubrietia Cottage*', and reluctantly I used some more of Sasha's money for bedding and mattresses and kitchen appliances.

* * *

Simon was improving. With each of my visits he was looking less haunted but there were still times when he seemed to be in another place altogether and the doctors seemed as unable, as I was, to reach that final part inside him. On this particular day the sun was bright in the sky and I arrived at St Judes feeling in a very good mood. Simon too, was on better form and had been told that we could leave the grounds of the hospital for a few hours; this was a very big step.

He sat in the passenger seat and looked more like his old self in the familiarity of the car. He wasn't ready to visit the cottage yet so I drove along the road just enjoying having him with me away from hospitals and restrictions. We headed out past Woodstock, and as time moved on, stopped in a village I didn't know. I parked in the car park of The Red Lion pub so we could have lunch. Simon said he was enjoying being out of the confines of St. Judes and we should walk a while first if I was up to it.

"If I'm up to it!" I teased. "What a pair we are Simon," he laughed slightly nervously, like a stranger. I pushed my hand into his and we set off in the direction of the river. The day was chilly, but walking soon warmed us up. Wildflowers were starting to bloom in the hedgerows; primroses peeped cautiously out from their wrinkled dark, cabbage-like leaves, and smiled with yellow faces as we passed. It felt good to be outside. For this little while to set aside all cares and worries and enjoy the end of the winter becoming spring, and enjoy each other too. A footpath led down to the dark water of the river Glynne. We ducked under the low hanging branches of hawthorns and rowans, which were just starting to bud. Simon broke off the end of a twig and twiddled it in the fingers of his other hand as we walked. I chatted inconsequentially about the children, about the cottage, which I was in the throes of painting, ready for Simon's homecoming; whenever that might be.

"You're doing too much," he told me.

"It's only a quick coat of emulsion; I managed to get away with just washing the gloss with sugar soap."

"I don't just mean the painting, I mean everything. I don't want you making yourself ill as well." It was the first reference in a while that Simon had made to his illness in my presence.

"Simon, I'm fine. Let's just concentrate on you and get you home shall we?"

"I'm not ready yet," he answered quickly a hint of panic in his voice, his fingers squeezing on mine.

"No," I tried to soothe him. "Not yet, but when you are, I want everything to be nice for you." I felt his fingers lose some of their tension. We walked on. In the distance there was the sound of shouting and laughter, the sound of children playing. I smiled at Simon as we both took in the noise and we walked on, rounding the bend in the bank to reveal where the happy din had come from.

A boy, his voice not yet broken, shouted out in excitement to one of his friends, "Don't 'e let go, its bloody cold for swimming!" His friend was swinging out over the river on a long rope with an old tyre attached to the end. As he swung he let go with one hand and leaned back, letting out a long scream of exhilaration as the rope stretched out across the icy water and arced back toward the bank.

"I aren't gonna let go, am I?" he called loudly to the other boy as a third caught on to the back of his jeans and the edge of the tyre and kept him from swinging out once more.

Simon had stopped stock still as we watched them, I gently tugged him forward but he did not move. His eyes were glazed with that look which told me he was there but he wasn't there. I had seen it often the past months.

"Simon, come on," I urged. He did not move. He just watched the boys on the long rope as another took their turn.

"What you looking at?" one shouted over. "You wanna turn?" and they all laughed loudly and raucously from the opposite bank.

"Simon, come on love, come on." I pulled gently on his arm and automatically he came with me keeping his head turned all the time toward the river as I pulled him away. When we were out of sight of the boys we stopped. I straightened his lapels, smoothed his coat, and wiped back his hair, mother actions, whilst all the time puzzling over his sudden change of demeanour. Then he started shaking. His whole body was trembling, and his eyes were flooded with tears. "Simon, Simon, what is it?" I pleaded, grabbing his lapels in each of my hands as I tried to get him to focus on me and not on the place his mind had turned to.

When he spoke it was barely more than above a whisper. "I've done something awful Donna."

"It's all right Simon," I reassured him, "it's all right, whatever you did it's over and we must think now about getting you fully better."

"No," he screamed out, pushing me away. "You don't understand."

"Don't understand what?"

"You don't understand. There are things I haven't told you and I can't tell them," he jerked his head to indicate the direction of St Judes. "I can't tell anyone." His face was screwed up in anguish.

"You can tell me," I said softly, reassuringly, understandingly. "You can tell me anything Simon, we have been through the worst and I'm still here with you."

"I wish I could believe that," he said his voice full of despair as the tears fell thick and fast down his cheeks. He came back to me, his eyes focused on mine and I saw him searching in their depths, looking deep beyond what he could see on the surface. I stood quite still and let him look and I hoped he could read my willingness to listen to him and help him and love him regardless. Suddenly he seemed to make up is mind. "She came to that house." I knew *she* was Sasha and *that house* was '*Dreams*'. I listened, I did not speak. "She came one day, she wanted to move in, she wanted me and her to be a couple, be one. I didn't want to Donna; I swear I didn't want to. I told her to go. I told her to leave me alone. I wanted to leave that house. I never wanted it. I told her to go, told her I was going and you and me were married and I didn't love her. I loved you. You were my wife, I told her." He was becoming agitated as he spoke and I patted his arm and nodded my understanding. "She seemed to accept it. I was so relieved. I wanted rid of the place, I threw everything over the banister. I was going to burn it all down."

"What stopped you?" I asked, shocked.

"She did. I had it all there, thrown all over the stairs, papers, pictures, bedding, I had collected the petrol from the shed and I was started to unscrew the top and she was there. I didn't know at first what it was. She came at me from behind and leapt at me, she clawed me, bit me, fought me like a mad woman, she was possessed. I was knocked off my feet. She was like a wild animal, spitting and snarling at me. I fought her as hard as I could. Then she was there on the floor. I had knocked her loose and for a moment I think she was winded or something and I was the one in control. I was the one who was going to make *her* see sense."

"What happened?" I asked quietly, dreading the answer.

"I don't know. It was so unreal. One minute she was fighting me like a tiger and the next she was underneath me and I wanted her to know she couldn't do that, she couldn't beat me. Oh God Donna! Oh God forgive me!" He hung his face in his hands and sobbed uncontrollably.

"Did you ...?" The question went unfinished.

He nodded, slowly, between his anguished sobbing I saw him nod. I felt sick. I pressed my fingers to my mouth to stop myself from crying out. He slowly raised his head and looked at me. "I never meant to do it, she made me do it."

"Made you do it?" I snapped. "She made you do it?" My voice was rising. I tried to stay calm, in control, I tried so hard to understand that Simon was letting out his demons and I should be supporting him not berating him, he was laying himself bare. I forced myself calm. "Do what exactly?"

"I don't know how it happened, she was there. She kissed me. It was different. I don't know how it happened. I wanted to make her sorry. At that moment I wanted her to suffer as I had suffered. I ... attacked her. I suppose it was rape. I thought it was rape, but afterwards she was different."

Part of me flooded with relief that it hadn't been what I had naturally thought and another part of me was repulsed by his confession. "What happened next?"

"Are you sure you want to know?" I nodded mutely. "She went away. I was stunned, shocked, repulsed, I didn't know what to think or do. Donna I'm not violent, you know I would never hurt a fly, would never step on an ant if I could avoid it, I couldn't face myself, but then she came back. A few days later she breezed in as if nothing had happened and she said she was going to look after me, she said I was hers now."

I was feeling violently sick, but I took deep breaths and waited for him to continue.

"She did look after me, I was ill by then, I hadn't moved in several days. She fed me, let me sleep, in a few days I was well enough to get out of bed and go downstairs."

"Did you sleep with her?"

"No! I never did, apart from what I've just told you I never did. I think she was afraid, I don't think she could."

"But you would have done if she had said yes?"

"I don't know, probably, yes, in the beginning, maybe, I don't know, but not then, not afterwards."

I digested this piece of confession.

"Then what happened?" I asked again.

"There was a row, a blazing row, for a minute I thought she was going to kill me, we both looked at the knives and I know the thought flashed through her brain. I told her about the baby. It seemed to break her. I told her I loved you; there was no-one else for me but you. I told her she had been a terrible mistake and she must accept it. I told her there was no future that I wanted you and no-one else but you. It had really always been like that."

"Was that true?"

"Yes, it was true." I felt he spoke honestly.

"So then?"

"I left. I stayed at The George to give her time to clear out and when I went back I thought she had gone. Her car had gone. I was so relieved. I wanted to go back and just clear out my things and leave, never go back again."

"And had she gone?"

"Yes ... and no." The look of wild eyed terror which he had had in the early days of his illness was back; he was looking left and right, rapidly scanning around as if he thought Sasha might at any moment creep up upon us, his hands twisting around each other in a continuous motion.

"What does that mean?" I demanded.

"I went back to the house and I opened the door." His words were stilted as he dragged his confession out. "She was there ..."

"I thought you said she had gone?"

"No. She was there. She was there in the hall. She was ...." He tailed off and I waited with an enquiring look. His voice was a whisper. "She was dead. She was hanging in the hall, from the banister, just hanging. She looked like a ghost. She wasn't beautiful any more, she was hideous, she was everything evil and wicked." It had cost Simon everything to tell me and I felt the deepest, deepest pity for him.

"What did you do, you didn't tell the police?" I queried.

"I was going to. Believe me I was going to. I was horrified, I couldn't think straight. I couldn't get away fast enough, I ran to the car and they were there all around me."

"Who? Who was there?"

"Black spirits, evil intentions, I don't know, they came seeping out of the ground and made shadows all around and chased me. I drove out of there as fast as I could, like a bat out of hell, I was in hell, but then, when I was away I stopped. I didn't know what to do. She, Sasha, she had done this to spite me, to revenge me for rejecting her. I never knew much about her but no-one seemed to be missing her ... so ... I ..." he couldn't go on.

"Did you get rid of her body Simon?" I asked tentatively.

He nodded. Again his words came thick and fast, having started his confession he was determined he was going to tell it all. "I went back. I could hardly cut her down."

"The gouge in the banister?" I spoke with realisation dawning.

Again he nodded. "She danced on the end of the rope as I cut and I felt she was dancing with joy at her revenge. It was grotesque. When she fell to the floor the noise was awful, such a crack, but by then she must have been dead a while because she didn't bleed. Just that awful crack of bone on stone. The smell! She smelled of lavender. I will never smell lavender again without thinking of that moment. The smell was cloying as I wrapped her body. She was so cold." He looked at me for understanding, silently pleading with me to understand. I took his hands and held them but he pulled them away looking at them front and back as if seeing things which weren't there. "Such bad hands I have now Donna. I took her in the car and buried her in some woods. I don't even know where. I was panicking. I was scared. I was so scared. I didn't know what I was doing."

"Could anyone have seen you?"

"No. I'm sure they couldn't. If they had I would have heard something by now."

I walked a few steps away, pacing back and forth, looking at Simon occasionally. He stood with his head bowed. Tracking back I took his hands in mine again and held tight as he tried to retract them. "These are not bad hands Simon," I told him. "You are not a bad person. You know she was mad, you know it, don't you?"

"I suppose so."

"There is no suppose about it. She was mad and she drove you to do things which you wouldn't normally do, the stockings and everything, but it's over. It's over Simon. Do you understand what I'm saying?"

"It's not over," he replied slowly.

"You mean there's more?"

"When I went back to that house I began to pack up my stuff, to get ready to clear out. I was going to tell you as much as I could, about meeting *her* and everything and then you wouldn't want to stay in *that* house either. I knew I had to risk it in order to get away from the place. She never left. When I went back she was still there - haunting me. It was so strange, she had hung as white as a ghost, even when she fell she didn't bleed and yet all my nightmares are full of her blood, it seeps around me like poison, all my dreams are red."

"Even more reason to leave then."

"I couldn't. She'd seen to that as well."

"What do you mean?"

"As I cleared out the desk there was a letter. She said she knew me, knew I wouldn't go to the police, knew I would risk hiding her body and that if I tried to leave "*Dre...*", that house, her solicitor was to open a letter and I would be exposed as a murderer. Oh, she was very clever, the letter was written in such a way as to leave no clues for anyone else, but I knew what she meant and anyone else who saw it would see me implicated."

This was a twist I hadn't needed.

"So you see; I can never leave the house. I am tied to it and I can't go back to it. So must I stay at St Judes forever?"

"There must be a way, there has to be a way."

"Don't you think I've puzzled round it? I've thought of nothing else for months. There is no way out, she's won."

"No!" I shouted, "She will not win!"

"She already has."

I would not let Simon's defeatist attitude rub off on me, there had to be a way and I would find it. Neither of us felt much like eating after that. We retrieved the car and I drove Simon back to the hospital.

"Simon, don't lose hope," I told him as I left.

* * *

Inevitably at some time I had to go back to '*Dreams*' to clear out the rest of our things. I packed the children off to school, the cottage was quiet. It ached with the quiet. I missed Simon. His revelations had stunned me, shocked me, but somehow now I had had time to think through all he had told me I found that forgiving him was easy. He had been weak, he had been stupid, but I believed him when he said he hadn't killed her and had been panicked into hiding her body. When I thought about it I felt so sorry for him, for the guilt he had been carrying had been a heavy burden and he had certainly paid the penalty. I even felt that his attack, I could not bear to think of it as rape, had been manipulated. He had been so weak. So today was a new day and I would start to clear out '*Dreams*' and when I visited Simon later I would talk to him about coming home in a few days and we would be together, start afresh. I wanted to look after him, I wanted to hold him close and protect him. He would get better and I would be by his side. He was so much a part of me that the thought of life without Simon was unbearable. The months we had been apart, whilst he was in St. Judes, and before, were proof if proof were needed that I did not exist without him. For better or worse, and it really couldn't get any worse, from now on it was going to get better. So it was I left from our new home in a very positive frame of mind.

I was nervous as I pushed my keys into the lock at '*Dreams*'. Since Simon had confided in me I found I was looking at it through his eyes and the house did indeed feel evil. I pushed open the door and looked into the hallway, a thin layer of dust coated the floor and motes floated in the air which stirred as the door swung back. There was a slight resistance and a swish of paper as the door pushed back the pile of post which had built into a small heap. I looked over to that part of the hall which Simon had avoided, the area where Sasha had swung, my stomach lurched and my nerves jangled.

"Don't be stupid!" I told myself. "It's just a house." I stepped inside, but I left the door open behind me. I picked up the post and headed to the kitchen dumping the armful of letters onto the counter to be dealt with later. Like Simon and even Rosa, I found myself skimming the hall and avoiding *that* spot.

I was not going to take anything away that had come with the house. I started piling our old bits and pieces on the side. There was very little. Most of what we had brought had been binned at some time; there had been no need for brown stained, chipped mugs when we had been given a whole row of shiny new ones. Our old battered saucepans had made way for gleaming stainless steel, thick bottomed, designer replacements. The same had applied to plates, dishes, almost everything. There was still the antique, blue, papier-mâché jugs which had belonged to my grandmother, the few glass dishes which had been a wedding present all those years ago. There was the children's artwork which was magneted to the fridge. I collected together all the little bits of everyday paraphernalia which shore up the foundation of family life.

I was getting into my stride. I collected boxes from the car which I had thought to bring and in those I stacked books and DVD's from the family room off of the kitchen. I would not have been human if I hadn't looked with some small regret at what we were leaving, the huge plasma screen, the deep cushioned sofas, the space and luxury, but my regret was easily outweighed by wanting to put behind us all the catastrophic events of recent months. The silence in the house was oppressive, I found myself humming a little tune just to break it. When I felt there was no more I looked carefully all around to check I had forgotten nothing. In my condition the boxes were too heavy for me to lift alone, I would have to find help to load up the car, but at least if it were all just in piles that would be a very quick visit. I might find someone up at the farm that would help, I didn't want to bring the children back to this evil house, they were confused enough as it was by their sudden change of fortune.

Then I heard it - a noise in the hall. I stopped in my tracks, hand outstretched to pick up books as I froze. My breath held and my humming caught abruptly silent in my throat as I strained my ears to listen. There it was again, a scraping noise. My heart was pounding. I didn't believe in ghosts but my nerves were already stretched taut as I heard footsteps coming across the hall.

'Ghosts don't make footsteps,' I reasoned. A dark shadow loomed in the doorway and a small scream escaped me.

"I'm so sorry," a deep, extremely well spoken voice intoned. "I didn't mean to startle you."

I said nothing as I waited for more explanation and took in his appearance. I had had money enough recently, to recognise a bespoke suit when I saw one. Time to take in a silk tie and manicured hands, but more than the material trappings there was an air about this man, an aura of confidence. I felt he was a man used to getting his own way. He was definitely good looking but had such a supercilious air about him that it marred any attraction. Silently I thanked goodness that my own clothes although casual were of good quality, although the size of my bump suddenly seemed to be magnified tenfold as it protruded between us. He introduced himself, my hand came to my chest as I fought to calm my breathing, and find my lost voice, but all I could do was stare as I took in the import of standing face to face with Sasha's husband. I must have swayed, or looked as if I were going to faint, for he spoke again, "are you all right?" his voice wasn't one of concern, but of the pompous upper class ass which I so despised. Irrationally I blamed him for all Sasha had done to Simon. His tone did more to revive me than anything. Taking a deep breath I straightened up to face him.

"What can I do for you?" I asked, trying to sound braver than I felt.

He gave me a look of such condescension that I had to fight not to recoil under his gaze. I could feel my jaw tighten and my nostrils flare as I stood my ground and stared at him full on.

"It seems we have a bit of a mess here."

"A mess?" I queried.

"Don't play games with me Mrs Koweski; I assume you are Mrs Koweski?" I half nodded assent. "I have been contacted by the police, several times now, and that is not something I appreciate. I gather from their information, and from some subsequent discreet enquires I instigated, that there appears to have been some sort of liaison between your husband and my wife." He said the last word as if he did not want to soil his mouth by using the term 'wife'. I still said nothing, but my chin tilted upwards in defiance, and for a moment I could almost feel sorry for Sasha and understand what had driven her to find comfort in the arms of another man. Then I remembered the other man was my husband and sorrow for her was not an emotion I was going to waste.

He went on. "We seem to have a situation here; a criminal situation."

I tried not to betray emotion, but my mind was racing, how did he know? He knew about Simon burying the body – how the hell did he know that?

But then he spoke again, "It would appear that this property has been purchased with monies which my wife procured in a way that was not entirely ... shall we say ... ethical." It took me a moment to register that he was not talking about her body, he was talking about money. I looked at him with a mixture of relief and loathing and understanding, for this was a man that only dealt in money, he wouldn't understand anything which was not connected with money. Still I did not speak.

"Do you understand what I am saying to you?" He questioned as if he were talking to an idiot.

"I'm not sure I do."

"My wife stole from me. She used money that she procured from my account to fund the purchase of this property. I am here to see what can be done to recover that money."

"What are you going to do, beat it out of me?" I asked sarcastically.

"That, Mrs Koweski, is not my style."

"No, I don't suppose it is, but coming here to collect doesn't seem your style either, if you'd pardon me saying so. You look more the big city lawyer style I think." I did nothing to keep the sarcasm from my tone.

He eyed me carefully. "Yes, you're correct, although I rather feel the fewer people who know of this ..." he hesitated, "... situation, the better. I am not a man who likes to be made a fool of. I have a prestigious company and bad publicity could be very harmful. I do not court bad publicity. I do not seek to make this matter public. Do you understand?"

"Oh Yes," I responded. "I understand perfectly." His whole persona was guaranteed to rub me up the wrong way and I couldn't help but go on the defensive against him. I was not the same person who had entered this house all those months ago. Back then I had been as unworldly as a sainted virgin, but not any more. After all that had happened, after all the crap I had had thrown at me I had found strengths I didn't know I possessed, and I wasn't about to be messed about by yet another repercussion of Sasha's strange fantasy.

"Good. Then that will make things easier." His eyes scanned the pile of belongings stacked on the kitchen unit. "You appear to be clearing out?"

"No," I lied. "I'm just spring cleaning, it's the nesting instinct you know," I indicated my pregnancy. His nose twitched in disgust.

"Mrs Koweski, I will seek to recover my losses, I will salvage what I can from this unsavoury mess that my wife has perpetrated. I would prefer it if you would cooperate and that would make things easier for you and simpler for me."

"Are you threatening me?"

"If you like."

"You would do well not to. You should remember that I am also a victim here, and I am not about to be threatened by you or anyone else. There is nothing that can be done now that could hurt me more than I have been hurt, certainly nothing you can do." I stared him down.

"I understand that you moved here from a house in Fallgrove," he cocked an inquiring eyebrow, I did not reply. "Your husband worked for Rowley Max, which has since gone into liquidation. I assume from your original humble circumstances you have very little money of your own. He is now an in-patient at St. Judes, which inevitably implies he does not at present have a regular income. Given your condition I think I am probably right in suggesting you too are not currently employed. Your husband and my wife developed a relationship which it appears she sought to sustain by ensconcing him and most probably herself in this house in due course. Your husbands whereabouts is a given, my wife, I neither know, nor quite frankly care."

"You seem to know a lot about us."

"I pay people, I pay well. I pay for information and I pay for discretion and silence. I am willing Mrs Koweski, to pay you for your discretion, not to mention your silence."

"What do you mean?"

"I am suggesting Mrs Koweski, that you vacate this property, you ask your husband to sign papers I have had drawn up which state the house, grounds, contents, etc. revert to me. I believe my wife also made a settlement of one million pounds, of which you have spent approximately £43,500 to date. I will reclaim the sum of £500,000 and the reminder, and any interest accrued, will be your reimbursement for any inconvenience."

"Why would you do that?" I asked.

"I have told you already, I don't believe I can make it any plainer. I pay for silence. Call it damage limitation."

"And if I don't agree?"

"I am trying Mrs Koweski to do this the nice way. There are other ways if you prefer."

I walked to the table and pulled out a chair. I had not expected this. One of the biggest problems I had been facing since Simon had been ill was money and how we were going to cope once he was home. It would be a long time before he would be able to work properly again. I had been using *her* money to pay for the hotel, to eat, and even the rent on the cottage, telling myself all the time that it was justified, that we deserved it, for although it was tainted money it was all we had. I had tried to keep our spending to a minimum, taking as little as I could conceivably get away with, but nevertheless using what I had to so that myself and the children had not been homeless or starving. It had been distasteful. I had hated using it and so had tried to close my mind to the implications. Besides I had a million worries and using some of her money had been the least of them at that time. Now here was her husband, standing before me, so sure of himself, so sanctimonious, but also I sensed a little worried. Bad publicity would indeed hurt him, and he was such a bloody arse that he probably thought that all people like *us* would do that, would go shouting to the tabloids. I could see that he had me marked down as common as muck, with his disdainful look and his attempt to buy my silence.

On the other hand I had four children and one more so very nearly on the way. The house I had rented was tiny, as small as we could manage in, with the smallest rent I felt I could possibly pay, using Sasha's money. The strain of thinking how we were going to cope was taking its toll. It wasn't as if we could claim any benefits, (and it would go against the grain to do so), for they would only have to investigate our bank account and Social Services were hardly going to give handouts to a family which had a million quid in the bank.

All these thoughts raced around in my head, banging into one another, being considered and dismissed and reconsidered. This supercilious prig standing in the doorway was offering me a way out. It would be one less worry. It would cushion us against the world for a long while as Simon recovered. I wouldn't need to tell him, not immediately, I could wait until he was stronger and would see the logic of it. At present he hadn't seemed that interested anyway, he was still convinced he had no escape from this house. Not only would this provide us with money to live on but it could get Simon away from '*Dreams*', get him home where he belonged, with his family.

"Your wife left a letter," I told him.

"What letter?"

"She left a letter with her solicitor, Sylvester, Markham and Tweed, do you know them?"

"Yes, I know them, they are not my solicitors, but I know them."

"Well, you are a man of influence; if you want to seal this deal then you must retrieve the letter and return it to me unopened."

He looked puzzled. "What could possibly be in a letter which would give you such cause for concern?" he asked suspiciously.

"It ties my husband to this house. I don't know the details; I only know that without the letter I cannot get him to sign the papers."

"But the house is mine, bought with stolen money," he reasoned.

"Then perhaps you can use that as your argument when you secure the letter. You people," I spoke slightly sneeringly, "you people operate an old boys network, I'm sure you can pull some strings. If the letter is returned unopened I will see that Simon signs your papers. You will have your house, and you will not hear another word. I too do not seek publicity, whatever you might think to the contrary."

"Who did she deal with?"

"Mr Markham."

"I'll see what I can do."

I'm not sure how hopeful I was that he would be able to pull such powerful strings, but I had no choice. Without the letter Simon would not come home. I needed '*Dreams*' gone if I stood any chance of getting my husband back.

It felt despicable to be arranging such a sordid deal. I was being sucked into something I neither understood nor wanted and the realisation of that helped me to see that perhaps Simon had been more innocent than I had given him credit for and he too had been lured by circumstances snowballing beyond his control. This was a rolling stone gathering moss. It was now my rolling stone while Simon was in St Judes, but I would not be broken by it. My survival instincts were strong. It hurt me to stand and face this obnoxious man and do a deal with him, but I thought of Simon, of Suki, Peta, Ronnie and Ryan. I thought of the baby inside me, who for once seemed to be sleeping peacefully. I thought of the months ahead, facing Simon's home coming, and the worry of where the next meal was coming from being one less concern.

Sasha's husband held out his hand and with a small glimmer of hope I held out mine and we shook.

Our bargain was sealed.

* * *

I heard nothing from him for more than a week. During that time P.C. Duncan visited 'Aubrietia Cottage'. I was busy whitewashing the final wall in the sitting room. The front and back doors were open creating a through breeze. The stove was constantly warm, the cast iron holding the heat from one day to the next and working so close to it was hot work. I was dressed in an old pair of Simon's jeans. Since leaving '*Dreams*', leaving my designer clothes behind, I had taken to wearing Simons clothes a lot, it made me feel closer to him, and besides, not many of mine fitted me any more.

The radio was playing music from the sixties and I was happily singing along with Del Shannon as I 'nested'. I didn't hear the knock at the door. I jumped sky high when the deep, round voice of P.C. Duncan broke over the sound of the music.

"I'm sorry, Mrs. Koweski, I didn't mean to alarm you."

"P.C. Duncan, what are you doing here?" my words must have sounded ungracious; I quickly tried to make amends. "I mean, what can I do for you?" I wiped my hands on an old piece of rag as I spoke and walked to the radio to flick it off.

"I heard you'd moved out of the big house," he said.

"Yeah well, it was never really ours in the first place."

"Really, whose was it then?"

I tried to cover my mistake. "When I say it wasn't ours, I mean it wasn't really our style, this is much more our type of thing." He looked around as I gestured our surroundings and I was aware of the stark contrast.

"It's very nice," he said, "cosy."

"I like it."

"Will your husband be coming home soon?" he asked.

"I don't know." I was still answering cautiously, still not entirely certain why he was here. "Can I offer you tea?" I said to fill an uncomfortable silence.

"Tea would be lovely, thank you."

"Take a seat, I'll fill the kettle." I went to the kitchen to put water in the large old fashioned kettle before returning to put it on the hotplate.

"You don't see many of them old things any more," he nodded toward the stove.

"No," I laughed nervously. "This house is a treasure trove of antique appliances."

"I remember my granny had one of those, she was always on her hands and knees with the black lead, you could see your face in it she shined it so much."

"Well, I don't think you'll ever see your face in this one." I made tea in two mugs as the kettle boiled and handed him one. "I'm sorry," I said, "I don't have any biscuits or anything."

"That's fine, I shouldn't anyway." He patted his large round tummy, it would have been a hard call to say who's was biggest, his or mine.

"When's the baby due?" he asked conversationally.

"Well, I had thought the end of May, but after my last scan it seems I got my dates wrong," I laughed at myself depreciatingly. I was still puzzled how I had been so far adrift. "Out by a couple of weeks, so hopefully before the middle of the next month."

"June's a good time for babies. Do you mind if I ask you a few questions Mrs. Koweski?" Here it was, the reason for his visit, he dropped the conversational tone to something less friendly, more official.

I was suddenly desperately nervous, as I smiled and I had to put my hand to my mouth to ease my top lip from my dry teeth.

"I know this can't be easy for you, but I need to ask about the woman, Sasha, with whom your husband developed a relationship."

"Had an affair?" I spoke defiantly, my chin raised.

"Quite."

"My husband did not have an affair. He told me as much and I believe him. That woman was obsessed, obsessed to the point of madness, she stalked Simon and she scared him, scared him to a breakdown."

"Then where is she now?"

"I neither know nor care." Even as I spoke I heard echoes of her husband's words. "She went to '*Dreams'* and they had a row, Simon told her about the baby, she left."

"Did your husband see her again after that?"

"Well I suppose he must have done."

"How's that?"

"P.C. Duncan, you must know this is both painful and humiliating for me, but I will tell you what he told me." I was thinking fast, trying to concoct a reasonable explanation which was both feasible and believable. "She must have gone back for there was that night." He sat forward a little as he listened. "The night when they ...." I broke off and covered my face, squeezing tears from my eyes. "The stockings, the underwear, all that. You understand how humiliating all this is for me?" I looked at him appealingly. "The thought of my husband with that woman ... but even then, even then nothing more happened. She came back and trapped him, tricked him, lured him with her seedy games and when she had him trapped she left. Is it any wonder that he broke down? Apart from spending days secured to the banisters he knew Rosa was in the study suffering. He didn't know if he would be found or not. I had left with the children because of a row over *that* woman and she had made a complete fool of him." I cried openly.

"So he didn't see her again after that, she never went back when he was trapped?"

"No. I don't believe she did."

"It's just I have a witness that says he saw her."

"A witness?" My heart was thumping loudly. It wasn't possible. I knew Sasha had been dead by that time and that Simon had been held some sort of captive by the warped imaginings of her ghost.

"Aye. So you see it's still a mystery."

"What does your witness say?" I asked cautiously.

"He went to the house early one morning, says she was there, says she's an angel," he said on a laugh. "He says he saw her floating across the hall."

I laughed a forced unnatural laugh. "Sounds like your witness was on the moonshine," I joked.

"Well, I will admit he gets a little confused about times and dates, but he is convinced he saw Sasha there."

"Well no-one is denying she was there. Even I cannot deny she was there, much as I might like to."

"No, well I thought I would just check it out and seeing as how I cannot ask your husband I just wondered if you might know something. The woman seems to have just disappeared off the face of the earth and that bothers me." He looked at me and I wasn't certain if it was there, or if my guilty conscience made me see, an element of distrust in his countenance.

"Well I'm sorry I can't clear up your mystery for you, but quite frankly I hope none of us ever see her again. She has been beyond destructive in our lives and I just want a chance to rebuild."

"You're a very forgiving woman Mrs Koweski, not everyone would be as understanding as you."

"I love my husband Constable. I don't know yet if I can forgive him, but I think he has paid a heavy price for his error of judgement. I have my family to think of and myself. I want him home with me and the children. I want him better."

"So this is home now is it?"

"Yes." I stood, indicating this interview was terminated.

"I may have a few questions for your husband when he's home."

"P.C. Duncan, my husband has been very ill, he is still ill and a long way from a full recovery, your questions can only serve to hinder that. I hope if you have anything you need to know you will come to me first and not bother him."

"I'll do my best, Mrs. Koweski, good day to you." He replaced his cap and left. I closed the door and sat heavily on the sofa shaking violently.

***

It was the following day when Sasha's husband appeared. I had let him know the address of '*Aubrietia Cottage*' for when he had completed his part of the bargain. I really hadn't been too hopeful, but here he was, a sheaf of papers in a file and an envelope with an artistic sloping handwritten instruction upon it.

I slit the envelope open and skim read the words. "The evil, vindictive bitch," I seethed to myself. The letter seemed to be genuine. I had power of attorney to sign on Simon's behalf, I had been to the court in Oxford when he had first become ill to swear the oath and be appointed as his signatory. I read through each sheet carefully whilst that man stood impatiently waiting. I was not going to hurry; I wanted to be absolutely certain all was as it should be. I had no legal brain and I did not want to involve another solicitor so had to rely on my own judgement. I read very slowly and very carefully. When I was satisfied I signed where he indicated and watched as he too signed his sections. He gave me one set of papers and pocketed the other.

"Now there just remains the business of the money," he said pompously.

I reached for my handbag and my cheque book and wrote a cheque for half a million pounds to a name he gave me, which wasn't his own. There was no satisfaction in doing so, not even any relief - if anything, it felt grubby.

I handed it to him; he checked it carefully, before sliding it into his inner pocket. He held out his hand to be shaken, I kept my hands firmly by my side.

"I believe our business is concluded," I said.

He lowered his hand, gave me a last black look and left.

It was over. '*Dreams*' the thing of nightmares was gone. This was a new start. I couldn't wait to tell Simon. I read and re-read the letter which Sasha had written and hated her more than I ever felt it was possible to hate anyone. No wonder my poor, naive, innocent Simon had been so trapped, she had been evil beyond words.

When I showed him the letter and told him it was over, he cried.

"I don't know how you managed," he said. "I can't believe it's true, that I'm free of her wicked shadow. Donna, I will never ever give you cause to doubt me again. I love you so much. I still can't believe it's true, it's over."

"Yes it's over. She's gone. Maybe now we can think about you coming home?" I told him.

There was still a degree of hesitancy about him, but now it was mixed with some relief and some belief that yes, maybe he could.

That was the turning point. Maybe it's true what people say about a problem shared is a problem halved for from that point, each time I visited, I saw a new and improved man. My Simon was coming back day by day. He even started to tell little jokes and asked if the children might visit him. Up to that point he had refused point blank to see them.

The doctors said he might come home and so I scrubbed and cleaned the house from top to bottom, changed beds, washed everything that moved, hung pictures which had stood in stacks against the wall up to that time. I filled the house with jugs of wild flowers and stocked the fridge with Simon's favourite foods. The children made a banner saying "*WELCOME HOME DAD*" and strung it across the front of the house. The neighbours came to wish us well. There were no secrets in a tiny hamlet and they knew Simon had been in hospital, although I had refrained from filling them in with all the details. Mrs. Green from next door baked us an apple pie and presented it golden crusted and sugar dressed.

I left Peta with the boys while I drove to St. Judes. Simon was waiting in his room, his bag packed. He looked rather nervous, but excited as well. I sat on the bed beside him.

"It's going to be fine," I reassured him, taking his hand in mine. "Everything is all right now."

"The nightmares have gone," he told me.

"Oh Simon, when, why didn't you say?"

"I wanted to be sure. The nurse taught me some breathing techniques, they seem to have worked, but really it's down to you Donna. Without you being so strong, so faithful, sorting things out, it would never have happened. I still don't know how you managed it, but I will be eternally grateful. I'm ready to come home Donna." We hugged tightly.

"Come on then, what are we waiting for?" I whispered into his neck.

We left the room hand in hand. Simon had to check out and he wanted to say 'goodbye' and 'thank you' to his doctors so our progress was slow, but eventually we were in the car and heading home. Home, it sounded good, it sounded real and very wonderful.

SIMON

It felt so good to be going back to my family, so good to finally put it all behind me. Since Donna had arranged everything I hadn't had the nightmares. Mind you it was a bit hard to have nightmares given the quantity of Nitrazepam I took every night which knocked me into oblivion. I was scared to give them up just in case the bad dreams started again, but I would, in time. The doctors assured me I would be able to manage without, maybe cut down from two to one and then half; little by little I would finally stop. I just had to regain my confidence and know that imaginings couldn't hurt me and it would all be all right. But for now I would rather rely on a little help to get me through the night. The worst time was the last minutes before waking, when I struggled through the foggy mist of a drug induced sleep to awareness. That was when I was at my most disorientated. The ward sister had taught me some deep breathing exercises which filled my body with fresh oxygen and brought me back to the surface much quicker and made me more lucid, they seemed to work. In the last weeks I had managed to sleep peacefully and Sasha had not invaded my thoughts in a negative or frightening way for some time. Of course I was scared of what might happen when I was away from the hospital. It was a safe place. The doctors assured me it would be all right; after all they said laughingly, I couldn't stay at St. Judes forever.

Donna brought me home to Peta and the boys, and their bright coloured, homemade banner strung across the house. I was looking forward to seeing Suki at the weekend when she came back from university. I loved the cottage Donna had chosen; it was small, cosy, but so warm and welcoming. I felt safe and such a long way removed from what '*Dreams*' had been. Donna had made it nice; there was not a single reminder of the false, rich life we had left behind. The white wooden gate had creaked on its hinges as we crossed from the lane to the small garden. The early bees floated around the purple aubrietia and the late tulips. All that was missing was a dog coming to greet us. Maybe when I was stronger, mentally stronger, we could get another dog, but not a golden labby; I couldn't bear to look at another golden head resting on my knee. Perhaps a black one; a black one would be all right.

The day passed.

Donna did her best to make everything appear normal. We ate a leisurely lunch, the children, who had appeared wary at first, soon settled to chattering and squabbling, and it felt good to be around them. We managed a short walk along the lane and back, I was surprised how quickly I became tired, so we returned to a much needed cup of tea. In the afternoon I helped Donna unpack some baby clothes she had bought a few days previously. I cut out the price tags for her, before she folded the tiny babygrows into small piles, storing them in the cot, which was in the corner of our bedroom. Donna had arranged that the boys and Peta would stay with friends for the night. Although it had been a joy to see them I was actually quite glad, their constant chatter had tired me more than I wanted to own up. Donna drove them whilst I rested for a while.

Much later, tired but happy, we got ready for bed.

I almost felt shy, it was the first time in months I had seen Donna naked and she was now heavy with the baby and this one was going to be an acrobat I thought. As she stood at the mirror creaming her arms and shoulders with moisturiser; little arms or legs were pressing her stomach out. I watched fascinated. She saw me, caught my reflected gaze in the mirror, and smiled at me.

"Wanna feel?" she asked. I nodded dumbly. I stood behind her and placed my hand flat on her stomach, almost immediately it was greeted with a fierce right hook. I smiled at Donna and she smiled back. She covered my hand with her own, slightly tacky with cream, and whispered down to her swollen stomach, "Go to sleep now baby, time to sleep." Then looking me in the eyes through the mirror she asked, "Do you want to cream the baby to sleep?" I nodded.

She left the circle of my arms and walked to the bed, lying back among the pillows with that otherworldly look of the happily, pregnant woman. She held out the bottle of lotion to me. We had done this with Suki, with Peta and with the boys, it made me feel a part of her pregnancy and so it was again, I took a squirt of the rich, white cream in the palm of my hand, warming it before I placed it on her stomach. Gently I rubbed it over her, round her tight abdomen, moving in smooth circles over her skin, now lined with blue veins, her belly button turning outwards, feeling the new life inside her rotating under my touch. It seemed it was presenting its back to me to be rubbed as well. Donna watched my hand lazily stroking the two of them and I felt closer to her than I ever had in my life. We had been to hell and back, Donna and me, and maybe we weren't all the way back yet, but it felt like we were going to be; it felt wonderful to me. I was full of renewed hope; this baby being soothed beneath my touch was new hope for us all.

"If it's a girl, can we call her Hope?" I asked.

Donna lay relaxed and dozy, with a contented smile on her face, she nodded her acquiescence. She gave a deep sigh and a small moan of warm pleasure. I pulled the covers up over her.

In the bathroom I brushed my teeth, pee'd, and washed my hands. I hardly recognised myself, so far had I seemed to have travelled these last months.

"You're home," I said quietly into the mirror. "You're safe, you made it, you're home." I nodded my assent at such simple words which I knew now to be true. Taking my tablets from the cabinet I looked at the label, considering. Was I strong enough to stop? "One thing at a time, Kid," I told myself, "one thing at a time." I pressed down and twisted the lid and took the prescribed two pills from the pot. I jiggled them in the palm of my hand. No, I knew I could not do without, but maybe one would be enough, putting one back in the pot and ducking under the tap in the hand basin, I rinsed the other down with a swig of water. It wouldn't work for half an hour or so. I padded back up to the bedroom; Donna was asleep, breathing deeply, a vision of contentment. It was a bright moonlit night, a full moon. I padded down the stairs to turn off the lights. Through the open curtains I was caught by the glory of the silver disc in the sky, shining so splendidly. A mist of clouds framed it in beauty. I had come a long way in a short time.

In the beginning, back when I had first been admitted to St Judes, I couldn't stand the dark, had been terrified of it. The nights had come at me blood black, as they had all those nights I had been trapped on the staircase at '*Dreams*'. I had feared to shut my eyes as the shadows had closed over me, saturating me in the inky, seeping river of Sasha's wickedness. I had felt as long as I kept my eyes open it would stem the flow, so I had fought sleep, fought against the blackness, fought against her evil as she had tried to swallow me up. I had waited in shivering despair for the light to come inching over the horizon and release me from my purgatory. But Sasha had been clever, she had held all the cards, she had even made the light evil. As it crept into the house, as it peeped over the sills, and tipped into the hall, and through the open doorway of the kitchen, it was as if it was opening old wounds, and they began to seep anew with fresh, red blood. The light brought no relief, just more of her malevolence, her wicked, tainted malice, creeping over the floor and always threatening to engulf me. I don't know how long I had been held prisoner by her on the stairs; even now, although the doctors told me it was days and days, I cannot capture a sense of time. There was no sense of time; there was only the sense of wanting to die, but not that way, not drowning in Sasha's crimson tide. Even at my very worst moments, I knew that I hadn't wanted to die that way. The psychiatrist said that was how I had stayed alive beyond all possible human endurance, because I was determined not to lose to her. He said I was the winner and I must accept I was stronger than her. I had come a long way. I could now turn off the light and look at the silver moon, and the darkness behind me and the silver light above me held no fear. It was just light and dark, black and white, with not even the faintest tinge of pink to taint it and make it something it wasn't.

The pill was beginning to take effect.

I moved quietly through the house and back up the stairs, sighing one last time at the brilliant moon which lit my way. I pushed the door shut behind me and climbed into bed beside Donna. It felt a mile wide after the confines of hospital beds. Donna's body was warm and reassuring. I put my arm across her and she turned away from me, pushing her bottom back into me, like spoons we linked, curled together as one, warm and reassuringly comfortable. As my eyes grew heavy I let a huge yawn escape and Donna mumbled, "I love you."

"I love you so much," I whispered into her back, "so very much." It was good to be home. Donna was my home, where my heart was. As I snuggled into her back I sighed contentedly, cradling the mound of her stomach where our baby rested warm and snug.

"Not long now," I whispered, as we were both toppling over the edge of sleep.

"Longer than we thought," she murmured almost indistinctly.

"How's that?" My eyes were heavy as lead, I knew the signs, I was about to fall into the black abyss of lost consciousness.

"Baby's not coming now 'til the fifteenth of next month." As she spoke she pressed back closer to me, placing her own hand on top of mine as my hand tensed on her stomach. "Don't know how I got it so wrong," she murmured. Through my sleepiness I comprehended the implication.

And then I heard *her*.

She whispered into my black night. *"That's our day, that's our day, the anniversary of when we met, that's our day, I'm coming back."*

Sasha's voice was softly caressing me toward the edge of sleep. I clung to Donna to keep her safe, but I could not do more; the drugs had hold now. I cursed myself for falling. My arms and legs felt as heavy as lead, I could not raise my head from the pillows. I was falling.

* * *

I didn't know where I was when I awoke.

It was those minutes of heavy eyed disorientation which come after a drug induced sleep, the minutes it takes to focus back to reality. I lay quite still and tried to summon my wits. There wasn't the background hubbub of quiet noise I was used to. No distant clattering of a trolley along a long corridor. No mumble of voices as nurses changed shifts. No crying out of a patient in distress or disorder. My lids were heavy, drug heavy; I scrambled with my foggy brain to get my bearings.

I did the deep breathing thing which the nurse had advocated. I felt my body shiver involuntarily as I recalled my nightmares. Even through my sleeping tablet I had felt Sasha winding into my red dreams. My baby, our baby, our 'Hope', had been in my dreams. But not the baby I had expected. Not the baby Donna and I had anticipated with such joy. Not the baby we had talked of and I had lulled to sleep under my creamy massage. The baby in my tainted dreams had emerged smiling enigmatically, repulsively wrapped in a curtain of long blond hair, her body streaked red with blood. She had not been a baby at all but a tiny, miniature of Sasha, her echoed laughter tormenting me, her whispered words promising that she would *"be with me always"*.

I had struggled with her through the foggy darkness, tried to protect my Donna. Donna was my safe place. I had held her tight in my arms, trying to protect her. I had gripped her tighter, harder. I had tried to stop Sasha from coming between us – nothing would ever be allowed to come between us again. I promised Donna, I would do all I could to make sure of that.

* * *

The smell was the first thing I noticed; a metallic tang assailed my nostrils, different from the stink of an institutional breakfast and the cheap cleaning products which had combined to fill my sense of smell each morning for the last few months. This was like the smell one got as a child from the taste of sucking the lead in a pencil. I willed my eyes open, but although they fluttered they refused to perform to my demand.

"Open," I demanded of my blind eyes. "Open."

I wished they had not.

Nothing in the room was as it should be. The curtains were pulled shut but there was enough light filtering through for me to register the chaos. I closed my eyes again and breathed once more, deeply though my nose hoping that I was still lost in a vivid and horrifying dream. But dreams did not have smells.

I knew from the smell it was not a dream.

* * *

P.C. Duncan surveyed the room. It was only an hour since he had been called. He knew Simon Koweski was now home. The neighbour, Mrs. Green, had come bustling from her front door, her words tumbling over themselves as she had told him about the amount of noise coming from Simon's house in the night. She had been worried, but being a woman on her own had not wanted to interfere. She had a spare key and she gave it to P.C. Duncan.

He had pushed back the front door, all was quiet, it looked as if they may not even be awake; the stove was barely warm. Calling up the stairs he had received no reply, so cautiously he had climbed the narrow treads, aware of his bulk in the confined space. The doors to two of the bedrooms were ajar, the rooms unslept in, obviously the children's rooms. He cautiously pushed back the door to the third room. It was in semi-darkness, the curtains still closed, but thin enough that light shone through. Furniture was tipped this way and that, the remnants of a baby's cot, smashed into pieces. The wall mirror hung crookedly, cracked into fragments, small items of clothing dripping from the light shade, from the upturned dressing table; little ghostly whispers of white in the darkened room. In the midst of the scene of total chaos, Simon sat naked in the middle of the bed rocking, his legs tucked beneath him, his arms wrapped around himself. Beside him lay Donna, her face a white mask, her lips dark in the half light. She was streaked with blood; multiple wounds puncturing her body, trickles of her life had oozed from the gapping holes and seeped into the sheets, gathering in dark pools. In her stomach, in the round protrusion of her pregnant belly, a large pair of black handled kitchen scissors, so recently used to cut price tags from small clothes, stood proud.

Simon never took his gaze from her face, never stopped the slow rocking. "She came," he told Duncan in a hoarse voice. "She was stronger than both of us, even together."

Duncan said nothing; he stood in appalled horror just inside the doorway. He could not take his eyes from the mutilated body of Donna, lying naked on the stained sheets. He fought to keep both his breakfast and his anger at bay.

Simon slowly raised his eyes. "She came," he said again. "I couldn't stop her."

THE END